CHASING YOUR DREAMS CAN GET YOU KILLED.

Liz Hanlon strives for success as a musician. But family se-crets come to light when she discovers the body of her young cousin at the foot of the stage where she is about to perform, nearly ruining her career, and putting her life in danger.

"Barbara Reed's *High Notes Are Murder* features a heroine as smart and likable as any in crime fiction today. Singer Liz Hanlon's voice remains strong and pure throughout this refreshing debut novel."
>   —Martin J. Smith, author of *Time Release*, *Shadow Image*, and *Straw Men* (release date January, 2001)

"*...High Notes Are Murder* is an inspired murder mystery that exposes the tainted side of the music business on the way to solving who-done-it. This is a sound story that will keep you guessing to the end."
>   —Chris Enss Author, *Women of the Gold Country* Falcon Publishing

"...Reed strikes a chord of terror in this musical whodunnit which will leave you guessing even after the last bar is played!
>   —Billie Raven Author, *A Most Personal Look* Markham Publishing

FIRST EDITION

HIGH NOTES ARE MURDER

by

Barbara Reed

Rare Sound Press • P.O. Box 15028, Long Beach, CA 90815

ISBN Number: 0-9700024-0-8

Library of Congress Card Number: 00-190436

Cover Art & Design by Eddie Young. www.EddieYoung.com

Cover Layout by Nikki Matthews, Access Print Design. www.authors-n-music.com

Acknowledgements

I always believed this page would be easy to write but it has not turned out that way. Considering the number of friends who repeatedly offered help and suggestions along with continued encouragement to keep going, I find myself overwhelmed by their kindness and depth of genuine friendship. It's difficult to thank them properly but below are some who deserve special mention. My appreciation goes to:

Nikki Matthews, for countless computer skills required in the design and production of this book, for editing and marketing suggestions, and endless phone calls at all hours. Mostly, for a tenacious spirit.

Billie Raven, for the exhaustive hours of reading and editing with insightful feedback, unwavering friendship, and an uplifting attitude that continues to help keep me on track.

John Anello, Jr., for brainstorming, and for running with the ball. For a steady and compassionate way of proving that anything is possible, and for always being there.

Llew Matthews, a true musical treasure. For arrangements of music that went far beyond my own imagination, and for immeasurable friendship.

Mollie Gregory, a terrific editor, an accomplished, gifted writer, and an all-round great person.

Eddie Young, for introspective and beautifully crafted artwork, and a generous outpouring of good-natured support.

Denise Bloch, for reading and brainstorming during the tedious early stage of rough, unpolished drafts. For the laughs and the perspective.

Chris Enss, for helping to pull it all together and reminding me why it matters.

Nancy Weiss Lampert, for sensitive photography with a personal flair.

Dennis Oliver from Colt Security Service in Palm Desert, California. For details in the personal security business.

Doug, Tim, and Bobby at DGC Digital Recording Studio in Orange, CA. For both web site and musical help, and thoughtful suggestions.

For Bill

NOTE TO THE READER

Music is magic. As a toddler I would pull myself up onto the piano bench and derive great glee from the sounds I'd make by pounding up and down the keyboard. Over the years, I've continued to be fascinated by the infinite nature of music and by the power it has to take us into a state of deep reflection, and to set our imagination in motion. As a piano player, I've always wanted to know more about the combination of tones, as if I might be able to understand these magical properties if only I could get inside the harmonies or bathe in them as they washed over me.

I believe music truly is a "universal language" as it carries its listener to his own unique position on the emotional spectrum—exactly the effect a composer strives for when he paints his musical canvas with melody and rhythm.

In **High Notes Are Murder**, Liz Hanlon is a masterful composer with the rare ability to captivate her listeners in the hypnotic glow of lyrics that evoke cherished memories or hint of sweet things to come. She is compelled to follow her dream, even to sacrifice personal comforts in her quest for a lifetime of creativity. A trade-off she can live with, she calls it, for to deny her passion would be to endure a life not fully lived. The songs on *High Notes Are Murder*'s companion soundtrack are the culmination of her passion.

Barbara

One

The thick, humid air in Brogino's Bar & Grille smelled of smoke, beer and bodies. By early evening, sixteen of the club's regulars had staked out the stools in the lounge. Late-comers who wanted to be part of the bar action had to stand three-deep around them while Rocky, the night bartender, kept them entertained by demonstrating his ability to slide a mug of beer the length of the bar with enough backspin to keep it from slipping off the edge. The ten tables spotted across the dingy lounge filled up quickly as diners left the adjoining restaurant and settled in as if it were their own living room. Couples with dancing on their minds arrived before the music started, ordered the one drink they would nurse for hours, and nabbed seats at the piano bar, waiting impatiently for the piano player to begin.

Liz Hanlon thought the phrase "piano player" in this joint was a joke. She didn't feel much like an accomplished musician whenever she reached for a chord on the decrepit instrument in the corner and had to work around the four broken keys. A five-year-old couldn't plunk out a version of *Chopsticks* on it without hitting a clunker. When Liz took this gig, she knew she'd have to sideline her classic repertoire of Cole Porter and Michel LeGrand songs. This crowd wanted pop radio hits, "regular music" as owner Sam Brogino called it. But it was the piano that bothered her most. No matter what the song, she had to force her fingers into unnatural positions just to get any sound at all. She felt awkward and clumsy as she struggled to keep the rhythm steady, like racing for a bus wearing one five-inch high-heel, and one running shoe.

Singing and playing at the same time, a technique that requires two rhythmic patterns to be performed together, had never posed a problem for Liz, but on this piano it was damn near torture. No wonder she went home with aching muscles from neck to waist.

The piano was deceptive. It looked like a grand, but that was another joke. It was a cheap spinet pressed against a makeshift wooden table which had been cut into the shape of a full grand, and painted black. To her ear, it sounded like a bad soundtrack from an old western movie, and although she flashed her congenial smile with its distinctive dimple to encourage friendly chatter and more requests—part of the gig—she longed to be singing from the stage of The Hollywood Bowl. Four years at Berklee College of Music in Boston, and ten more on the L.A. musical roller coaster of one-nighters, but the steadiest gig she'd found so far was Brogino's Beef and Barf. Another beer joint that looked, sounded, and stunk like all the rest. Even her smile couldn't completely hide her discontent.

The room felt hot and muggy. She wore a dark red silk tee supported by delicate shoulder straps, not because she wanted to dress provocatively, but because by midnight the heat in her crawl space behind the piano was oppressive. A brass wall lamp above her threw off such intense heat the tips of her auburn hair fell against her bare shoulders in limp ringlets. The amber light created a golden glow around her full, round face, and more than one drinker had commented on her "halo."

"That's me," she joked, "Saint Liz."

An elderly man drinking brandy called out, "I surely hope not, 'cause we ain't lookin' for no saintly activity when we come here!"

Customers close by joined in the laughter.

She'd had other gigs, of course, but Brogino's kept Liz Hanlon from living in her car. Four nights a week she pounded out "drinking songs" that kept Sam's cash register ringing.

"What would you like to hear?" she asked over the microphone.

Requests bombarded her: "Snowbird!" "For The Good Times!"

"Neil Diamond!" a woman with stiff, yellow hair shouted from the dance floor. "Something slow and sexy."

Liz set the drum machine to a rhythm with a "headache beat," and watched the dance floor fill up, reminding herself of why she was here: she was broke. Piano bars didn't pay much, but short pay was better than no pay.

Sam Brogino sauntered out of the kitchen with a blood-stained apron tied around his potbelly and a pissed-off pout on his lips. He squeezed between two drinkers and leaned his sweaty face close to Liz's microphone.

"How come it doesn't sound like the record when you play it?" he snarled.

Her eyes snapped open. The dancers stopped.

"They're called CD's now, Sam, and did you ever think it might be your piano?" she said, noticing the hairs protruding from his nose. "Half the keys don't even work!"

"Use the other ones," he said.

"Why don't you do us both a favor and turn this thing into firewood?"

Sam waddled back to the bar, and she watched him wipe his palms on his greasy apron and shake hands with Corky, a regular who insisted on the same bar stool each night. Corky kept two beer mugs overflowing at all times. His nose and cheeks were bright red, and Liz had nicknamed him Rudolph.

"You ought'a lighten up on her, Sammy," Corky said. "She sings like an angel."

Sam laughed. "Give it up. You'll never get her in the sack."

"All's I'm saying is that it's her we come to hear every night. You give her a hard enough time, maybe she takes her music somewhere's else."

"Piano players're a dime a dozen," Sam scoffed, returning to the kitchen.

Liz finished the song just as Rocky, the bartender, picked up a white envelope from the bar and squinted to make out the writing.

"Hey, Liz!" He held up the card.

She started toward him. "What's that?"

"Got your name on it."

"Okay, who's the smart-ass?" she said, before noticing the

same slanted handwriting she'd seen a few nights ago. She grew uneasy as she tore it open.

Rocky continued placing damp-dried glasses on the shelf. "I turned around and there it was."

She looked at the men inhabiting the end of the bar. "Anybody see who left this? Corky?"

They shook their heads. "Better not be from another guy," Corky said. "I hate competition."

"The world is your competition, Corky."

His friends broke up.

"Hey, you gonna play or what?" someone shouted.

Liz squeezed back behind the keyboard and slid the card out of the envelope. The cover was a glossy photo of a sleek, black grand piano with a single red rose on top. The same handwriting was inside:

Ignore Sam. I will rescue you from him soon.

A chill slithered through her. Two days ago, she'd gotten a similar card: *I always get what I want. And I want you.*

Someone's idea of a sick joke, she'd told herself, and she'd tossed the card in the trash. She reminded herself to have Rocky walk her to her car when she left.

"C'mon! Let's hear somethin' we can dance to," a man yelled, clicking the heels of his cowboy boots.

She dropped the card into her purse and set a drum beat. Couples bolted onto the dance floor, but Liz had a hard time concentrating. She was certain a pair of eyes watched her maliciously. Her hands trembled as they moved across the keys by rote. She stared deep into the crowd, wondering which of them might have sent the card, and why.

The smoky haze stung her eyes. She felt relieved when she spotted Danny Amata's shiny, blue-black hair. Danny was a close buddy, and a twenty-eight-year-old musical success story.

He was a first-call drummer for movies and television recordings, and always the top choice of any arranger. Usually, a sexy young bod clung to his arm, but tonight he was alone. Liz watched him order a beer with the same flirtatious flip of his hair he'd perfected on pretty girls in his teens. He wore a black silk shirt that matched the sheen of his hair, and his face exuded a tenderness when he smiled. *No one should be born that cute.*

He leaned over the piano bar and pretended to flash the seductive smile of a guy on the prowl. "Hey there, gorgeous, what time d' you get off?"

"Hey, Danny! What brings you out on a rainy Wednesday night? And dateless at that."

"Thought I'd see how you were doing," Danny said. "And to give you the news before it hits the streets—I've met someone special. I think she might be the one."

Liz looked skeptical. "With you they're all 'the one'."

Danny took a corner table, and she played for over an hour, working the crowd into a dancing frenzy as they shouted for more.

"Do Billy Ray Cyrus!"

"No! Dolly Parton!"

She sang until she was hoarse and her back ached. "Back in fifteen," she announced, and hit the taped music button. She grabbed her purse and headed for Danny's table.

He pulled out a chair for her. "This place, it's—"

"Early cave man. Good recommendation you had there, buddy."

He shrugged. "You were broke. Come on, you can slum it for a few weeks. It pays the rent."

"I've been paying the rent for ten years. When do I get to move on to health insurance?"

Danny was the most flamboyant member of her band, and Liz marveled at how well-informed he was about the city's music scene.

"Don't get a swelled head over this," he said, "but I hear people talking about you all over town. Not just about your voice, about the music you're writing, too. You're getting hot."

"Really." Trying to be supportive, sometimes Danny came off sounding like he was full of it.

"Really. It's just a matter of time. You're in that gray area."

"What's that, the ozone?"

"You know what I mean," he said. "Our group's played some good showcase nights, and now the big clubs know your name. It's going to pay off soon. Besides, don't you always say it's better to be playing than sitting around talking about it?"

"Yeah, yeah. I love singing, I love composing, but I'm thirty-six, and I'm working in an upholstered toilet!"

"You see upholstery in this joint?"

His good mood made her laugh at herself.

"C'mon, you're being negative," he said. "You do a damn good single."

A single. "One person struggling to do the job of three or more. I played singles in Boston. I came to L.A. to put a killer band together."

"You did!" he said. "What 'd ya call the three of us, chopped liver? What's the matter? I've never seen you so down. You ought to be glad you can accompany yourself. Lots of singers can't work unless the club can afford a group."

"I guess I'm just afraid that places like Brogino's are as far as I'll ever get in the music business."

"We're all afraid of waking up someday and finding there are no more gigs," he said. "With so much music being recorded by computers now, my studio gigs are fewer all the time."

"I didn't know that."

"Hey, you won't believe who called me awhile ago," he said. "Gina. She told me to meet her here."

"Gina?" she said, astonished. "Gina McCurdy?"

"Yeah." He frowned. "C'mon, you two aren't still giving each other the silent treatment, are you? She's your cousin, for godssake."

A year ago, Gina moved to Los Angeles, and stayed at Liz's apartment until she found a job and a place of her own. By the end of the second week, she was hitting dance clubs till dawn and sleeping all day, not even pretending to look for work. Liz asked the owner of a club called Germaine's West to give Gina a job, but soon Gina was bringing customers home and sleeping with them on Liz's hide-a-bed in the living room. One night Liz took Gina out for dinner, hoping to settle their disagreement, but after several drinks, Gina began making sexual advances toward strangers. Liz was embarrassed, then infuriated. Finally, she'd yelled "slut" across a crowded bar. Gina and her clothes were gone when Liz woke in the morning.

The next call she had from Gina was three months later from the L.A. County jail. Gina and her new boyfriend were charged with running a scam on elderly couples, bilking them out of $50,000. Liz's brother, Carl, a Los Angeles attorney, worked to get the money returned and the charges dropped to keep Gina from having a police record. Liz and Gina hadn't spoken since then, but in recent months, Liz had begun to feel badly about the way they'd left things.

"What's she coming to this dump for?" Liz asked.

Danny shrugged. "All I know is there's some good news in the works, and she wants to see the look on your face when you hear about it."

"Gina's idea of good news is a rich guy with a vasectomy."

"Hey," he said, chuckling, "she told me to meet her here, I'm here. Really, Liz, I think she's trying to patch things up with you."

Liz nodded, thoughtfully. "I'd like that, too."

Danny squinted at the puffs of smoke hanging in the air. "They could rename this place Brogino's Smoke and Choke. It's so thick, your baby-blues don't even show from back here."

"Sam's not big on fans," she said. Her allergies to smoke, dust, mold, and other unknown substances had been in high gear since her first night. She reached into her purse for a tissue. The white envelope fell to the floor.

Danny picked it up. "What's this? Fan mail from one of the toothless drunks at the bar?"

"Some weirdo," she said, looking into the crowd. "Take your pick around here."

"Really? A secret admirer from here sent you a card?" he asked, reading the inscription.

"More like a fruitcake who wears tin foil to bed to ward off invaders," she said. "Last week I found another card in my teaching room."

"Someone snuck into Walter's studio?"

She nodded. "At first I figured it was for another teacher. No name on the outside, but inside it announced that he's used to getting what he wants, and he wants me."

"That takes balls," he said. "You think this dude's here now?"

Her eyes scoped the room. "It feels like it."

"I'll keep an eye out while you're playing. Don't worry."

She tucked the card into her purse. "So who's the new sex kitten?"

His face lit up. "The new bartender at the Stop." The Midnight Stop was a local hang-out for musicians and night club workers. "Her name's Tiffany, and she works days."

"Sounds like you're dating a lamp. How long have you been seeing her?"

"About a week."

"Forsaking all others, I see. Watch out, you'll be meeting the family soon."

"Okay, be a wise-ass," he said. "It's easy for you, you've got a sure thing with Ben." As he spoke, he took his eyes off the crowd and noticed her fingers wrapped around a glass. "Hey, where's your ring?" he asked, making a quick search of her hand, then her face.

Ben Parkhurst had been the steadiest lover she'd had in years, pursuing her relentlessly, and making no secret of his desire to marry her.

"What happened?" Danny asked.

"It's hard to explain. I guess we were both wrong. For each other, I mean."

"What the hell does that mean? Ben's nuts about you."

"He was. I'll never find anyone like him, but it's about music," she said, "my career. He can't stand it."

"He decides this now? You were a musician when he met you."

"I guess he thought he could convert me to Harriet House-wife."

Danny frowned. "Or he's afraid people will call him 'Mr. Hanlon' if the spotlight's on you, and not him. What a stupid move."

"He said he wanted a 'normal' life, not one where reporters are parachuting into the backyard for a sneak photo. He wants a wife to follow his career, not the other way around."

"Macho bullshit." Danny's hand patted hers. "Don't worry,

either he'll come around or he's not the right one. 'Cause you," he said, shaking his head, "you gotta make music."

"He won't come around."

His eyes narrowed. "Why? What happened?"

She sighed. "We were in a restaurant, and he explained that since I've been knocking around 'all these years' and I haven't made it yet, I should throw in the towel and marry him!"

"Uh-oh. That temper of yours. You didn't slug him or anything?"

"I thought about it. I threw the ring instead. It landed in his shrimp scampi."

"And?"

"I walked out."

"I thought he understood the music business better than that," Danny said. "Some of the most accomplished names are in their forties before they're recognized. Even their fifties."

"There's a rosy picture."

"It'll never take you that long. You'll be kissing these third-rate dives goodbye soon."

She wanted to agree with him, but telling him about Ben re-ignited an old, tormenting fear. "I keep seeing myself as a feeble old woman sleeping alone in an abandoned car."

"He's nuts! So are you! Have you talked to him since?" he asked, his eyes roaming across the room.

"I started to call him a couple of times, but—"

"Hey, Liz! It's for you," Rocky called from behind the bar.

She looked up; he was holding the phone in the air. She checked her watch. "Quarter to twelve. Who's calling me now?" She pushed back her chair.

Rocky stretched the phone cord across the bar for her. "Guy says he's your manager."

She took the phone, relieved. "Hi, Marty. What's up?"

Marty Steinhauser spoke slowly and formally, starting every conversation by clearing his throat. "Forgive me for calling so late, Liz, but I got a call from the owner of Germaine's West."

"Sonnie?"

"Yes. He's got some exciting news. I told him you'd stop on your way home tonight. Is that a problem?"

"What's this news that everybody in town seems to know but me?"

"He wants to tell you himself."

"At least give me a hint."

"You'll see," Marty said, merrily. "Pick up the contract, and we'll talk tomorrow."

"Contract? C'mon, Marty, don't leave me hanging."

"Have a good night." He hung up.

Germaine's West was one of L.A.'s most prestigious night spots, a room known for showcasing talent. Last year, shortly after Marty became her manager, Liz and her quartet had performed there for one week, but they'd never received the hotly desired call back.

She hurried back to Danny's table. "The owner of Germaine's wants to see me. What's going on? How come Gina knew about this?"

"Ask her yourself when she gets here."

She looked at her watch, then at the crowd. "I've got one more set to do. Why don't you two stick around and come with me?"

"He asked to see you, not me."

"Don't be ridiculous. Sonnie's not interested in me. Not that way. And besides—"

"Besides, what? Sonnie's a cool guy. And he's in a position

to do you a lot of good."

Her jaw dropped. "Are you saying I should sleep with him just to get a good gig?"

Danny chuckled. "No, but he's obviously interested in you, and he's not exactly a nobody. You blow him off like he's pond scum."

"I do not," she said, starting back to the piano. "You're missing a very important point. Well, two, actually. First, Sonnie is married, and second, he's a club owner. My God, he's not even—"

"Not what?"

"Not even my type."

"Uh huh. In that case, Gina and I'll tag along."

Back at the piano, Liz was singing about horses and old trucks while she pictured herself on the stage again at Germaine's West.

At the edge of the dance floor, two couples moved to the beat. Looking beyond them, Liz saw Gina come through the battered door. She walked up behind Danny, threw her arms around him and greeted him with a long kiss that nearly knocked him off his chair.

Gina looked different to Liz. Her dark-haired beauty was intact, but she had gray circles under her eyes, and her cheek bones were more prominent. She wore tight black jeans, black boots, a white lace shirt, and carried a handbag trimmed with tiny white faux pearls. Her cousin always did have exquisite taste, Liz thought. Liz played her last song glad she'd have a chance to clear the air between them.

She gave Gina a hug, then began packing the last of her music. "You look great, Gina," she said, nodding toward the white handbag. "What a beautiful purse."

"Thanks. I've got to admit, Liz, you're still the best singer around."

Liz smiled at her. "I'm really glad you came in. I guess I should have called you before this."

Gina waved her hand in dismissal. "Wasn't your fault. You just need to lighten up on people a little. Let'em be what they are."

Liz stopped. "Excuse me?"

"Like me, for instance. You were always on my case about how much I drank, or who I drank with."

"That's not how I remember it!"

"That's exactly how it was. Admit it, you're a great musician, but you're a tight-ass. Music's all you care about. You ought to have a little fun sometime."

Danny saw Liz's annoyance flash. "Hey, come on, you two. We've got to get to Germaine's."

"Yeah, Gina, what's all this good news stuff?" Liz said.

"You mean how come I heard about it before you?" Gina countered. "Because I'm not afraid to hang out with folks. I don't rush off after the gig like you do. I relax with people, let 'em talk if they want."

"You let 'em do plenty of other things, too," Liz said under her breath as she turned back to unplug her equipment.

"You'd kill to have my social life!"

"That's not a social life," Liz yelled, "it's a reputation!"

Gina stepped forward, starting to swing. Danny jumped between them and caught her arm in the air. He looked down and noticed Liz's fist poised to return the punch.

"Knock it off!" he cried. "What's the matter with you two? You've got the whole room staring at you."

Liz spun around. Several regulars gawked at them. She cooled down and looked at Gina, remembering the childhood secrets they'd shared and wondering what had become of them.

"I'm sorry. We just see things differently."

Gina's fist unfurled. "Yeah. Come on, let's forget this crap."

Liz packed her microphone and picked up her keys. "Right. I could use some good news. I'll take my car and meet you there."

Liz waved goodbye to Rocky and they headed for the door. "You probably won't believe this, Gina, but I really am glad you came in tonight."

Two

At twelve-fifty-five that night, Liz cruised through the
puddles in the back parking lot of Germaine's West on
Melrose Avenue. The lot was empty; Danny and Gina
had not arrived yet. She was about to lock the door when she
spotted the plane ticket for her trip to Boston on the seat. It
had taken the last of her savings, and she could not replace it.

She grabbed it, locked the car, and walked across the lot.

Camden Street, perpendicular to Germaine's, was lined with overgrown trees hanging over the sidewalk. The roots cracked the concrete. A row of well-kept shrubs divided the parking lot from an empty lot of weeds. The band had often told Liz about a man living in the bushes. She'd never believed it, but she hadn't walked in to check it out either.

High above the club, a huge neon sign flashed:

"TONIGHT: Saxophonist, Dino Marcel."

For one week last summer it had read:

"THIS WEEK: Vocalist, Liz Hanlon."

Her band had played shows to packed houses. Seeing the sign brought back a whisper of the old excitement.

As she walked through the back entrance, familiar bass rhythms pounded overhead, the volume low and constant. She followed the sound of voices.

Even after hours, the lounge vibrated with energy. Tiny lights glittered around the dance floor giving it the depth and shine of a night-lit swimming pool. From the doorway, a long glass and chrome bar extended the length of the entire left wall. Liquor bottles were displayed in long rows, each one lit by bulbs built into the edge of the shelf.

Liz's doctor had warned her that people with certain allergies sometimes had a keener sense of smell. As she stepped inside the lounge, the scent of perfume and after shave made her eyes water.

"Hey, Liz," Sonnie called out, "over here."

He unfolded his six-foot frame from a bar stool and engulfed her in his long arms. "Damn, it's good to see you!" He stood back to look her over from head to toe. "You look great! You cut your hair. Very sexy."

Amiable and outgoing, Sonnie Tucks could put even the

most timid people at ease. Musicians called him the most personable club owner around. His sandy blonde hair was graying, his small greenish eyes were often lost in deep laugh
lines. Tonight the puffy bags beneath them showed his age
and fatigue.

"This is like old times," Sonnie said.

"Marty asked me to stop by, but he wouldn't say why," she
said. "Then Gina showed up at my gig out of the blue. She and
Danny are right behind me. What's going on?"

"I'm glad you and Gina had a chance to settle your differences before we all start working together," Sonnie said.

"If that was her mission tonight, we failed miserably. What's
this about working together?"

Sonnie led her to the other end of the bar where a vigorous-looking man turned to greet her.

"Liz, I want you to meet an old childhood buddy," Sonnie
said.

She gazed into a pair of chocolate-brown eyes large enough
to make her think she could jump into them. Inviting enough
to make her want to. His radiant smile drew his cheeks into a
merry, self-confident expression.

"This is Tony Perdusian."

Tony took her hand. "Sonnie's been bending my ear about
you. This is truly a pleasure."

His skin looked healthy and fresh, as if he'd just had a
professional grooming job. His dark eyes hinted at an intensity beneath the surface, a fire kept at bay. "The pleasure is
mine," she said, feeling a flutter of arousal. Her mind became
a jumble of senseless phrases.

"Sonnie's bragged about you," Tony said, "but he left out
the eyes. Crystal blue eyes. Like the ocean on a moon-lit night."

Sonnie placed a glass of wine in front of Liz. "Yup, Liz and her water-blues. They're gonna sizzle all across the world."

"Is anyone going to tell me what the hell's going on?" she cried.

"Live TV concerts," Sonnie said, stressing each word with the excitement of a child at Christmas. "We're going to broadcast live shows from the stages of all three of my clubs in the chain."

She blinked, getting her thoughts around an idea that seemed hard to believe.

"We've made a deal with CBS for the first one-hour concert," he said. "If that's successful, we'll do one show a month. Each broadcast will come out on video. On the Internet, too."

"My God," she murmured, "you're serious. Sonnie, this could be—"

"Spectacular! Worldwide recognition."

"All three clubs. How will that work?"

"We'll start off the show here in L.A., then switch to the Miami stage, then the New York stage, and back to L.A. for the finale. All in one hour."

"How did you manage something like this?"

He gestured toward Tony. "Meet our own in-house concert promoter, Tony Perdusian."

"Oh, you're *that* Tony Perdusian," Liz said. She'd heard the name over the years, but big-time concerts had never been part of her daily routine, so the name hadn't registered. "This'll certainly put Germaine's on the map," she said.

"It'll put your whole band on the map," Sonnie said, "because you're the headliner, Liz. The official Germaine's house band. You'll open the show with one of your originals, then do one or two more in the middle, depending on time, and end with one more when we cut back to you to close. Send the world off to sleep with Liz Hanlon in its dreams. Any of this ringin' your chimes?" he asked, beaming.

"You kidding? I'm hearing chimes in keys that don't exist!" she said.

Sonnie topped off her wine glass. "Now, I know you're busy, Liz. You've always got a million things going."

She thought of her gig at Brogino's. "I think I can fit this in."

"I was hoping you'd feel that way."

"Did you really think I'd refuse?"

"I thought you might be a little miffed," he said. "The truth is, I always felt bad about not having you back after that one week," he said. "But I wasn't jivin'. It was just as I told you. Money's been getting tighter and tighter. I had to go with the names I knew could pull in a crowd. It was economics, never a slam on your talent. Believe me," he said, earnestly, "I want you back."

"Don't you need a big name now that will attract attention? What about the sponsors?"

"Tony and I have worked that all out. Two minutes into your first song, sponsors are gonna be coming out of the woodwork," he said.

They heard laughter as Danny and Gina came through the back door.

Sonnie looked up. "Hey, Danny! How's it going?"

Danny gave Sonnie a warm handshake "Awesome, now that Gina finally filled me in about the concerts. Very slick, man!"

Sonnie beamed. "It'll be great. We'll have Liz and your band back," he said, turning a smile at Gina, "along with our lovely waitress and resident airhead. What could be better?"

Gina dragged a stool and placed it between Liz and Tony.

"Somebody start at the beginning," Liz said. "How did all

this come about? And what about you, Gina? I thought you worked at the King's Row now."

"I did, but—" Gina smiled devilishly. "I'm back here now. Sonnie and Tony made me an offer I couldn't refuse." She pressed her hand around Tony's arm. Her eyes rained seductively down his body. "After all, this is where the action's gonna be."

"Our fair-weather friend," Sonnie cracked, good-naturedly.

"Damn right!" she said, posing like a model with arched back and one hand behind her head. "An exquisite package such as myself, I gotta go where I can get full value for my services." She fluttered her eyes again, drawing laughter from everyone.

"Sonnie, this is fantastic!" Liz said. "I feel like I could overcome gravity, and lift right up into the air—and it's not the wine!"

"You never could drink," he teased.

"This is pretty heady stuff. One minute I'm pounding the keys at Brogino's Swig & Swill, and the next minute I'm gonna be on TV!"

"Thank Tony," he said. "He showed up here couple of weeks ago after who knows how many years. When we were kids, my Uncle Booker owned this place, and Tony and I'd hide behind the beer coolers to hear the music. Remember, Tony? What were we then, ten?"

"About that," Tony said.

Gina's glossy fingernail traced down Tony's arm. "Tell us some of your juicier memories, boss. The ones about you and Tony when you were very bad."

"Naw, that's ancient history," Sonnie said. "We're onto the future. I predict that Liz will be offered a major recording deal the minute those suits see the show she puts on. And me," he said, rapping his knuckles on the bar, "my place will be so famous, I'll be fighting off bus tours and foreigners with cameras. Just like the Lighthouse in the '50s. A whole generation of jazz lovers grew up on those concerts."

Excitement shot through Liz. "When do we get started?"

"Tomorrow," Tony said. "I've got a construction crew coming at six a.m. to start knocking down that dilapidated old thing." He pointed at the red brick wall that extended from the end of the bar, running to the edge of the small stage. "We'll enlarge the stage, make it look more professional."

Sonnie disappeared into the office, and came back with a camera. "Everybody move in closer," he said, focusing. "This is a moment in Germaine's history."

They leaned in together. At the last minute, Danny brushed a kiss on Gina's cheek. The camera flashed.

"One more," Sonnie said. Just as he focused, Gina threw her arms around Danny. The sudden move threw her off balance, and she crashed to the floor, taking him down with her. Tony broke out laughing, and shifted his stool out of the way as Sonnie snapped pictures.

"Oh yeah, these are keepers," Sonnie said.

Danny and Gina brushed themselves off. Tony moved his stool back into place. "It's obvious you've all been friends a long time. I'll bet you guys know how to party," he said. "I've got the place if you've got the time."

"Ooh, a party at your house," Gina said in a come-hither tone. "I like that."

"I never turn down a party," Danny said.

"Middle of next week?" Tony asked.

"I'm in," Liz said. "I'll call the other guys."

"Sounds like a plan," Sonnie said, beginning to refill glasses. Liz covered her glass with her hand. "No more for me,

Sonnie. I should be going. Marty said you had the contract ready."

"Yeah, come into the office."

She followed him around the corner. The office was crammed with another computer, fax machine, scanner, an extra phone line was being put in. Paper covered the desktops.

"Excuse the mess. Tony's moving a few things in."

"A pair of shoes, a tooth brush, and he could live here."

"That's the idea. It'll be easier for him to have his office here during the construction, rather than running back and forth to Malibu. Where the hell is that contract?" He closed a file cabinet and moved to a desk drawer.

"That's where this party will be? Malibu?"

He shoved papers from one spot to another. "Yeah. It's a helluva place. Here it is." He pulled out the contract. "Can you swing around here with it tomorrow night?"

"Sure. Assuming you're not going to change your mind and hire Samantha the Snake Woman instead. It'll be late, after my gig. Will anyone be here?"

He yanked open a drawer, withdrew a key, and handed it to her. "Here's an extra door key. Keep it."

"So I can tell Samantha she's out?"

"Wise guy. By the way, can you handle wardrobe and a makeup artist for the band? Ratty tee shirts aren't going to make it on this deal."

"Sure. I'm going to Boston for my mother's birthday. I'll set up the appointments before I go."

His fingers fidgeted through his hair. "You're going to take off now?"

"Maybe I could shorten the trip, fly in for her party and come back the next day. That'll leave the rest of the week for preparation."

Sonnie looked unconvinced.

"The group's tight, Sonnie. We've been together for over a year. Believe me, I have no intention of getting on that stage unprepared."

"You're right," he said. "I'm just nervous." He lowered his voice. "Keep this under your hat, but my nerves are frazzled. You may get another chance, Liz, but this is my last hurrah."

"You've kept three clubs going through all kinds of rough times. Other things will come up."

"Not for me. My finances are stretched to the max. These broadcasts are going to make or break the Germaine's restaurant chain."

"But the club is so well-known, and the crowds are still coming—"

"It's been a growing thing; I'll explain it to you sometime," he said, as he stepped back into the lounge. His tone changed as he called out, "Hey, everybody, listen up. I got a joke. You guys ever hear the one about the two invalids and neither of 'em could get it up?"

Gina groaned and stood up. "Another Viagra joke. Come to the dressing room with me, Liz. It'll save you from Sonnie's sick humor, and I've got something to show you."

Liz followed her into the dressing room. Costumes overflowed from closets, hung from the back of the doors, and the vanities were piled high with makeup, brushes, combs, curling irons.

Gina opened a drawer. "This one's yours. We got it organized so everyone's got one of their own. And over there," she said, pointing to the large closet, "I'll make a spot for you to hang up things. The vanities belong to whoever gets here first."

"Thanks." Liz sat on the edge of a love seat. "I'm sorry we got into it earlier. Guess we can't do that if we're going to be working together. So, how have you been, Gina?"

"Good. I got a nice place on La Perla street. Nice room-mate, too. You should come by sometime."

"I will. I always felt bad about the way we left things."

"It wasn't your fault," Gina said. "I was knocking back the booze pretty hard."

"I always thought it was the influence of that guy, what was his name—?" Gina didn't respond. "Anyway, that's all behind us now. Working together will be fun."

"Yeah," Gina said. "When we were kids, it was always you and me, remember? Carl was usually off in another room deciding which pranks to pull next."

Liz smiled at the memory. "Mostly on me. Hey, how's your mother? Are she and Jerry still in Chicago?"

Gina shook her head. "Nope. She had enough of him about a year ago."

Gina's father had passed away when she was very young. Liz had a shadowy memory of being told that Gina was going to have a new father when Aunt Irene married a man named Jerry McCurdy. After that they moved to Chicago, and Liz rarely saw Gina until she came to live in Los Angeles.

"Mom moved out here about a year ago," Gina said.

"In L.A.?" Liz asked, amazed. "I never knew."

"Yeah. What about your Mom? She still givin' you attitude about being a musician?"

"Constantly. She practically disowned me when I insisted on jazz and modern styles instead of classical. Now she wants me to do the husband and kids thing."

"What'd 'ya think she'll say when you tell her you're going to be on television?"

"I'll find out soon enough. Her friends are giving her a surprise birthday party Saturday night. I'm the surprise."

"She doesn't know you're coming?"

"Not yet."

Gina turned a sideways glance at her. "This ought to be good."

She watched Gina move costumes out of the way. "Hey, how's the love life these days? You seeing anyone?"

Gina shrugged. "Kind of."

"Anyone from the old crowd I might know?"

"No."

"Boy, remember how some of those guys could drink?"

"They weren't so bad."

"You kidding? I remember one guy who went through a case of beer a night. Of course, we were all younger then—"

Gina leaned her hand on her hip. "Hey, if you're gonna keep raggin' on my social life like you did before, this'll never work. I know how much I can party. And I know how to land on my feet."

Three

Bullets of rain battered the roof. Suzanne Becklin sat on the edge of the bed watching Liz pack. Since their teenage years, Liz had referred to her friend as "tall, stunning, traffic-stopping Suzanne." Her bright red hair tumbled in thick waves over her shoulders, and she managed a commanding height of five-foot-ten with elegance. Liz always joked that she, too, could make a grand entrance, it just took a lot more mirror time.

Suzanne peered into the bulging suitcase. "I thought you shortened this trip to three days."

Liz folded another blouse and placed it on top. "Two. But you never know about the weather in Boston."

"You're going to give your mother some notice, aren't you?"

"I'll call her tonight."

"Maybe hearing about your new break will make her ease up about your career."

"Don't count on it."

"I don't know, Liz, when I got the job as Musical Director for Amy Renoir, your mom was pretty thrilled. She even sent me a nice bouquet of flowers."

"That was you, Suz, not me. She was ecstatic when you married Rob, remember? To her, if it doesn't involve a husband, it's not the real thing."

Liz and Suzanne's friendship went back to grade school, when they'd taken their first piano lessons together at six. Suzanne was already tall enough to reach the sustain pedal, while Liz was still sitting on a phone book to reach the keys.

"I thought she'd be excited when I told her I'd landed Marty Steinhauser as my manager—the same manager who's turning your boss, Amy, into a household name. You know what Mom said? That being famous was okay for Amy, but it's no life for a married lady."

"She's just scared for you. Once you're successful, I'll bet it'll calm her fears."

"I hope it'll calm mine," Liz said.

"There's no security in the creative world, that's for sure."

Liz flopped down on the bed. "I know. But I still replay these damn fears late at night. Ben's words painted a scene that isn't far off the mark. The years are racing by, and I've got nothing saved. Even if the concerts last, there's no guarantee I'll get a recording contract, or that I'll earn enough to build a nest egg." She jumped up. "Oh, listen to me! I'm letting my mother's cynicism get to me."

"That's fear talking," Suzanne said, peering into the suitcase. "Got your ticket?"

"Picked it up yesterday." She rummaged through her purse. "Where did I put it? Oh no. No! I left it at Germaine's. Dammit! It was in my hand when I walked into the office with Sonnie."

"Next time try an electronic one, Liz. We can run over now and get it."

"No, it'd take all night in this rain. I'll stop by on the way to the airport in the morning. You want some coffee?"

"Do you have any of that orange spice tea? I'll have a quick one, then I've got to go. I can catch the end of the game with Rob."

"Ah, marriage." She pulled two cups from the cupboard.

"Quiet nights behind closed doors can be a lot of fun."

"I know, and I want that someday too, but right now I've got to get four new songs ready every week. And they'd better be hot. If I blow this, no record company this side of the moon will give me a second shot."

"I'll bet you've got at least two hundred songs you've never done anything with."

"I'll be dusting those off for sure," Liz said. "But my career—my whole future is riding on this."

"You're up to the job. You've got all the ingredients—a great band, killer songs. What's to be nervous about?"

"I know I'm lucky to have the guys in the band. They've stuck with me through some hard times."

Suzanne let the tea bag bob up and down in her cup. "Your wave is rollin' in, Liz. Relax and ride it."

"You're talking logic; I'm talking real life." Liz stood in the doorway and looked across the living room, making a mental checklist of things to be done before she left. Her music case next to the piano reminded her that she'd promised to choose some new songs for her precocious seven-year-old piano student, Sherice Williams. She withdrew a book of popular songs and set it on the kitchen counter.

"You're not taking your music to Boston, are you?" Suzanne asked.

"No, I told Sherice I'd find some new songs for her. It's always a challenge to be ready for her next lesson."

A small pink note card was wedged inside the book's binding. Liz pulled it out and stared at it. Was this someone's deranged idea of a love affair? She gaped at the words:

Soon you and I will share the harmony of eternal peace.

Her knees went weak. She dropped into a chair.

"What's wrong?" Suzanne said, looking first at Liz, then at the card. "Eternal peace? What's this all about?"

Liz's words were barely audible. "This isn't the first—"

"Tell me."

Liz described the card she'd found at the studio, and another left for her at Brogino's. "This jerk says he always gets what he wants, and he wants to save me from Sam Brogino."

"For all eternity," Suzanne said, nodding toward the card Liz had dropped on the table. "Jeez, Liz, you'd better call the police."

Liz stared at the card, not moving.

"You going to call?"

Liz glanced at the clock and sighed. "I have to be up at four o'clock to make the plane, and with the time change I'm going to be dragging as it is. I can't spend the next three hours at the station. I've got to get a little sleep."

"How much sleep are you going to get knowing there's some screwball out there with his sights on you?"

The color drained from Liz's face. "Good point."

"You want to come home with me and leave from there in the morning?"

"No, I've got to wash my hair and pack a few things. I'll be lucky to get to bed by midnight. But how would you feel about crashing here? You can have the bedroom. I'll take the couch."

Suzanne nodded. "I guess I could do that. I'll call Rob."

"You'll miss the game."

"Like I care about a football game. What about the police?"

"I'll go as soon as I get back." She walked to the cupboard and pulled out a bottle of red wine. "On the bright side, I'm getting out of this garbage heap of a town for a few days."

●

The second storm began around midnight, blowing into a cloudburst by the time Liz tossed her bags into her car at five-fifteen Friday morning. When she pulled in front of Germaine's fifteen minutes later, the wind was howling. Rain hammered her umbrella as she stepped out on the curb. She used the key Sonnie had given her to let herself in.

The smell of dust and plaster mixed with a heavy musky fragrance. Once her eyes adjusted to the darkness, she passed the photos on the wall and turned to enter the lounge. She was able to guide herself by a narrow stream of light coming from the bar area. The cleaning crew must have already arrived, she thought, glad to know she wasn't the only one who worked offbeat hours. In the lounge, she cut a path between the tables, heading toward the office in the back.

She flipped on the light. Her ticket lay on the table by the desk. *Way to go, Hanlon.* If scientists figured out a way to remove the brain from the skull and leave it somewhere, she was in trouble. She packed the ticket inside her purse, and was looking around for a pen and paper when she heard an odd scraping noise. Workers moving furniture around? She scribbled a note to Sonnie, telling him she'd booked the hair stylist from the David Letterman show for the guys, hoping that would soothe his nerves.

Something was being dragged in the lounge. She started out from behind the desk, forgetting she'd left a drawer open. Her knee crashed into it, she fell backward against a metal typing table, knocking it against a wall.

"Ugh!" she cried out. She rubbed her knee, dropped the note on Sonnie's computer keyboard, tossed her purse over her shoulder and limped toward the lounge.

Something dropped with a thud. As she entered the lounge, the back door clicked shut.

The room was dark. The night light that had lit her way in was gone. She moved slowly, cursing herself for never noticing the light switches in the lounge, following the curve of the bar, inching her way forward. Her next step sent her stumbling. She felt bricks beside a pile of two-by-fours at the base of the partially dismantled brick wall. As she started to step over them, the tip of her shoe hit something soft.

The darkness blinded her. She bent down and reached around until her hand bumped against a grainy chunk of wood. She groped sideways, searching in the dark until her fingers skimmed a long mass of smooth, ribbon-like fibers, the silky texture out of place in the construction debris. Reflexively, she brushed her hand against something round, fleshy, warm.

She yanked back her hand. It was sticky, damp. Her breath caught in her throat. She struggled to her feet, groped her way back to the bar, and retraced her steps to the office doorway. Inside, she fumbled for the light switch, snapped it on, and gaped at the blotchy dark stain on her palm. She spun around, and stepped into the lounge again where the light shone on a small area of the bar and a few tables. Her eyes cut across the room.

A woman's body lay in the rubble, her arms and legs draped unnaturally, her dark hair caught in a heap of plaster and nails. Blood oozed onto the debris.

Slowly, Liz realized she was looking at the body of her cousin, Gina McCurdy. A strangled sound erupted from Liz's throat, a scream that would not resound. She reeled backwards. Her hand caught a bar stool for support. She sucked in her breath and pushed her voice into action.

The sickening stillness wrapped around her. The rain pounded the roof. "Is anyone there?"

Paralyzed, yet afraid to stay where she was, she felt trapped by what seemed like an ugly nightmare. A phone. Where was the phone? The office. She backed away from the body.

At Sonnie's desk, she reached for the phone and dialed 9-1-1.

In the seconds she waited for an operator to pick up, shocky tremors rattled through her body. When she spoke, her voice quivered as she recited her name, the name of the club, and the word, "body," before doubling over with nausea.

Four

Detective Tim Milleski parted his black hair low over his left ear, and plastered the few remaining strands over the top of his bald head. His bulging, brown eyes gave him the look of an inquisitive bulldog. His pronounced lisp made his speech difficult to understand. His partner, Detective John Robbins, was a rotund three hundred pounds, a girth that made him appear shorter than his five-foot-eight height. His breathing was labored as he rose from examining Gina's body.

Members of the Crime Scene Unit hovered around the body, taking samples and photos.

Robbins pulled off his gloves and nodded toward Milleski. "Did anyone get ahold of the owner yet?"

"He's on his way," Milleski said, looking around the room. "Hell of a wake up call for him."

The front door burst open. Lt. Medorie Wahlberg strode in, announcing her jurisdiction with quick, abrupt steps. Her straight blonde hair, pulled back from her face, was held in place by plain bobby pins. Her face had a youthful plumpness to it, and her smile—on the rare occasions when she did smile— was sweet and pleasing, the opposite of her brusque manner.

Medorie Wahlberg had graduated from the police academy with high marks. The criminal matters of mystifying details were her forte, the arenas in which she honed her powers of detection. Her impeccable record had shot her to lieutenant ahead of her peers, but when it came to diplomacy and "people skills," she relied on her detectives who showed more aptitude in dealing sensitively with actual people.

She conferred with the CSU, then moved into a corner where Milleski filled her in on details he'd jotted in his notebook.

"Did you locate the family yet?" she asked.

"Thtill working on it," Milleski said.

Lt. Wahlberg turned toward the far end of the bar where Liz sat stiffly, her face turned away from the body. "That the woman who called it in?"

"Yes," Robbins said, "the victim's cousin."

"She see anyone?"

"No, Lieutenant. Just said she heard noises," Robbins said.

Wahlberg started in Liz's direction just as the front door opened. Murky light from the street lit the walkway as Sonnie hurried toward them, arms pumping. He spotted Liz at the end of the bar and headed toward her, then drew back when he reached the body. "Sweet lord." He knelt close to Gina.

Milleski hastened toward him. "Don't touch anything, thir. Are you Mr. Tucks?"

"Yes. What happened here—?"

"Gina McCurdy worked for you?"

"Yes." Sonnie pushed past Milleski, draping his arms around Liz. "My God, Liz, are you alright? This ... how did this happen?"

"Mr. Tucks, we have to ask you some questions," Milleski said.

"Yes, yes, anything." Sonnie took a bar stool, then jumped off it again.

"Over here, please," Milleski said, indicating a far corner where Lt. Wahlberg and Detective Robbins stood. "The lieutenant would like a word."

"I'll be right back," Sonnie said to Liz, then followed Milleski.

Lt. Wahlberg didn't wait for an introduction. "Mr. Tucks, are you the sole owner of this establishment?"

"Yes," he said, his fingers tracing through his hair.

"Are your employees in the habit of staying in the club after hours?"

Sonnie frowned. "Of course not. I know the law."

"Why was Ms. McCurdy here at five-thirty in the morning?" Wahlberg asked.

"I have no idea."

"When did you last see her?"

Sonnie hesitated. "Night before last. She was off last night."

Milleski scribbled in his notebook.

"What's the relationship between Ms. Hanlon and the victim?"

"Liz and Gina are cousins. They were cousins."

"They get along?" she asked.

"What? Of course," Sonnie said, "they were family."

"Families fight."

"That silly thing the other night wasn't a fight," Sonnie said. "Liz never would have hit Gina. It was just a spat. We were all drinking together an hour later, happy as pigs in—"

"What was the spat about?" Wahlberg asked, stone-faced.

"Oh, who knows? They're just different, the two of them, but believe me, it wasn't anything." Sonnie rubbed his arms. "It's freezing in here. Is this going to take long? I could turn the heat on."

"It will be awhile," Milleski said. "The CSU has a lot to do."

"The 'thee-eth-you?'" Sonnie repeated, trying to decode Milleski's words. He gave up and went to adjust the temperature. He stopped at the service bar, filled the coffee pot with water, and snapped the button to 'on', then went to Liz and took her hand.

"Oh honey, you're like an ice cube," he said.

Milleski joined them. "Where have you been this morning, thir?"

Sonnie looked up. "Me? Home."

"Anyone with you?"

"My wife, Marilyn. Look, what happened here?"

Milleski turned back to Liz. "Ms. Hanlon said she heard noises, and came out of the office. Why don't you go on, Ms. Hanlon?"

Liz felt numb, as if encased in cellophane, distanced from the room. Time seemed sluggish, sounds distorted. Any second she expected to wake up in her own bed.

"You thought you'd heard workers, is that right, Ms. Hanlon?" Milleski prompted. "Then the back door closing?"

"What workers?" Sonnie asked.

"I thought it was the construction workers, or the cleaning crew," she said.

"Heavy rain causes all kinds of thounds," Milleski said.

"It wasn't the rain."

Robbins took the stool near Liz. "What about a purse?" he asked. "Car keys? See anything like that?"

Liz shook her head. "I really didn't look."

"Where were you when you heard the back door close?" Milleski asked.

Being asked to dissect the scene moment by moment brought brutal clarity to Gina's death. Tears filled her eyes. "I ... I was out here by then. I came into the dark lounge and I heard it shut."

The coffee pot spurted. Sonnie poured the entire pot into several cups. Steam wafted up, the aroma of fresh coffee filled the room. He came around the bar and handed a mug to Liz.

"Here, this should warm you up. At least it covers up that perfume smell."

"Perfume—" She raised her eyes as the steam encircled her face. In a moment, she began to shiver, a contrast to the warm liquid she was holding. The shaking grew more violent. She held the mug out in front of her to keep from spilling on herself.

Sonnie grabbed her cup and set it down. "Detective, she's losing it. Could we do this later?" He pulled her into his arms. "Oh, Liz, I'm so sorry you had to be the one."

"It's imperative we get the details while they're fresh," Milleski said. "The killer may still be out there."

A stretcher was brought in. Liz watched Gina's body being placed on it. "Look!" she said, pointing to the lines in the powdery construction debris. "I told you. Drag marks. Someone dragged her. That's what I heard."

Milleski examined the marks, conferring with Robbins and the medical examiner.

Early morning grayness shone in the room as Tony Perdusian rushed in. The door slammed behind him. He drew up abruptly in front of the stretcher. "My God."

"Excuse me, sir," Robbins said, hurrying toward him. "Who are you?"

Tony's face was ashen, his eyes bloodshot. He dabbed a handkerchief at the perspiration on his forehead.

Sonnie stepped between them. "This is my partner, Tony Perdusian. I called him from my car on the way over here."

Robbins' eyes narrowed. "You said you were the sole owner."

"I own the restaurant, but Tony and I are involved in a new joint venture here at the club. Music shows."

Robbins looked at Tony. "What's your relationship to the victim, Mr. Perdusian?"

"Just business."

"Where were you earlier?"

"Home. In Malibu."

"Wait here." Robbins moved off to speak with Milleski in private.

Tony whispered to Sonnie, "They're not implying that Liz did this, are they?"

"No. That's crazy."

"I can call a friend of mine. A criminal attorney."

"Liz's brother is an attorney."

"I said a criminal attorney."

"She doesn't need a damn criminal attorney."

Lt. Wahlberg dragged a chair, placed it in front of Liz, sat down, and snapped open her notebook. She nodded for the detectives to join her, then gestured for Tony and Sonnie to take the bar stools nearby. "Sit, please."

"Ms. Hanlon," she said, "you were here to pick up a plane ticket at five-thirty in the morning?"

"Yes. My plane left at seven."

"Do you have the ticket?"

Liz withdrew it from her purse and handed it to her.

Wahlberg gave it a cursory glance, then went back to the notes in front of her. "Did the victim know you were going to Boston?"

"I told her, yes."

"You two agreed to meet here this morning?"

Liz frowned. "Of course not."

"When was the last time you saw her?"

"We started to get re-acquainted two nights ago right here."

"Tell me what happened from the time you arrived until the time you found the body."

Liz repeated everything she had already told the detectives.

"Where did you leave this note for Sonnie?"

"On his computer keyboard."

Lt. Wahlberg glanced at Detective Robbins, who nodded. "We have it, Lieutenant."

Wahlberg looked back at Liz. "Let me see your leg."

She raised the leg of her slacks. Wahlberg glanced at the blotchy red and black bruise.

"Then what did you do?"

"I walked into the lounge."

"Why did you use the pathway in front of the bar that time, instead of cutting across the room as you did on your way in?"

"The room was totally black. I had to use the bar as a guide."

Lt. Wahlberg pushed a pencil and paper toward Liz. "Sketch it out. Indicate the path you followed on your way in, then the one you took to leave."

Liz drew the bar at one end, the stage, the tables and booths, leaving empty the area leading to the back door.

Wahlberg studied the sketch. No one spoke.

Sonnie began to pace again.

Tony stared at the ceiling, the door, the carpet.

Lt. Wahlberg pointed to the open space leading to the back door on Liz's sketch. "Is this where you went to look for the cleaning people, Ms. Hanlon?"

"No. I never went beyond the bar."

The lieutenant's pencil tapped several times. "What did you and the victim fight about the other night?"

Liz looked up abruptly. "Fight? Gina and I didn't fight."

Wahlberg's eyes fixed on her. "You were ready to throw a punch at her."

The words between herself and Gina had been forgotten. "Gina found me...irritating."

"Why's that?"

"She thought I didn't approve of her friends, her lifestyle."

"So instead of slugging her then, you put it on hold till tonight?"

"Lieutenant!" Sonnie cried.

Liz blinked. "I could never do this," she said, her voice quivering.

Wahlberg turned toward the detectives. "You get through to the family yet?"

"Just now, Lieutenant," Robbins said.

Mention of the family brought childhood memories rushing back for Liz. Vivid images of playing on the floor with Gina, of sitting together at family dinners, of wearing each other's clothes, the time Aunt Irene had scolded them for painting the walls with her lipstick. "Poor Aunt Irene," she murmured. "Gina is her only child."

Lt. Wahlberg turned to Tony. "Mr. Perdusian, were you in your car when Mr. Tucks called you?"

"No. I was home, on the Internet with my business partners."

Sonnie started to interject something, then held back, easing onto a stool.

"Who are these partners?"

"Investors. Financial backers for the concerts Sonnie and I are putting on. Occasionally, we have to raise additional capital."

"How do you do that?"

"We might approach corporations that stand to gain from the advertising of their products. The manufacturers of musical instruments for example, or record companies."

"I'll need to see all records concerning those business partnerships as well as those concerning your partnership with Mr. Tucks." She turned to Sonnie. "Your club will be closed during the investigation."

"Closed?" He jumped to his feet. "We have to meet our deadline. Millions of dollars are at stake. The money's been paid, the acts are signed. I can't even describe what it's like dealing with network executives! Please. This deal is critical. If this thing doesn't go, I'll lose my business."

Lt. Wahlberg showed no signs of even hearing him.

"It isn't just the broadcasts, Lieutenant," Sonnie said. "My club's on shaky ground. See, I planned to keep Germaine's open during most of the remodeling, until we're ready to pull out that brick wall." He pointed to it.

The look on Wahlberg's face was rock-hard. "It's the law, Mr. Tucks. Do you have any enemies? Someone who might want to ruin your plans?"

"By killing Gina? That's crazy."

"Yes," she said dryly. "I'll need a list of all your employees, delivery people, everyone you deal with."

"Lieutenant, my employees are my friends. They've been with me for years. Nobody would do this just to get at me. I mean, who the hell would do something like this?"

Lt. Wahlberg said, "That's what I'm asking you." In a sudden move, she snapped her notebook shut. "You can go for now. We'll be wanting to speak with you again, Ms. Hanlon."

●

Liz stood on the sidewalk in front of Germaine's as Gina's body was put in the Medical Examiner's wagon. The doors slammed shut, making her jump.

A thin veil of brightness peeked through the clouds.

Sonnie glanced up. "It almost stopped raining."

Tony joined them as the wagon pulled away. "I imagine we could all use some sleep," he said.

"I'll drive you home, Liz," Sonnie said, then thought better of it. "Maybe you shouldn't be alone right now—"

Tires squealed against the curb as a black Mercedes slammed to a halt. The driver, impeccably dressed in a dark brown suit and silk tie, jumped out. "Liz!"

Carl Hanlon raced toward them, arms outstretched. His light brown hair was gray at the temples, and, unlike Liz, he had inherited their father's slenderness. A stroll through a law library was enough to keep his weight down.

"Liz, why didn't you call me?" His words trailed off when he saw her dazed expression. "Oh, Liz, are you okay?" He hugged her and slid a swatch of damp hair off her cheek. "I called Mom to see if your plane got in, and she told me."

"They let me call her so she wouldn't go to the airport."

"You should have called me. Our mother," he explained to the others, "she worries. Liz, you should have had an attorney with you."

"Can we get out of here now?"

"Of course," he said, turning to the others. He shook Sonnie's hand. "If there's anything I can do, Sonnie, let me know."

"I might need your help getting my place opened if this thing drags on." He gestured toward Tony. "This is my new partner, Tony Perdusian."

They shook hands. "Carl Hanlon. Terrible thing, this morning."

"Nice to meet you. Yes, awful."

Carl turned back to Liz. "Are you headed home? I think we should talk."

She withdrew her car keys from her purse. "Now? I just want to lie down."

"Just a few minutes," he said. "Why don't you ride with me? We'll pick up your car later."

Tony said, "I'll drop it at your apartment. Sonnie can follow me."

Carl nodded. "Thanks. 'Appreciate that."

"It's no problem," Tony said, taking Liz's hand and pressing it inside his. "This is a nightmare you've been through. If you need anything, I'm always around."

"Thanks, Tony, that's very nice of you."

Five

Carl Hanlon sat at the wooden table in his sister's tiny kitchen, watching her stare at the coffee-maker as it released puffs of steam. The carafe was full, and he wondered how long it would be before she reacted. It was not like Liz to be locked within herself.

"Did you cut your hair?" he asked.

"You noticed."

"Looks good. It curves around your shoulders."

"I was going for the sultry look," she said, flatly.

"Getting ready for Mom?"

"Bingo." She filled two cups, then reached up and pushed the pink curtains into gathers along the curtain rod. "Get some light in here."

The rain had stopped, sunlight streamed in.

"This is so unbelievable," Carl said. "Someone in our own family murdered. Do you think Jerry will fly out for the funeral?"

"He should, he's been Gina's father since she was eleven, but I don't know. Gina said he and Aunt Irene separated last year. Did you know she's been living here for nearly a year?"

"Aunt Irene? No."

"That's what Gina said. I'd have gone to see her if I'd known."

"Seems strange she didn't contact us."

"Maybe she didn't want us to know she'd left Jerry," she said. "You remember much about him?"

Carl shook his head. "No. We were too young. Tell me what happened when you found Gina."

"When I touched her, it was like my whole body was weighted down with cement. No matter what was going on around me, I was stuck for the longest time in that spot."

"What'd you mean, 'going on around you'?"

She explained about the noises she'd heard. "Sonnie said the cleaning service doesn't arrive till ten, and the construction workers were tied up on another job. They weren't expected till noon. I heard noises, though, and it wasn't the rain."

"What about the door itself? Did anyone check to see if it

was locked?"

"It wasn't. The police checked it."

"So that's how the killer got away. Which means—Jeez, you were in the office while the killer was still there! Liz, I told you before I think you ought to have a gun. With the hours you keep, and the crackpots out on the road—"

"I know, I know. I'm thinking about it."

He reached across the counter for the coffee pot, and divided the last of the coffee in both cups. "I feel strongly about this."

"Obviously. But then you always did drink a lot of coffee. Should I make another pot?"

"Ah, humor. You're doing better." He checked his watch. "No, I'll drink this, then I've got to get to the office. You'll need a permit to carry a gun," he said. "I'll talk to that Lieutenant Wallpaper."

"Wahlberg."

"Wallpaper's better."

"You know her?" Liz asked.

"We've met. She's got all the smoothness of alligator skin. I'll see if I can convince her. You're in danger if the killer thinks you can identify him."

"Boy, I never thought I'd be packing fire power in my purse. I wonder if things would have been different if Gina had carried a gun."

"We'll never know," he said, looking out at the sunshine. "Tell me about Tony. He seems kind of quiet. For a show biz person. Is he always like that?"

She shrugged. "I just met him, but Sonnie swears he's a genuine guy. They grew up together. They're very tight. He does seem to like to talk, though. Mostly about himself."

"Yeah? What's he got to talk about?"

"I only know him by reputation, and from the stories he and Sonnie were telling the other night. Something about him getting his start in the business when Sonnie's Uncle Booker owned the club, and how he built himself up from nothing. Twice, I think."

"Wait a minute," Carl said. "This isn't the same Tony Perdusian who handled all those rock stars when we were kids?"

"You were never a kid," she said. "Yeah, that's him. He started out managing rock 'n' roll bands in the '70s. He made a name for himself because he was so good, and because he was so young. How come you recognize his name? I didn't."

"While you were still into Barbie, I was following all the big names, and how their managers got them that way. The name Perdusian kept showing up in the papers."

Liz was amazed. "Gee, I thought I did a pretty good job of keeping up on the business."

"I had a collection of rock 'n' roll magazines hidden away in my closet, remember? I read everything about the stars."

"Stars like who?"

"Big Rockin' Martha was my favorite," he said. "Pepper Marvin & The Love Knots, too. Janey Sylvestri. I played their records all the time."

"I remember Betsy Forrester and some pretty steamy windows."

"Those songs are responsible for my best back-seat action."

"Spare me."

"So Sonnie grew up with this guy?"

"When his uncle owned Germaine's, Sonnie and Tony used to cut school to hang out at the club. His uncle would sneak them in the back, and let them hear the music all night if they wanted."

"So the idea of live shows was hatched way back then.

Well, it's too bad you had to lose your big chance."

"It's terrible all around," she said. "Tragic about Gina, of course, but I'll never get another chance like that if I live to be a thousand. And poor Sonnie might lose his whole business."

"You don't think Tony will be able to reschedule?"

"Not as long as Germaine's is closed. It's disastrous for Sonnie. He's broke. The concerts were going to bail him out."

"Germaine's? In trouble? I thought it was always packed?"

"He told me that two years ago the New York store— Germaine's East—had a huge fire," she explained. "The fire was set, but they never found the arsonist. It cost Sonnie hundreds of thousands to restore, and the insurance only covered about half. Then, just as they were having their grand reopening, the Miami store got hit big time with some kind of invasion robbery. Suspects came in and made off with everyone's jewelry."

"Oh, yeah, I remember that," Carl said. "A lot of famous people for an industry awards dinner, dressed to the max."

"Again, Sonnie paid out a lot. Some picky detail about the exact type of insurance he carried. He had to drain funds from Germaine's West to cover it. For the last few years business has been slower than usual, so you can see why he was so thrilled when Tony came up with this plan."

She put down her cup. "I suppose if the murderer is found quickly, Sonnie would have a chance to meet the deadline."

"Sometimes these investigations drag on for months, Liz."

"What if we did a little investigating on our own?" Liz said. "Remember that guy who did research for you awhile back? Maybe we could call him."

"Gabriel? He's still with me, but he's buried under with the case work we've got already."

"Not him," she said, "that seedy character who looks like

he never goes out in daylight. You always said he's the best."

"Enos. I had to let him go. He was too weird to have around the office. That long, greasy hair, and the constant chain-smoking—"

"You fired him because of his looks? Isn't that against the law?"

"The guy never bathed, for godssake!"

"Where's he working now?"

"Probably under a rock."

"Which rock?" She gave him an insistent stare.

"I heard he's on his own now."

"A freelancer."

"What else? No one'll hire him." He glanced at the wall clock. "I better get to the office. Oh, I almost forgot, I picked up that cell phone you ordered. I'll bring it by tomorrow."

"A cell phone in a thirteen-year-old car. What's wrong with this picture?"

"It's for more than your car. Keep it with you all the time. You're out alone at night. It's a necessity these days."

"A phone and a gun. I'll need a bigger purse."

He picked up his briefcase and walked into the living room. At the front door he stopped and took a long look around the room.

"Hey, I like what you've done with this place," he said.

"I got a few new glossies of the cars since you were here last," she said, indicating the framed pictures of classic autos on one wall.

"You and your passion for antique cars," he said, peering at a photo of a black 1933 Duesenberg with maroon leather seats.

"Granddad took that." She pointed to another photo above the television. "This is my favorite. Dad behind the wheel of his dream car, a '36 Auburn boattail speedster. Taken the day before he died."

"I always wondered what happened to this picture."

"I put it away till it felt right to put it up."

"Got any more?"

"Of Dad? A few. I'll dig them out for you."

"Why don't you come for dinner on Sunday, and bring them with you? Reggie's making your favorite."

"Italian calories?"

"The way they should be."

"I'll be there."

"You sure you don't want to throw a few things in a suitcase and hide out for the weekend? You've already got other players filling in for you at Brogino's, and Sam thinks you're in Boston."

"Yeah, until he sees the News."

"Why don't you catch up on some rest?"

"I want to visit Aunt Irene, and I should spend some time working with Sherice. Maybe Sunday I can get the band to rehearse. I've got a few new tunes we haven't tried yet."

"Okay, but if you don't want to be alone, we've got plenty of room."

"Thanks. I'm okay. I want to stay busy till the funeral."

Six

I rene McCurdy's thin frame nearly vanished when she sank into the deep beige cushions of the sofa. Liz perched on the end of a matching love seat, glancing around at the complimentary color arrangements of her aunt's small condo in Studio City. The decorative scheme used soft shades of green and blue to offset the beige sofa and love seat.

The smell of alcohol filled the room. Irene's face was puffy, her eyes swollen, her complexion mottled.

"Mom sends her love," Liz said, "and her condolences. She'd have come herself but, you know, she doesn't fly any more."

Irene barely nodded. "Your mom and I, we were close once. Before your dad died."

Liz recalled that her mother had withdrawn when her father died, cutting off almost all communication with the rest of the family.

"I was offended when she shut us out," Irene said, "but now, losing my baby, it all makes sense." Her eyes filled with tears. "You tell her I said that, Liz."

"I will. I know this is a terrible time, Aunt Irene. I'll do anything I can to help."

"Most times are terrible."

The bitter words stung Liz.

"Gina'd been living out here for two years now," Irene said, "but you two didn't spend much time together."

"We had different friends. But Gina stayed at my apartment when she first moved here," Liz said. "Then she found a roommate she really liked."

"You want a drink?" Irene asked. Irene rose and rocked backward, then sat back down on the sofa.

"No, thanks, I'm fine. Gina and I were about to work together again—"

She stopped, wanting to kick herself for reminding her aunt of what might have been.

Liz moved over and took her hand. The bones in Irene's hands were so frail Liz was afraid they might splinter. "She was a beautiful girl. Everyone loved her. And she was happy."

"Was she? It was too short, though."

"Yes. Way too short."

"You should have something. Soda? Coffee machine's in the kitchen, but I didn't make any. Gave it up for Lent." Irene managed to pull herself out of the cushions and onto her feet. Unsteady at first, she gained her balance and went to the refrigerator. She dropped ice into a glass, then took a bottle of V.O. from the counter and filled it. "Help yourself."

Irene returned to the sofa. "Tell me about her."

What could she tell a mother about her own daughter? "She was well liked, she had lots of friends—"

"Bull. She had a 'side' life. That's why you two weren't close. Didn't think I knew about it, did you? I've still got a few friends."

"Well, she worked as a waitress—"

"I know that. I also know she fooled around here and there, got herself in trouble a few times. Not that kind of trouble," she added, "no little ones, 'least none that I ever heard about. She drank too much, too, but then that's to be expected, considering the family genes."

Liz walked to the window and gazed out at the sunny morning, thrusting her hands in her jeans pockets as she leaned on the window sill. In her pocket, her fingers touched the edge of a photograph. She drew it out.

"A few days before ... uh, some of us got together at the club. Gina was with us, and Sonnie, the owner, snapped this picture. I thought you might like to have it."

Irene stared at the photo. After a few seconds, Liz started to slip it back in her pocket, but Irene reached out and took it. The picture shook in her hand; she gazed at it intently.

Outside, gardeners revved their leaf blowers. Ordinary life was all around them. Liz felt suspended in the silence of the room.

"Why'd she'd have to go back to Germaine's?" Irene moaned. "She was doing fine at the King's Row."

"Maybe she decided Germaine's was a better job after all.

She had a lot of friends there." Liz explained about the plans for the broadcasts. "I'm sure the TV exposure would have brought in a great deal of money."

Irene snorted, "Exposure! Never did a bit 'a good for anybody." She sipped her drink. "Gina was adopted, did you know that?"

Liz was astonished. "What do you mean?"

"Oh, she was my child, but when I met Jerry, she was almost eleven. That age, it's hard. There were things I couldn't give her, but being with Jerry made them possible. She liked him pretty well, at least in the beginning."

"And he adopted her?"

"Right. He said if he was going to be her father, he wanted it to be legal."

"Good for him."

"Good for her, 'else she'd 'a never had anything. Her real father, he never had anything. Not that he didn't try, 'cause he had talent. And he loved his daughter. Loved me, too. But he was just another musician with dreams. Always looking for exposure."

"I heard stories as a kid about Uncle Victor's wonderful voice. And such charisma."

"The family had high hopes for him."

Liz settled deeper into the sofa. "No one talked about Victor after he died, and I never really knew what happened."

"You were a kid; no reason for you to know. I got remarried, and at least we were done with music shysters after that. You'd 'a thought Gina would have steered clear of those types after what happened to her daddy, but maybe I protected her so much she couldn't spot 'em like I can."

"I wasn't aware of Gina being involved with any music business people," Liz said. "Do you mean Sonnie? He owns the club. He was a good friend to Gina."

"The whole phony bunch of 'em," Irene said. "Them and their made-up world of dreams. That's what got my baby killed."

Liz waited for Irene to explain, but she became silent, sunk in her thoughts.

"Aunt Irene, maybe you'd like to get out for awhile. I saw a nice little cafe on Ventura Boulevard. We could have lunch."

Irene held up her glass "I'm having it," she said. Then, to soften the edge in her voice, she said, "I know what you're trying to do, Lizzie, and I appreciate it, but I've got to deal with this my own way."

"I'm sorry I didn't see you before this, Aunt Irene. I didn't know you'd moved here, or even that you and Jerry had split up."

"It's been over a year."

"Well, you're not alone any more."

"Yes, I am," she said, staring hard at Liz. "You'd think I'd be used to it, wouldn't you? I've been alone for a long time.

Seven

Enos Kaperstein remained seated and rolled his chair across the linoleum in his studio apartment. His long, thick hair fell in matted, greasy clumps, unwashed for weeks, maybe months. His skin was sallow and heavily pock-marked. Even his eyes looked dirty. His shoulders, parked on his thin frame, sank inward, giving him the emaciated look of a person who'd rather work at his computer than eat.

Liz stepped back as Enos rolled from a small computer to a larger one near the window. It occurred to her that she had never seen him standing, only sliding this same leather computer chair around as he worked.

Close to him, she smelled the sweet and sour odor of his body. No wonder Carl stopped working with him.

Enos's apartment was one large room crammed with computers and electronic equipment, a single unmade bed with stained sheets crumpled on top, and a tiny kitchenette. Dirty coffee mugs, plastic glasses, and fast food containers filled the sink. On one wall, a built-in bookcase was stuffed with papers, files, computer manuals, and gadgets she could not identify. The place smelled of dust, nicotine, and spoiled food.

Enos spoke without taking his eyes off the computer. "So, blue-eyes, your cousin was snuffed, you're getting death threats, your whole career's about to fall in the dumper, and you come to Enos because you know I'm the only one who can make sense of it all."

"Something like that," she said. "The police are investigating Gina's murder, but I was hoping there'd be something more you could do."

"There's always something more I can do," he said. He turned and let his gaze trail down Liz's entire body.

"I meant about the murder."

Enos ignored her last comment. "You remember the story that broke last month about the phony doctor in Orange County? Cops had been trailing this guy for two years; couldn't get him. Who d'ya think wrapped that one up?" He focused on the computer screen again. "Tell me something about your cousin you forgot to tell the cops."

She'd already told him much about Gina, Sonnie, the new

concerts at the club. "I can't think of anything more right now."

"What about Gina's friends?"

"She had a roommate she was pretty close to. I could talk to her."

"How about her family?"

"There's just Aunt Irene, and Jerry McCurdy, Irene's ex-husband."

"Previous employment?" Enos asked.

"Gina worked at the King's Row before coming back to Germaine's."

"I'll start there. I like to dig up background info on everyone concerned. Here," he said, pulling a pad of paper out from under a pile of disorganized files. "Write down their full names. Make sure you spell 'em right. Even family. Especially family."

Liz began to write.

"Now tell me more about the cards. Anything remarkable about this creep?"

"It's the 'eternal peace' thing that turns my stomach."

"It does sound like our boy resides on the far end of the bell curve. What else?"

"I was hoping if you found Gina's killer the cards would stop."

"Assuming they're related to the murder. Are they?"

"Enos, if I knew that, I wouldn't be coming to you! I found the first one a few days before she was killed, but that's the only connection I can see."

"I'll start with her private life."

"Thanks for doing this, Enos."

"There's the little matter of my fee."

Her pen froze. "I should have asked what you charge before we started."

65

"But you didn't." His droopy eyes lifted to look directly at her. "Your brother know you're here?"

"No."

He looked off. "Let's see, you're a musician so you don't have any dough."

She started to object, then stopped. "I'll get Carl's help."

"'Course, this is family," Enos said, his hand flipping back and forth as he considered the many sides of the issue. "Naturally, a person of my breeding and unique understanding of such sensitive issues deserves to be compensated. These special characteristics are what set me apart from your grade-B-type researchers."

"Bottom line it, Enos."

"This murder happening at the place of your new employment, well, that creates a kind of dual need where you're concerned. You don't get this murder cleared up fast, you lose your big chance."

"I meant, bottom line your price."

"On the other hand, if I let Germaine's close up just because L.A.'s finest can't solve this thing, you'll never be able to afford me, and we both lose. So I'll tell you what. With the exception of any large, unexpected expenses that may pop up—"

"Which you will inform me of immediately."

"Without question. That exception in mind," he said, "I'll do this one as a favor."

"Oh, Enos, that's great. I really appreciate it."

He held up a hand. "But I want something in return."

Her eyes snapped to the filthy sheets waded in a ball on the bed.

"You get your brother to throw me some work. The meaty stuff, not the grunt work any beginning researcher can do. I'm a consultant now. I charge well for my services because I deliver where others fail."

She wondered what magic she would have to perform to get Carl to go along with this. "It's a deal."

She wrote three phone numbers on a slip of paper and handed it to him. "Being alone at my place is starting to get to me so I'll probably split my nights between Carl's and Suzanne Becklin's. Both numbers are there. The last one's my cell phone."

As she opened the door, a large cockroach scurried across the floor.

"Pleasure doing business with you, Enos." She hurried out.

●

Liz sat in her car outside Enos's apartment, thinking of how few details she'd been able to tell him about Gina's life. She listened to the birds fluttering in the trees beside her, their songs sweet and clear, their lives so free and uncomplicated.

She'd always thought of Gina as a free spirit. Gina had had a knack for reading her customers, too, knowing just how far she could entice them with her feminine charms, but she never seemed to think beyond tomorrow. She was the first one out the door if someone yelled, "party!" Liz wished she could be as uninhibited, and live only in the moment.

She realized she knew little about Gina. Had her basic impression been wrong? Maybe she'd been too judgmental after their disagreement. It was time to find out more. She'd told Enos she'd talk to Gina's roommate. She dialed information and got the number.

●

Liz's tires crunched on the hardened berries that had fallen from an overhanging tree as she pulled into the driveway of the two-story house on La Perla Avenue. The first story was faced with red brick; a narrow balcony ran along the second, decorated with flowers. A large mound of household items were piled at the edge of the sidewalk waiting for a trash pick-up. She wondered if she had the right address. She headed for the front door, but before she reached the porch, the door swung open. Detective Milleski stepped out, followed by his partner, Detective Robbins.

Paige Alvarez was dressed in jeans and a long button-down shirt with rolled-up sleeves. Her black hair was cut in a short 'bob'. She held the screen door open. "Thanks for checking the place out," she said.

Robbins handed her a card. "If you notice anything missing you can call us at that number."

"It's probably a good idea to stay with family while—" Milleski stopping when he saw Liz.

"Hi," Liz said. The detectives stared at her. "I just came by to see if Paige needed any help."

"Do I know you?" Paige asked.

"I'm Liz Hanlon. Gina's cousin."

"Oh, yes. You called."

"Looks like you're moving."

"I probably should. I've been robbed."

"A break-in," Milleski said. "Doesn't seem to be anything taken."

"They just tore the place up," Paige said.

"Why?" Liz asked.

"Hard to thay," Milleski said.

"Is it connected with Gina's murder? If they bothered to break in, why not take anything?"

"It's possible they found what they were looking for,"

Robbins said, "but Ms. Alvarez doesn't realize the item is gone."

Milleski started down the walkway. "If you need us again, you've got our cards. Ms. Hanlon? One question. Do you have a key to this residence?"

"Me? No."

"Just wondering, the victim being your cousin and all."

"No, I've never been here before."

Liz waited until the cops walked to the sidewalk, then she faced Paige through the screen door.

"This is a terrible way to meet," she began, "but let me start over. I'm Liz. I was hoping we could talk about Gina."

"Let me finish putting these things out," Paige said, wrestling a large box of broken dishes. As she struggled through the doorway, Liz grabbed the bottom of the box. They sidestepped along the walkway and hoisted the box onto the pile, then stood back to look at the heap of broken household goods.

"You want to come in for awhile?" Paige said. "I think the bums left me some coffee. Cups might be optional."

"Thanks." Liz followed her into what had been a well-decorated home. The sofa cushions were ripped, picture frames smashed, drawer contents tossed on the floor.

Liz gaped at the mess. "Did the police have any clues at all?"

Paige pushed things around in the cupboard and found two unmatched cups.

"The old man upstairs told the cops he heard noises early this morning. That's all."

"So you didn't stay here last night?"

"No. I didn't want to be here by myself. I went to my Mom's, came back awhile ago, and found this."

"No one should lose a friend like this," Liz said, thinking how devastated she would be to lose her life-long friend,

Suzanne.

"I miss her," Paige said.

"You were close a long time?"

"Since she moved to L.A. Gina was something."

Liz smiled, settling into the kitchen chair. "Tell me about her."

"You probably knew more than me."

"No. We were close when we were kids, but then she moved away, we both grew up, and we grew apart."

"Everybody liked Gina," Paige said. "She was a smart cookie."

"She was more fun than almost anyone else I knew. Sometimes I wish I could be that carefree, you know?"

Paige gazed at her a long moment. "It's true, she liked to party. But carefree? I don't know as I'd call her that. She was actually quite serious."

"Gina? Well, everyone's got a serious side, but I remember her being more fun-seeking than anything else."

Paige's lips curled into a knowing smile. "Had you fooled, too, didn't she?"

"She probably changed a lot without me knowing it."

"I don't mean that," Paige said. "I'm talking about the airhead act. That's what it was. An act. She did it to get favors, or make more tips. It worked, too."

Liz recalled being embarrassed a few times when Gina had put on an act for a man she'd just met.

Paige went on, "You know how comedians say they 'work a room'? Well, Gina worked her customers. She developed a believable dumb broad act when she got hired as a waitress. She'd flirt a little, give the lonely guys a hint that maybe she'd be interested, just maybe she'd go home with them—kept 'em all hanging. It made her a small fortune as a waitress."

"Surely she could've made as much money being herself?"

Paige shook her head. "Not a chance. I know what Gina made; I did her taxes. Believe me, she had it down to a science."

"She had a sharp tongue when she was pushed in a direction she didn't want to go. Did you ever have trouble determining when she was herself and when she wasn't?"

"I knew her pretty well."

"Did Gina ever talk about being in danger? Maybe some jerk at the club who wouldn't leave her alone?"

"Not many people gave Gina any crap. She carried a gun and she made that fact well known."

"She did? I didn't know."

"You weren't a threat. She let the news out to certain types so they wouldn't mess with her. She wouldn't have told her mother, either."

"What kind of relationship did they have?"

"Kind of unusual. Gina went a long time without talking to her mother. Then, recently, they started talking on the phone late at night for hours. It was almost too much."

"How so?"

"After those talks, Gina was in a gloomy mood all the next day. It happened over and over. Like they shared some private melancholy all their own. Very heavy."

"She never told you about it?"

"She said I wouldn't understand. I didn't press her. More coffee?"

She looked at her watch. "No, thanks. I should be going," she said, getting up. "If I can help you get things back together, let me know."

"Thanks. It's been nice meeting you. Gina always talked about you and your music. She was going to nab us front row

seats at the first broadcast."
   "It would have been great."
   "Maybe I'll get to hear you another time," Paige said.
   "I'll let you know when something good comes up."

Eight

Liz leaned in the rounded archway of Carl and Reggie's newly remodeled kitchen. To her, the house looked like something an ambitious artist might plan, yet it clearly reflected Reggie's talents. Copper utensils hung from the kitchen's dark-beamed ceiling. They had extended the space beyond the kitchen by adding a sunny conservatory with dozens of timber-framed windows.

Reggie was a highly-trained soprano with an established Los Angeles choir. Each Easter, the choir master featured his top three vocalists, and each year Reggie was one of them. She also sight-read choral music. Liz used to joke that if she only had one line to read at the piano, maybe she could sight-read at a glance too, but after trying to perform each other's music a few times, they had both admitted to a newfound respect for the other's abilities. "You can't get further apart than we are, and still be in music," Liz said.

Reggie hummed softly as she glided around the kitchen. She had an ageless beauty: long blonde hair, the golden-bronze skin of the perfect California girl in the '60s surfer songs. And Reggie had substance. Liz had admired her even before Carl married her.

Reggie filled her arms with salad vegetables and bumped the refrigerator door closed with a roll of her hip. "This is your first visit since we remodeled, Liz. I know the music business is crazy, but—"

"I keep hoping someday I'll have a real schedule, and I can make plans."

"The choral society is putting together a new women's chorus. I'll help you with your voice if you're interested."

There it was again, Liz thought, another dig implying "traditional" singing was real singing, while other styles did not command the same degree of skillfulness.

"Gee, Reg, things're pretty busy right now."

"I'm not suggesting you should sound like an opera singer, but developing a strong head voice will save you from losing your voice after just a few songs."

"The chops are not a problem anymore. That technique of imitating Julia Childs really works," she said, a little surprised.

"Of course you have to temper it some."

"My coach used to say, 'think of your voice like water running through a garden hose. If you squeeze the hose, only a trickle comes out, but all the pressure is behind it, and that's your breath support."

"High school music teachers spout off these terms, but they never tell you how to do it. I don't think they know themselves. Took me years to figure it out on my own."

"They always say, 'Put it in your nose!'"

Liz scoffed. "I could tell'em where to put it."

Reggie gave her a crooked smile. "You're not interested in the choir, are you?"

"Not a bit. No offense, Reggie, but I need music with a groove. Jazz and blues, ballads with drop-dead lyrics—that's the sound that does it for me."

Reggie chuckled. "Okay, hint taken." She eased an oblong baking dish from the oven and pulled back the cover. The aroma of Italian food filled the room.

"Lasagna!" Liz cried. "My all-time favorite."

"It needs a few more minutes. Take a look around the house. See what you think of the remodel job."

Liz strolled through it, drinking in the rich colors and luxurious paintings. Real paintings, not ten-dollar photos of fancy old cars. Skylights let the setting sun stream in across shiny-leaf plants.

It struck her how different she and Carl really were. Carl had always been conservative, carefully considering the outcome of every decision, while she had been the radical risk-taker. He was only four years older, but since childhood they had pursued completely different dreams. This home was Carl's elegant display of his accomplishments. In her world, it was her music that demonstrated her endeavors, determination, and her accomplishments. Her own display included a light blue hand-me-down sofa, a plain pine bookcase overflowing with music, and her most valued possession: a vintage upright piano built in 1912. She'd composed dozens of songs on it.

"Hey, Liz!" Carl called out.

She went back into the kitchen. Carl was setting plates on the table.

"Everything's ready," he said.

"And so am I," Liz chirped, taking a seat near the wall. "Thanks for letting me barge in on short notice."

"I wouldn't think you'd want to be alone until a suspect is brought in," he said.

He cut several pieces of steaming lasagna and placed them on the plates.

"Carl, you've got friends at the police station, right?" Liz asked. "Are there any details yet? Any reason for Gina even being there at that hour?"

"Not really, although I heard there are so many prints around the lounge they're having a hell of a time. They're still checking into Gina's private life."

"That ought to be interesting," she said. "Her roommate, Paige, told me Gina carried a gun."

He looked up. "She did? What else till she tell you?"

"Just that Gina played her customers for bigger tips, and she let the word out about the gun so no one would mess with her."

Carl put his fork down and looked into the distance.

"Why is that suspicious?" Reggie asked.

"May not be," he said, thoughtfully.

"But why did she have it?" Liz muttered. "Was she worried about some sick-o, but never got the chance to tell anyone?

We gotta find out more about her."

"My guess is we're going to discover her teenage years weren't exactly the Brady Bunch experience."

"How do you figure that?"

"I was thinking about Jerry," he said. "He isn't even coming to the funeral."

"He's leaving Aunt Irene to do this alone?" Liz said. "What a jerk. When I saw her, she was in such a state, slipping into the past, then snapping back to the present."

"What was she saying?" Carl asked.

"Something about music shysters bothering Uncle Victor years ago, and how the whole business is full of crooks. I think she meant Sonnie, but she'd had a lot to drink so it's hard to tell."

"You think she blames him for Gina's death?" Reggie said.

"Not really, but I think it's all blurred in her mind. They were a happy family once, so when she thinks of Gina, she remembers Uncle Victor."

"Poor lady," Carl said. "She's been though a lot."

"She sure has. It'll be interesting to see what Enos finds out."

"Enos? You went to see him?" Carl asked, surprised.

"You said Gabriel was tied up."

"How much are you paying him?"

"He cut me a deal."

"What kind of deal?" he asked, suspiciously.

She hedged. "He's the best, Carl, you said so yourself. He's working on his own now, and he's got every piece of equipment imaginable. The place is loaded with surveillance gadgets, high tech computer stuff, closets full of spy gear."

"What kind of deal?"

"He said he understands that this is family—"

"You don't make the kind of money he charges, Liz."

"No, but—"

"Uh-oh. What does he want?

"I ... sort of promised him you'd throw a little work his way."

"Oh, no!"

"He just wants in on the interesting cases, and that won't be hard to do. You're always saying Gabriel is overworked. Enos works at home now so he won't be in the office. Throw him a bone; bring him in on one case."

"This guy'll hang on till the next ice age."

"He's the best, though, isn't he?"

"He tell you that?"

"Several times."

Carl tossed his hand, resigned to it. "What the hell. He's right, he is the best. Okay, I guess I can find something for him. What's he doing so far?"

"Just background checks on everybody. I'll call him tomorrow for an update."

"The funeral starts at ten in the morning," Reggie said. "Should we all go together?"

"Not me," Carl said. "I'll be coming from the office."

"And I'll want to stick around afterward," Liz said. "See that Aunt Irene is alright. I'd better take my own car."

"Three cars it is," Reggie said. "What about tomorrow night? Any plans?"

"I promised my student, Sherice, I'd fit in some practice time with her. She won't admit it, but I think she's a little nervous about this recital coming up."

"You're putting on a recital now?" Reggie asked.

"This is Walter's baby. All his students are involved. I'm just helping out."

"I think it's wonderful that you donate your time like that," Reggie said. "Not many people would bother."

"They would if Walter McCain had gotten to them," Liz said. "It's a good thing he uses his powers of persuasion for good, 'cause that man knows how to pull on the old heart strings. A million times I've heard him say, 'Every kid should have the opportunity to explore the excitement and freedom of music whether their parents can pay or not.'"

Carl cut another slice of lasagna.

"Walter's one of a kind," Liz went on. "He's been running Musicland for years, taking in any kid who leaned his curious eyes against the glass window. So, when he asked me to donate one evening a week, how could I say no?"

"How'd you meet him?" Reggie asked.

"All the big band players talk about him," she said. "One day I stopped in to see how much sheet music he stocked, and we got to comparing stories."

"I'll bet he's got some good ones."

"They make my piano bar tales look like Amateur Hour. Walter was a hell of a sax player during the big band era. I think his name is on every recording of the Dorsey band, the Stan Kenton Orchestra, Count Bassie's, too. About twenty years ago, he decided he'd had enough of the road, so he opened MusicLand. Half his students are freebies, and some are pretty far advanced," she said, "although, I think Sherice is going to wind up being the star of this show."

"How can you get her ready with so much going on?" Reggie asked.

"She's almost ready now. She's such a inquisitive kid. Most people run away from challenge, but she thrives on it. By next week she'll know every inversion of the chords in each song, and most of the scales that run through them."

"Didn't you say her mother is in jail? Is there even a father on record?" Carl asked.

"No father, but Mom is out of jail now and working in a convenience store. I don't know where Sherice gets her influence. It sure can't be her brother."

"What's wrong with her brother?" he asked.

"I told you about him. Eighteen, and he's already fully into weirdom."

"Weird how?" Reggie asked.

"When you speak to him, he stares at you with this hungry look before he answers. *If* he answers. Maybe he fried his brains on something."

"A musical virtuoso growing out of that environment," Reggie said, shaking her head.

"Can you imagine being that precocious at seven?" Liz said.

Carl laughed, arching a thumb in her direction. "Yes. I can."

●

After dinner, in the living room, Reggie looked over Liz's shoulder while she paged through the new book for songs Sherice might like.

"You mind if I try out a few of these?" Liz said, walking toward the piano.

"Not at all," Reggie said. "I'd love to hear you play."

"How 'bout a few requests?" Carl said, stretching out in his recliner.

"Stop in at Brogino's Grease Release any time. Requests are my specialty."

As Liz set the book on the piano rack, a light blue envelope fell onto the floor. Carl leaned forward and picked it up.

"You getting love letters from students?"

He held the envelope out, gesturing for her to take it but she felt frozen.

"What's the matter?" he asked.

The natural pink of her face paled.

"Should I open it?" Carl asked.

"No ... I don't know."

He shook the envelope, studied it, tore into it. "It's not a bomb. "Three small snapshots fell onto his lap. He glanced at them, then at her, waiting for an explanation.

She took the photos. A morbid shock spread through her. "They're pictures of me, taken last Wednesday."

In the first photo, Liz was entering a beauty salon. A purse hung from one shoulder, while she pushed the door open with the other. Her red-brown hair reached the middle of her back.

In the second, she was unlocking her car, her hair shoulder-length, set in loose waves that framed her face.

The third was taken outside her apartment door, snapped from a few yards away as she opened the door.

"Someone followed me inside the gate!" she cried. A locked, iron gate stood at the entrance to her apartment building. She'd always felt relieved to hear it click behind her late at night. "This means anyone can get into my apartment!"

"How do you know when they were taken?" Carl said.

"Look," she said, handing him the first photo. "My hair is long there." She showed him the others. "Shorter here. They were taken a couple of days before the murder. Someone followed me home," she said, her voice shrill with tension.

Carl read the inscription inside the card aloud:

You will never cut your beautiful hair again.

"What's going on? First Gina, now some jack-off is sneaking around taking pictures of you?" he said.

"The cards started before Gina was killed."

Carl kicked the foot rest on his recliner and flew forward in his chair. "You mean there are more?"

"Three others, all within the last week. My God," she muttered, lowering herself onto a corner of the couch. "Maybe that's why Gina had a gun. This bastard could have been tormenting her too—before he killed her. Now he's after me."

"Start from the beginning," Reggie said.

"It started a few days before the murder," Liz said. "There's always some little flirtation going on at the studio. I found a card stuck inside my teaching book, and thought it was meant for someone else. It said, 'I always get what I want. And I want you'."

"What about the others?" Carl said.

"On Wednesday night, I got a card from someone in the bar. At the time, I thought it could be one of the drunks who'd overheard Sam's snippy comment about my playing and used it to make points with me. The card said I should ignore Sam because I was going to be 'rescued' from him soon."

"Damn!" Carl cried.

"When I was packing, I found another one stuck inside a music book I'd taken from the studio. It was really repulsive. 'Soon we will share the harmony of eternal peace'."

"Didn't you tell anyone?" Reggie asked.

"I told Enos. I was going to talk to Walter about keeping people out of my room at the studio, but I haven't been back since the murder."

"Did you save the cards?" Reggie asked.

"I've still got the last two." Her stomach tightened into a knot. A shiver ran through her, as if someone had drenched her with ice water. "I'm going to take them to the Lieutenant."

Reggie took the card from her hand, and placed it on the

coffee table. "You're safe here, Liz. Nothing can happen to you."

"This all seemed like nothing at first," Liz said. "A lot of teachers use that piano room. My name wasn't on the first card."

"But it was in your music book."

"Sometimes those are shared, too. But this book is brand new," she said, tapping the songbook. "I ordered this one myself."

"Tell us about Sherice's weird brother who gives you the creeps," Carl said.

"Jeffrey. He drives Sherice to her lessons every Monday night when their mother is working, so he's usually around. I'll be walking out of the piano room at the studio, or rounding a corner to the office, and there he is. I've bumped into him at least twenty times, and he just glares at me. Sometimes I catch him leaning in a doorway, watching me. On the other hand, he's so passive, he's more like a drip of water than a torrent strong enough to do any harm."

"Let's give Wallpaper a call, Liz," Carl said.

Liz reached for her purse and pulled out her keys. "Better still, I'm going in person. I'll be back before you go to bed."

"Mind if I tag along?" he said, slipping his shoes back on and following her to the door.

Nine

Lt. Wahlberg examined the three cards Liz spread across her desk without a word. The quiet seemed endless to Liz. When she could stand it no longer, she blurted, "This proves it, doesn't it?"

"Proves what, Ms. Hanlon?" Wahlberg asked.

"That this bastard wants me dead! It has to be Gina's murderer!"

Wahlberg finally looked up. "Why do you say that?"

"Because of the timing," Liz exclaimed. "I got three of them *before* she was killed."

"Maybe all four."

"What do you mean?"

"You aren't sure how long the card with the photos had been in your music book," Wahlberg said. "You hadn't been back to the studio to pick it up."

"What difference does it make if he wrote them before the murder or afterward? He's still trying to kill me."

Carl stopped pacing and faced the Lieutenant. "What about the gun permit? Shouldn't we have heard about it by now?"

"It's still under consideration, Mr. Hanlon."

"Gina had a gun, Lieutenant," Liz said. "Her roommate told me she let that fact circulate among people she met. She thought it would keep someone from messing with her."

"Who?" Wahlberg asked.

"Well if I knew that, I'd know who the killer was!" Liz snapped. Lt. Wahlberg was unmoved by Liz's exasperation. Liz rose and turned toward the door. "Let's go, Carl. This isn't getting us anywhere."

Wahlberg called her back. "You have no idea who could be sending these cards, Ms. Hanlon? No patron of your music? One of your students with a teenage crush?"

"You didn't tell her about Jeffrey," Carl said. "You said he scares the crap out of you."

"Yes," Wahlberg said, "have a seat. Tell me about Jeffrey."

●

Cars snaked along the narrow lane that circled the Crestview Mortuary. Smooth lawns and brightly colored flowers were set

in patterns to inspire a feeling of peaceful, eternal rest. Illu-
sion, Liz thought with a shudder. Thirty-year-old Gina McCurdy's
final resting place would not be witnessed by her at all, but
only by those she'd left behind. A few pretty flowers weren't
going to make her untimely death any less tragic.

Looking for a parking lot, Liz cruised past the parked cars
on the curving road which led up the hill from the chapel. She
would have to walk down that long hill alone. Would she find
another eerie note stuck under her windshield wiper? A spooky
pursuer crouching between two cars, waiting for her?

She parked, surveyed the area, and got out. She'd gone
only a few yards down the hill when she spotted Danny Amata's
familiar van pulling in. Relieved, she waved. Elliot and Miles,
the other two players who made up her quartet, stepped out
at the curb. They were dressed in conservative dark suits and
ties, and even from this distance she could see Miles' long
pony tail had been hidden neatly beneath his jacket collar.
They waited for her.

"I can't believe you guys actually own dark suits," she
said, as she joined them on the narrow sidewalk.

Danny's blue-black hair glistened in the sunlight. Usually
jovial and easy-going, today he was somber and introspective.
He did a once-over of Liz's skirt and jacket. "Nice threads yourself," he said. "I've never seen you in anything this subdued
either."

"Something from the back of the closet. Thanks for coming, guys."

"We wouldn't let you do this alone," Miles replied.

At forty-three, Miles Aulander was the oldest in the band,
and, like Danny, had been highly successful in the recording
industry. He'd arrived in Los Angeles from Canada a decade ago
to infuse the musical score of a low budget film with his imagi-

native harmonic mixtures of sound and rhythm. Expecting to stay four days, he'd packed only a small bag, but his musical concepts interested orchestrators and musical directors. By the end of the week he was sending home for more clothes. He'd joined Liz's band two years ago, and stayed because it allowed his imagination freedom, something not always possible in precisely-timed film scores.

Bass player Elliot Reinberg walked behind Liz without a word, his eyes on the sidewalk.

"You're more quiet than usual, Elliot," she said.

"Yeah, we could use some of your pungent wit today," Miles said. "A little dry sarcasm, a few counter punches."

"I could come up with plenty if this didn't all feel so damn personal," Elliot said.

Elliot usually pointed out negatives, earning him the nickname "wet blanket" by the group.

"It's not that we knew her that well," Elliot said. "It's just that she was so young. I'm pushing thirty, and I feel like I'm just getting started. Gina was the same age."

"I know," Liz said. "People are supposed to die when they're old, not be cut down by some demented killer. And for what?"

Elliot looked up. "That's right. They never said anything about her being robbed or anything. Do you think she was..."

"Raped? She wasn't. Cops said the cause of death was trauma to her head when she fell."

They stepped inside the sedate foyer of the chapel. Across the room, Tony stood alone with Sonnie. Sonnie's wife, Marilyn, rarely attended any gatherings with him, and Liz didn't expect to see her here today.

When a high-pitched bell sounded overhead, they moved toward the doorway where the service would be held. "I'll catch up with you guys later," Liz said. "I'm going to sit with my aunt."

She spotted Irene near the entrance, standing with Carl and Reggie. Irene was a small woman, dressed in black, and dabbing continuously at her tears. Her sagging shoulders gave her the appearance of having been beaten by misery.

"Aunt Irene," Liz said, coming up to her.

Irene threw her arms around Liz and held onto her for a long, silent moment.

They sat together near the casket which was centered in the front of the room and adorned with white flowers. Liz found she had trouble looking at it at first, then later developed a curious fixation, and could not take her eyes off it. She kept running the murder scene over in her mind. The police report stated the time of death at approximately 5:00 a.m. She had discovered the body around 5:30. If she'd left her apartment a few minutes earlier, could she have prevented Gina's murder?

She felt bombarded. She closed her eyes, tried to blot out the drone of the minister's voice.

The tiny nerves inside her nose signaled an allergy attack. The flowers, she was certain. In seconds, her sinuses swelled, and her head pounded. She reached in her purse for the drops that helped keep her symptoms down, and placed a droplet in each eye. She was about to step outside when the minister called Paige Alvarez to the podium.

"I was Gina's friend and roommate," Paige began, fighting for control of her voice. Her notes shook in her hand. After a moment, she pushed them aside and improvised. Her words were the kind people are driven to say in moments of crisis, but they told Liz more about her cousin than she'd ever known. Gina had been a college student, which seemed incongruous to her fun-seeking, late-night party image. Paige talked about

Gina's sentimentality, a "soft-hearted gushiness" she called it, especially in her relationship with her mother. Hearing Paige's words made Liz wish she'd known Gina better.

When the service ended, they walked with Aunt Irene to the waiting limo. "I'll go with her," Liz whispered to Carl and Reggie.

In the distance, she spotted Sonnie pacing across the lawn toward them.

"I've been thinking," he said, catching his breath. "We should go somewhere and have a toast to her, don't you think? Some kind of send off."

"We should," Liz said. "Where are you headed? The Stop?"

"The Stop, it is," he said. "See you in fifteen."

"Wait! What am I thinking? I can't leave Aunt Irene. You go ahead. Explain to the guys."

"We'll stay with her awhile," Carl said. "You come over when you're through. It'll do you good to be with your friends."

"You don't mind?"

"No, go ahead."

She looked back at Sonnie. "One drink."

"Grab the big table in the back if you get there first."

●

The Midnight Stop was a small, unpretentious night club on Santa Monica Boulevard with an easy-going atmosphere and a crowded bar. Al Russell, the owner, designed the place for bar and restaurant employees who worked late hours, offering "happy hour" specials between midnight and two in the morning.

Liz rarely stopped in during the day, and was surprised to find a big lunch crowd. She spotted Al behind the bar. He didn't tend bar often, and he did not look happy about doing it now.

"What are you doing, Al?"

He double-poured, a bottle in each hand. "My day bar-tender wanted time off to go to the funeral. I'm expecting her back any minute. Sorry I couldn't be there myself. How was it?"

"Very nice—as funerals go. The minister talked about what a wonderful person Gina was, but couldn't pronounce her name."

A young woman with a fresh face and bouncy blonde curls walked behind the bar and began filling Al's drink orders. The advertisement across the chest of her snug T-shirt announced *The Midnight Stop* with a horizontal stretch that enlarged her breasts. She had to be twenty-one to work as a bartender, but she looked more like a high school cheerleader with breast enhancements.

Al dried his hands. "Liz, you met my day bartender yet? This is Tiffany."

"Hi, Tiffany. I'm Liz Hanlon. Guess we've all just come from Gina's funeral. Did you know her well?"

Tiffany shrugged. "Sure. She came in here a lot. I couldn't believe what happened to her. It's like ... I mean like ... you know, no one should like get killed, or anything."

"Right. Did you know Gina's roommate, too?"

Tiffany's curls bobbed on her shoulders as she shook her head. "No, she usually came in with her boyfriend."

"Oh, yeah, what's his name?" Gina had not mentioned a steady boyfriend.

"Um, I never knew his name," Tiffany said, serving a mug of beer to a customer.

"You work days, right?" Liz asked. "I guess Gina must have stopped by in the afternoons, before she went to work."

"Oh, yeah. Like a lot of days."

"If I drank in the afternoon, I'd be asleep at the keys by the second set." Something worth considering if she was going to be at Brogino's much longer, she thought.

Sonnie, Miles, and Elliot arrived, but there were three empty chairs at the table. "Where's Danny?" she asked.

"Waiting for you to get out of his way," Miles said with a gesture toward the bar.

The sheen of Danny's hair was obvious under the bar lights as he leaned forward, honing in on Tiffany with a magnanimous smile.

"What about Tony?" Liz asked, looking around. "Did anyone tell him we were here?"

"He's very upset," Sonnie said. "Not in the mood for conversation."

"He was doing some pretty good storytelling the other night," Liz said.

"Oh, yeah, Tony can go on non-stop sometimes," Sonnie said, apologetically. "When we were kids, he had my parents convinced he was a conservative little book worm." He rolled his eyes. "A 'good influence.' Whenever we'd want to stay out late for something, Tony would lay it on, and boy, he was good. They bought it every time."

"I'm getting a real spicy picture of these puberty years, Sonnie," Liz said. "Let's hear some details."

He laughed. "Oh, no. They're just dumb memories that seemed like a big deal back then. You know, hookers around the club, that sort of thing."

Danny pulled up a chair, saying, "Hookers? Is this club history, or something from the private archives?"

"Oh, no, you don't," Sonnie said, and chugged his beer.

They all looked at each other and nodded in agreement. "Okay, so we're talking about Tony, then," Danny said. "A very young Tony."

"We're not talking about either of us," Sonnie countered, "at any age."

"Yeah, I'll bet he boffed a few in his day," Danny said.

Sonnie chuckled, "His day? I hate to shock you punks, but you don't lose it the minute you turn forty."

"Let's hope not," Liz said, "It's only four years away for me! Worse case scenario? I'm still playing at Brogino's."

Elliot said, "With your luck, you'll still be driving that chug-mobile."

Liz's 1986 Chevy Impala wagon had been the recipient of continuous jokes for years.

"It's a good thing club owners don't have to pay for travel time," Sonnie joked. "With that car you drive, I'd go broke! Hey, speaking of cars, Tony's got quite a collection you might like to see."

Danny interjected, "Yeah, Liz, what does the old gas pig get these days? Three miles to the gallon?"

Laughter floated around the table. "Stuff it, you guys," Liz bantered. "I can fit my keyboard, my amp, a full sound system, and all the extras in the back of that buggy, and the best part—no car payments! Can any of you say that?"

"A minor point," Elliot said.

"Didn't Gina have a nice Firebird?" Miles asked.

"I don't know," Liz said. "I heard someone at the funeral say she was taking college classes, and I didn't even know that."

"She was," Danny said. "I bumped into her in the parking lot at City College one day."

Sonnie emptied the ketchup bottle onto his French fries. "I helped her get through a math class she needed for her entrance. It took her a little longer than most people, but she stuck to it."

"You know, I just didn't know much about my own cousin," she said.

"Did you hear the one about her famous waitress uniform?" Sonnie asked.

"No."

"Gina showed up for work one night with a uniform that could fit a ten-year-old," he explained. "She claimed the cleaners shrank it, but I figured she put it in the dryer on high. You should'a seen the skirt on that thing. With those long legs of hers, the hem line barely covered her butt."

Danny's eyebrows shot up. "Sorry I missed that."

"And the top," Sonnie added, breaking up, "the way she plumped out of the top—! I'll tell you one thing. It did the trick. Guys were scrambling over each other for her tables. Her tips hit an all-time high that night." Sonnie drained his beer mug. "I'll miss her."

"Me, too," Danny said. "You could always count on Gina to lighten the mood."

"Do the cops even have a suspect yet?" Elliot asked, looking at Liz.

"No," she said. "I was hoping to get an update from the Lieutenant when I brought her the weird cards, but she's got the personality of a snapping turtle."

"What about the club, Sonnie?" Miles asked. "You think you can move the starting date back and still do the shows?"

"I can't even estimate such a thing until I get the green light to open. I'm sorry, guys, but if I had to make a guess right now, I'd say don't count on it. Anyway," Sonnie said, pulling out his wallet, "you folks can stick around all night if you want, but I should get back. I'm hoping to hear something soon."

He was halfway to the door when he stopped, turned around, and walked back to the table.

"You know how they always say you should tell people how you feel when you've got the chance? Well, all of you—you mean a lot to me. You're the best musicians in town, but you're also good friends. I couldn't ask for more than that."

He turned to leave. "Wait!" Liz called out. "We feel the same. And you're right, we usually don't say anything till it's too late. But we say it behind your back, so this time we'll say it to your face—you're the best, Sonnie."

Heads nodded, murmurs of agreement went round the table.

Sonnie's fingers made a self-conscious run through his hair. "Thanks. Well, now I know why we don't say this stuff too often. Anyway, I'll see you."

Watching him walk away, Miles said, "There goes a class guy."

"I'll agree with that," Liz said.

Ten

Liz stayed with Aunt Irene until she fell asleep on the couch, then covered her with a blanket, and left a note saying that both she and Carl would be back the next day. She drove to Suzanne's house in West Hollywood andspentthe night.

In the morning, her first plan was seeing Enos. Squinting against the sunlight, she drove east on Santa Monica Blvd., turned south on LaBrea, and left on Melrose. Enos's apartment was a few blocks from Germaine's West.

Just past Paramount Studios, she saw the traffic backing up near the club. Media camera crews had staked out the main entrance of the restaurant and part of Camden Street. Throngs of onlookers packed the sidewalk. Had the bank next door been robbed? Had something else happened at Germaine's? She parked in the first available spot and began pushing through the crowd. Sonnie was outside the front door. His voice was tense, cutting through the noise.

"That's it!" he announced. "No more questions."

Moans went up, followed by shouts and more questions.

"I don't know what else I can add," he said. As he turned, he spotted Liz pushing toward him.

"Let me through, please," she called out. She was on the front steps when someone shouted, "That's her! That's Liz Hanlon!" The press swooped in around her, cutting her off from Sonnie.

"Are you the one who found the body?" a voice yelled out.

"What were you doing in the bar that early in the morning?"

"Are you a suspect?"

"Are you a suspect, Mr. Tucks?"

"Were you in it together?"

Liz tried to step around them, but she was surrounded by microphones and demands. Feeling the first stage of panic, she caught sight of Sonnie's hand stretching through narrow openings in her direction. She grabbed it, held it tight. He propelled her through the front door he was holding ajar with his foot, jumped inside behind her, and clicked the lock in place.

"So this is life in the public eye, huh?" she gasped, falling back against the door to catch her breath. "What's going on?"

"I got word that I can re-open this morning, so I hurried over. When I got out of my car all hell broke lose. Don't ask me how these vultures knew about it so fast."

"The police are done with their investigation already?"

"Already? You have any idea how much this place looses each day that its closed?"

"The broadcasts! Does this mean they're back on?"

"Come on inside, I'll tell you about it," he said. "You look like you need to relax the old nerves."

"Don't keep me hanging!"

He broke into a broad smile. "We're back on! I hope you're still up to it."

"Oh, my God," she said, astonished.

"Now you really look like you need to relax." He motioned for her to follow him.

"I should let Enos know I'm going to be late, and my aunt, too. Carl's with her now, but I promised to stay with her later."

At the archway to the lounge, she drew back. Her eyes fell upon the spot of the murder.

"Here," Sonnie said, putting an arm around her waist, "come this way."

In the office, Tony's belongings were still spread out on every desktop. Liz found a phone under a pile of mail. "How's Tony holding up?" she asked as she dialed.

"Better. It's funny, but the funeral really upset him."

Carl came on the line. "Hi Carl, it's me. I've got one more stop to make at Enos's, then I'll be there."

"No need," Carl said. "Aunt Irene's fallen asleep. She took something. I think she'll be out for the rest of the day."

"But if she wakes up and she's alone—"

"I'll stick around awhile to make sure, but I saw a bottle of tranquilizers in the bathroom, and she downed two or three of them. You can probably forget today."

"Okay. Thanks for staying with her," she said, hanging up. Sonnie glanced up. "Something wrong?"

"My aunt's having a hell of a time."

"Poor lady. This has got to be the worst thing a parent can go through."

"I want to reach out to her, but I don't even know what to say. I was right there, and still I don't know why it happened."

"No one expects you to." Sonnie looked down at his paper-work.

"Why do you think it hit Tony so hard? I didn't think he knew Gina that well."

"As a person gets older, death takes on a more immediate importance."

"And what about you, Sonnie? You and I haven't really talked about it. What part of it keeps you awake at night?"

"All of it. Mostly, the loss. She was only thirty. I feel for her mother. And, selfishly speaking, I feel for myself. I lost a good friend. It hurts."

"I know. It's so odd that I know her better in death than I did in her life."

"You two would have gotten tight again as these shows got going."

"The concerts," she said, easing down into a chair. A slow smile spreading over her face. "I feel like I've been on a roller coaster. But what about Tony? I mean, he's the money man--?"

"He's fine. There's no problem."

"You're sure we can make the schedule? God, how will I ever be ready? We'll have to get in some heavy duty rehearsals. Can we work here during the daytime?"

"Slow down. You said the band was ready."

"I was jivin'!"

Sonnie broke up. "Then you better get that group in shape fast, 'cause Tony's investors are expecting a show in less than a month, and we're going to give'em one."

"That's another thing," she said. "He mentioned these investors to Lieutenant Wahlberg, but that's the first I heard about them."

"Big concerts and festivals have several investors. Didn't think he was just going to whip out the old checkbook, did you?"

"Of course not, but he seemed so withdrawn at the funeral. He didn't join us afterwards, and he's not here helping you re-open."

"You're worried about the wrong thing, Liz. Tony's not the problem. Germaine's is."

"You said your finances were tight, but I thought the shows were going to straighten that all out."

"The problem's going to be holding on till they do," he said, leaning forward and dropping his head into his hands. "Under normal circumstances there'd be no problem, but I'm behind on every account I've got. When I think of what Uncle Booker put into this place, I feel like I'm letting him down."

"Don't do that to yourself. Things are different now."

"Booker opened in 1947, and he ran Germaine's like a friendly, corner tavern. It was just like that TV show, *Cheers*. In fact," he added, "Booker use to give out keys to his favorite customers, and they could be found hunched over the bar, already sipping their libations of choice when he arrived in the morning."

"Boy, things were *really* different then."

"Yup. Booker treated his customers like family, and they

loved him. It really rocked the neighborhood when a heart attack killed him in '79. That's when my dad, Joey, took over. But Dad never really liked the bar business. After awhile the neighborhood changed, and pretty soon Germaine's became just another joint with a small stage and a local band."

"Is that when you took over?"

Sonnie smiled, thoughtfully. "Yes. I jumped in; I loved the business. I worked here, learning everything I could from Dad. Then in '85 he announced he was turning the place over to me, and heading for Florida. Things were popping financially, so I added the other two clubs soon after."

"But business hasn't stayed that way?"

He waved a hand in disgust. "The people are here, but with the drinking laws they don't drink like they used to, and my expenses have tripled. I don't know if I can wait for the broadcasts to turn a profit."

"The crowds will be back once you re-open."

"That's just it. As long as the case is unsolved, I'm in trouble. I need to open as soon as possible, but opening the doors when nothing's been resolved still leaves a dark cloud over the place. Let's face it, public perception is everything."

"I suppose so."

"Ask yourself, would you go out for a drink at a place where someone just got murdered?"

"A lot of people love notoriety."

"Sure, one-timers. It's regulars who make this place go, and as long as the killer's still walking around, they're afraid to come back."

"What can I do to help, Sonnie?"

He forced a smile. "I've asked Tony to float me some extra funds. I'm going to buy us some good press."

"Buy?"

"Yes, buy. That feeding frenzy outside is free. Somebody got murdered here, that's news! But me struggling to get back on my feet, nobody cares."

"What are you going to do?"

"I'm going to throw one outrageous press party. I was hoping your band could play."

"Of course we'll play, but you're just going to call them up and say, 'Come on over, guys, and bring your cameras?'"

"Something like that. Fifty bucks a pop for gold engraved invitations, private limos for all the music business brass. First class doesn't come cheap, but I've got to do it. If things don't pick up fast, this club goes under."

"Don't say that, Sonnie, it'll never get that bad. What about good old word of mouth? Let's counter the negative press by spreading good news. All of us out there talking about the fantastic line-up of entertainment you've got? Appeal to the groupies, let them know this is a moment in history they shouldn't miss."

Sonnie looked doubtful.

"You've got a ton of friends," she said. "We could all help."

"I thought I had a lot of friends, but what I've got is a lot of hanger-on types who like to shake my hand because I'm the owner. The man. But since the murder, you see any of them around me? Anyone coming forward even as a character witness?"

"Then we'll have to do it ourselves. I'll talk to every musician who's ever played here, and a bunch more who've always wanted to. We'll pull on their heart strings, start circulating the news: Germaine's is back. Bigger and better than ever. Really, I think it'll work."

"Liz, you're a dreamer. A supreme optimist. Haven't you noticed how people-users never come around when the chips are down?"

She grinned. "Dreamers don't notice those things."

●

Liz headed east on Melrose, toward Enos's apartment. The thought of spending even a few minutes in his rancid place made her cringe, but if she could put in four nights a week at Brogino's Slime and Grime, she could certainly stand a visit to Enos.

Sonnie had painted a vivid picture of the nightclub business twenty years ago. As she sat at a light, she thought about the different atmosphere that existed back then. Musicians spoke about the '60s and '70s with reverence, as if the time had been magical.

She looked down the block and saw a sign flashing above a narrow storefront. Several bulbs were burned out, but she could make out the words "Used Records." She chuckled, remembering her high school days when she'd exchanged dozens of albums at secondhand stores, believing they would be available forever. Now she wished she'd saved some of them. The hiss and noise on vinyl records made her feel as if she were part of the live recording session.

She went through the light and pulled to the corner. Enos could wait another five minutes.

The store was one long, narrow room. Cardboard bins were crammed with record albums from the last fifty years. There were familiar names who were still popular now, and others she'd never heard of. She smiled when she came across a recording by Pepper Martin & The Love Knots, her favorite as a child. She set it aside, flipping alphabetically through the others with similar names. She pushed the stack back into place and was about to leave when one name caught her attention. She withdrew the album, and smiled as she stared at the face of Victor Markham.

Shadowy memories of her uncle came back to her. She let the impressions wash over her, remembering the sense of family unity she'd known growing up.

She paid for the albums and hurried out.

●

The chairs in Enos's large studio were piled high with newspapers and electronics magazines. Liz stood in the center of the room, ignoring the only available place to sit: a corner of Enos's unmade bed.

"What'cha got there?" Enos asked, nodding toward the package she held under her arm.

"Just a couple of albums from that used record store down the street. I thought they might warp if I left them in the hot car."

"Did you bring me those works of art from your stalker?"

"I had to leave them with Lieutenant Wahlberg," she said.

Enos rolled his chair back from the computer. "I have some rather tantalizing news for you. You want some coffee to wash it down?"

She watched him withdraw an unwashed cup from the pile in the sink. With a quick rinse, he dumped in a spoonful of instant coffee and filled the cup with hot tap water.

"No. Thanks," she said, turning away. "What's the big news?"

He rolled back and faced the computer while he spoke. "First, I'm still working on those background checks. It's taking awhile 'cause I'm doin' em on all of you."

"Who's 'all of you'?"

"Everyone close to the murder. Just broad, biographical stuff, but sometimes helpful things pop up. You should see what I dug up on you."

"This ought'a be good."

"Your credit rating is shit."

"There's a news flash. Why the hell are you nosing around in my affairs?"

"I'm not nosing around. I'm the best because I do a thorough investigation which may later turn out to be relevant. Don't get into a huff about it; I'm doing everybody. Your brother, his wife, Sonnie, Tony, even your Mother."

"My mother is a suspect?"

"If I'm ever called into court, I need to have the dynamic details."

"What kind of dynamite have you found so far?"

"Well, first of all, your boss, Sonnie, wasn't exactly forthcoming with the police about his whereabouts at the time of the murder."

"He was home! Asleep, like normal people."

"He *says* he was home. But his wife wasn't there to corroborate that."

"How do you know that?"

"The check-in register at the Ramada speaks for itself," he said.

"What are you talking about?"

"Actually, she signed the register with a phony name, but apparently the little woman was in such a hurry to get between the sheets, she didn't think about the name on her credit card. Marilyn E. Tucks paid for a suite that night. My nose says Mrs. Tucks is having an affair."

"This is more than background stuff. Sonnie probably doesn't know. Even if he does, is he obligated to reveal this to the police?"

"Only if he wants to have an alibi."

"I know he comes off like Mr. Saturday Night, but Sonnie really is a very private person."

"Here's a news flash for you, blue-eyes. Cops and lawyers aren't big on privacy."

She started for the door. "I 'spose. Anything else on the background checks?"

"Got a few more things to run down on Sonnie, then I'll start on his partner. Where are you running off to?"

"I want to see my aunt this afternoon, then I'm playing the Cristo Viejo Country Club tonight."

"Ooh, hoyty-toyty."

At the doorway, she stopped, pulling the albums out of the package. "I just thought of something. You'll be looking back a few years in the music business, won't you? There's a record company called HotRock Music that produced a lot of artists, including my uncle, Victor Markham. See if you can find out anything about them."

Enos scribbled on a slip of paper. "HotRock. Anything like what?"

"Who they were, how well they were respected by others within the industry, that kind of thing."

"Will do. Call me around noon. Or better still," he said, "come by in person. I'll take you to lunch."

"Uh, thanks, Enos, but I've got rehearsals up the butt. Could be weeks before I'll have a free day."

Eleven

Liz peered at the musical arrangement Suzanne had spread out on her dining room table. "What a job! Writing out every note for sixteen instruments," she said. "I hope when Amy gets up on that stage, she knows it's you who's making her sound so good."

"It could have been you," Suzanne said. "Amy offered you this job before me, remember?"

"Yeah, and when I see how much work you've got to do, I know turning it down was the right move."

"You're not sorry?" Suzanne asked. "You could be traveling through Europe instead of me."

"Suz, come on. That gig isn't right for me. Sure, I play the piano, but I'm not an accompanist. That's a distinct style of playing, and it's your forte, not mine."

"No, yours is coming up with songs and lyrics from scratch. Don't even talk to me about that!"

"Lyrics are no big deal," Liz said. "You just talk. Organize your thoughts."

"Yeah, right."

"How come you're not doing this on the computer?"

"Software problems," Suzanne said, "and no time to fool around with it. I need this chart tonight." She put down her pencil, and leaned back. "How about you? You been able to write anything lately?"

Liz sighed. "I can't concentrate since the murder."

"Your whole world has turned upside down."

"I'm worried. The broadcasts are back on, and Sonnie's hosting a big press party on Tuesday."

"Sounds pretty exciting to me."

"It is, but we need to prepare and all any of us can think about is Gina," she said. "Danny's been moody, Miles hardly talks. Even Elliot's caustic jokes have dried up. Sonnie worries me most."

"Why? Because Enos thinks his alibi is flaky? Obviously, the cops either don't know about Marilyn's affair, or they don't think it's significant. That's what counts."

"The tension with Marilyn must be killing him, but he brushes it off like it's nothing. He just won't talk lately, not like he used to."

"You said he's a private person," Suzanne said.

"Hey, didn't you tell me that Amy got pretty chummy with Marilyn during that long stretch of performances she did at Germaine's?"

"She and Amy tipped a few wine glasses together, but that was last year."

"Then it's time for a reunion."

Suzanne gave her a suspicious glance. "Are you going to do some spying?"

"Not exactly."

"Oh, you want me to spy?"

"Right. You're smooth, Suz. You can learn a lot from girl talk over a nice brunch on a sunny patio. Talk about husbands, passions, all that talk show crap. You never know what might slip out of her after a little champagne."

"Like what?"

"Like who she's having an affair with, and why!"

"And where are you going to be? Hiding under the table?"

"C'mon, this is about Sonnie not having an alibi."

"Marilyn having an affair does not translate into Sonnie killing Gina."

"No, but the cops might not see it that way when it comes out," Liz said. "What if this is all a set-up? Maybe she's trying to make trouble for Sonnie. They haven't been getting along for a long time. What if she used that credit card on purpose, knowing it would cast suspicion on his whereabouts?"

"Do you know what you're saying?" Suzanne cried. "That Marilyn is setting him up as a murder suspect!"

Liz's thoughts tripped ahead. "Which she couldn't have done unless she knew there was going to be a murder, which means—" She waved a hand. "Ah, you're right! I'm getting carried away."

"It's crazy. Absolutely nuts."

"It is."

After a few silent moments, Suzanne said, "Did I tell you Amy's opening the new Hilton Hotel downtown tonight?"

"No. A grand opening—that'll be spectacular. I'll bet the hotel will put on an outrageous champagne brunch in the morning."

"Probably."

"You and Amy will be exhausted after the late night. Brunch with old friends is always nice after a hard night."

●

That night, Liz turned into the parking lot of the Cristo Viejo Country Club, and slammed on her brakes.

A gleaming white Jaguar idled in front of her, then cruised slowly to the valet parking sign. She watched as other expensive cars clustered around the clubhouse, their drivers waving bills and demanding personal attention. Impatiently, she craned her neck to see the front of the line. A traffic jam in a parking lot on the one night she was running late. Perfect.

Eventually, a valet waved her forward. As she jumped from the car, he grabbed her keys and began a hasty move behind the wheel.

"Wait! I'm Liz Hanlon. I'm playing here tonight, and I have a lot of equipment to unload."

He raised a lazy eyebrow, letting his glance parade down the length of her station wagon. Road dust made the dark blue color look blanched and hazy.

She opened the back door, reached inside, and filled her arms. Without help, it would take several trips to unload everything. The valet stood stone-faced.

She crawled into the back on her knees and filled her arms

with microphones, wires, and music. Backing out, her head bumped hard against the metal door frame.

"Ouch! Ah, shit!"

The valet looked bored.

"You know, I could use a little help here, Dipstick." One look at her car, and he figured she didn't have the class to tip him, she thought.

Unsympathetic, the valet snatched the things from her arms and stomped to the entrance of the club. He deposited them in a heap on the doorstep.

"Hey!" she fumed at him, "when they're your cars, you can give me attitude. Until then," she tilted her head back to look down her nose at him, "park it!" With an exaggerated motion, she dropped her keys into his palm. "And be careful with it. Dude."

●

Liz carried a monitor speaker through the reception area and stopped in front of the information board. She had been told her band was to play in the club's lounge for a special party, but the board had her name listed in Salon A. She followed the signs down the hall, and turned into a huge ballroom. In the doorway, she stopped short.

All three walls were lined with enormous Off-Road vehicle tires mounted above even larger mounds of hay. Party guests were dressed in cowboy wear, the kind that comes from western shops in city malls.

Nothing was more nerve-jangling than being the wrong band for the occasion. She hurried to the bandstand where Miles and Elliot were setting up. "What's going on here? Marty said we're playing a country club, not a ho-down. We're not the right band for this crowd. Our music isn't even close to what they're going to want."

"Welcome to Southern California's annual Off-Road con-vention," Elliot smirked. "If you know any magic, Liz, this is the time to do it. These people are already screaming for 'down home country'."

"Oh, my God. Marty must have gotten the story wrong," she said. "We're in deep shit."

"These folks are gonna be throwing tomatoes after eight bars," Elliot said.

"I'll call Marty—see if he can find us some country play-ers. Meanwhile, can we come up with enough to keep 'em happy till they get here?" A few yards away a couple was practicing their dance steps. "Don't even answer that. I'll be back." Sev-eral fringed plaid shirts passed by while she stood in the hall dialing the phone. Rounded skirts with ruffles glided by. Boots everywhere.

"Marty!" she cried. "Thank God you're home! Listen, you've got to get a country band down here. Fast!"

"Slow down. What are you talking about?"

"I'm talking about this square dance you booked us for! What were you thinking? We play jazz. Pop tunes, Motown hits, blues, Latin. These people have their minds set for coun-try two-step. The closest we can come is our Willie Nelson swing rhythm, and that isn't going to cut it! Good God, Marty," she pressed, "they've got tires on the walls for decoration!"

She heard him gulp; probably brandy, she thought.

"I don't know what I can do at this hour," he said.

"Make some calls. At least get a guitar player who sings! Someone who can take the lead. We'll back him up. How the hell are we supposed to play country music without a guitar?"

"I don't know how this happened—"

"The hell you don't! Some slick-talking agent forgot to

book the right band, called you in a panic, and told you he needed a group for a country club. He'd failed to mention the client was having a private cowboy event!"

"Liz, I am so sorry. I'll make this up to you."

Anger took over. "Do you have any idea how embarrassing it is to stand up in front of people who hate your music?" she cried. "I don't want a box of chocolates, Marty, I want a country guitar player. Now!"

Her face was purple when she returned to the party. Danny and Elliot were connecting the speaker wires.

"Who's he calling?" Danny asked.

"Who knows?"

"Oh man! This is really gonna suck," Elliot groused.

"You got any better ideas?" she shot back.

"Wait a minute," Danny said. "Elliot, what about that country player you recorded with last week? You said he was great."

"Matt Blocker!" Elliot cried. "Perfect." He pulled change from his pocket and raced to the phone.

●

They made a list of song titles they thought the crowd would expect, then discovered that no one really knew the lyrics to any of them. They had only accompanied singers who'd performed the lead.

"Great," she groaned.

Elliot hurried in from the hallway. "Blocker said if he can make it at all, it won't be till after ten."

"We'll have to get by with the old schlopp I do at Brogino's." She snatched a folder from her leather bag, and checked her watch. "Let's do it."

They headed for the stage. Liz counted off the first tune, hoping for a little of the reverie she usually found with the band, but this time her muscles strained from tension. They played a few familiar titles, but halfway through the first set, dancers began shouting requests for newer songs.

"C'mon, you guys! Play something that's on the radio now!" She turned to the band with a pleading look. "Have you got any ideas?"

"I've got one," Danny said. "Follow me." He fell into a classic country two-step beat.

Dancers lined up on the floor.

"Great," Liz said, "but what's the song?"

"Anything," Danny called out. "Make something fit."

"Blues changes," she called out. "Twelve bar form, and whatever you do, keep it going."

She adapted the melody of a Blues song to the rhythm the band was playing. The crowd was appeased for the moment, and the tightness in her shoulders started to relax. Her thoughts drifted to songs she'd heard on the radio, and she began singing the sections she knew, dropping out of the others in time for the band to finish instrumentally. At the end of two choruses, she nodded for Miles to take a keyboard solo. He played through the song several times, keeping dancers on the floor. When Liz came back in for her last chorus, she realized she'd gone through every set of blues lyrics she could think of. She improvised the rest as the song progressed.

Miles was amused. "You're dangerously good at faking it, Hanlon," he called over the music.

"Years of practice."

They stepped down from the bandstand at the end of the first set, wiping nervous perspiration from their foreheads.

"I think we did pretty good," Danny said. "Not a single tomato."

"Don't let it go to your head," Liz said. "We're out of material."

Matt Blocker burst through the door pushing his amplifier, a music stand under one arm, his guitar hanging over his shoulder.

"Saved just in time!" Liz said, moving her things to make room for him on the stand. "I'm Liz Hanlon, and you have no idea how happy I am to see you."

Matt shook her hand. "Yes, I do. Last month my agent sent me out on a sixtieth anniversary gig. He failed to mention they wanted all Italian music." He flipped on his amp. "Does Blocker sound like an Italian name to you?"

Liz broke up. "Some things never change."

Back on the bandstand, Matt called the song titles, named the key, then started playing the familiar groove from the original recording. The band followed, and the tension in Liz's back slowly vanished.

Marty's guitar player never showed up.

●

When the night was over, Liz waved goodbye to the guys as they pulled out of the parking lot. She started her car, and looked up to find another notecard under her windshield wiper. Panic shot through her. Her eyes darted around. Was someone watching her? Waiting to follow her? She pounded on the horn hoping to alert Danny, but his tail lights were shrinking in the distance. She felt cold and alone. She grabbed the card and ripped it open.

Your music should not be wasted on these fools. Soon you will sing only for me.

She slammed the car in gear and tore out of the lot, glancing repeatedly in her rear view mirror, driving with one hand, and dialing Lt. Wahlberg's number with the other.

Twelve

Sunlight streamed in under the drapes as Liz woke, still groggy from the late night. Members of the Off-Road Vehicles Association had enjoyed the band so much with the addition of Matt Blocker, they'd asked them to play another two hours. When Liz crawled into bed, the clock's bright glare read 4:02.

She tucked the covers around her shoulders hoping for more sleep when Suzanne stuck her head inside the door.

"Don't mean to wake you—"

"I think I'm up," she said, pulling herself toward full consciousness. "What's going on?"

"You'll want to hear this," Suzanne said, sitting on the edge of the bed. "I didn't have to set up the brunch after all. Everything you wanted to know was displayed right before my eyes. She's having an affair, alright. A big, juicy one."

Liz sat up. "We're talking Marilyn, right? Sonnie's wife? You're sure?"

"I'm sure. While Amy was singing, I watched Marilyn crawl all over some dark-haired, Latin-lover for damn near two hours. Hands groping, hormones screaming. It looked like an old fashioned teenage drive-in scene."

"Out in the open?" Liz said, incredulous.

"Not a bit shy about being seen."

"You're sure it was Marilyn? It's hard to see much when you're looking out from the stage."

"There's no question. Amy sat with them between shows."

"I can't believe she'd do such a thing right under Sonnie's nose. What a bitch!"

"Maybe she wants to make sure he knows."

"Poor Sonnie," Liz said, starting to pull on her jeans.

"Don't get into it, Liz," Suzanne cautioned. "It's not your business."

"If my husband was having an affair, I'd sure want someone to tell me."

"Would you?"

Liz finished dressing and drove to Germaine's, still pondering that question.

●

Mid-day traffic on Santa Monica Boulevard slowed to a crawl. Liz reached for her phone and dialed Enos's number.

"Ah, blue-eyes," he droned. "You've reconsidered that lunch date?"

"Can't Enos. I'm on way to Germaine's right now. Lots of work to do. You told me to call this morning, remember?"

His nasal voice reminded her of a small ocean creature who'd been held out of the water too long. "True. Let's see, I just started on your boy, Tony, so there's not much to relay yet, except that he was the owner of that company on the back of your album jackets. HotRock Music. Guess you knew that, though—"

"Wait! HotRock Music was owned by Tony Perdusian? I didn't know that."

"You do now, thanks to the superior detective skills of one Enos Kaperstein."

The traffic moved in front of her. She caught up with it, easing into the left turn lane in front of Germaine's West. "Thanks, Enos. You're a brick."

●

The lounge inside Germaine's was empty. Sonnie stood behind the bar pouring a shot of whiskey into a coffee cup. Seeing Liz, he pulled down another cup.

"Why didn't you bring a lunch crowd with you?" he asked.

"If they're smart, they're still in bed."

"You look tired. You work a late one last night?"

She pulled the coffee closer. "We did, but I can't seem to sleep very well lately."

"Me neither," he said. "Marilyn and I had another fight at dinner. She stormed out, I tried to sleep, but by midnight I realized it wasn't gonna happen."

"This was last night?" she hedged, unsure about how to bring up Marilyn's affair, or even if she should.

He looked at her suspiciously. "She's having an affair. I suppose the whole town knows, huh?"

"Not the whole town. I won't tell anyone. How did you find out?"

"It's been going on for awhile," he said.

He rarely talked about his marriage, though he and Marilyn had been together for years with no signs of separation. No sign of real togetherness either.

"That's terrible, Sonnie. You think you and Marilyn can work it out?"

He stared into his coffee. "I'm not sure I want to anymore." He drained his cup. "What have you heard about the murder? I'm getting the big zero when I ask."

"Not much, but I hired an investigator who used to work for my brother. Strange little guy named Enos Kaperstein. There's nothing this guy can't find."

"Oh?"

"That's what Carl says."

"What's he turned up so far?"

"Just background mostly, things involving the night of the murder. I visited Paige Alvarez, too."

"Gina's roommate? You playing detective?"

She smiled. "Paige said Gina had this whole act going with her customers. Like she was a different person at times. You know anything about that?"

He gave her a look as if he doubted her sanity.

"I'm not making this up. I saw little indications of it when she lived with me, but Paige said she'd flirt with the guys, make them think she was interested, then keep them hanging."

Sonnie pursed his lips. "And they'd drop their pants for her."

"No, their wallet."

"Yeah, maybe."

"Maybe what?"

"Maybe there's something to it," he said. "I wasn't kidding when I said she put her uniform in the dryer to shrink it. She probably did. But she was a great girl, Liz. If she was leading them on a little, they wanted to be led. I don't see the harm in it."

"I'm not saying there was any."

"I mean, she wasn't hooking or anything like that."

"Hey, I'm not making judgments. But I did find it curious that her roommate says she had this whole 'act.' Everyone has sides to their personalities, but it doesn't sound like Gina shared much of her real self," she said. "I hadn't seen her since we argued, but her life is getting to be fascinating."

"She was never very forthcoming with me about her personal life. She always made me laugh, though." He sighed. "She got cheated."

"I guess that's what life's about," she said, "trying to get it all in before it's too late."

"See? That's you, the optimist. You dedicate yourself to something with no guarantee it'll lead anywhere. And it works for you," he said. "But it wasn't that way for Gina. It's not that way for a lot of people."

She began to wonder about his private world. Some people were only what showed on the surface; she sensed that Sonnie was more.

"What about you?" she asked. "Do you feel cheated?"

He shifted in his seat, drew a long breath. "Well, it's probably too soon to tell. The concerts will be the marker for me.

Tony's another story."

"We're talking about you."

"I'm just making a general point, and Tony's life is a perfect example. He's worked all these years, and what's he got? Nothing."

"Nothing? A powerful business magnate with the ability to get a show on TV? That's nothing?"

"Well, sure, but he's alone."

"Doesn't he have any family?"

"He had a wife back before the big blow-up, but after that," he shook his head, "nothing. He always had a young, sexy babe on his arm, but they just wanted his money."

"What's this big blow-up?"

"I told you, didn't I? When he was flat busted. No one in the business would have anything to do with him. He lost everything. Of course, he went on to build it all back and then some," he said in a tone of respect, "but he's had a stream of both good and bad luck."

"Do you remember when those bad years were?"

"Not exactly. Why?"

"I just got a piece of news that nearly knocked me over," she said. "Tony managed my uncle's career. You remember a singer named Victor Markham in the 70's?"

"Sure. A great singer. He was your uncle?"

"Gina's father. Gina changed her name to McCurdy when her mother remarried, but her father was Victor Markham. And Tony was his manager."

"Victor Markham's daughter! Who would have known? 'Course, I'm not surprised Tony was his manager. Tony managed everyone."

"That's what I mean. He may have lost love and success, but how can you look at what he's accomplished since then, and say he's got nothing to show for it? He's got a mansion in Malibu, and didn't you say something about a vintage car collection?"

"Oh, yeah. You ought to ask him to show it to you. There's nothing he likes more than showing off those cars. Matter of fact, it'd do him good to have someone show an interest. He's really been down in the dumps."

"I'm not good at playing shrink."

"I didn't mean that. I just thought since you both share the same interest, it might make him feel better."

She gave him a direct look. "Sonnie, is this guy having an identity crisis? 'Cause, if he is, I need to know."

"No, no. Gina's death did a number on him, that's all. That crackly laugh of hers and those rapid-fire jokes. She got to him."

"I have to admit my ears perked up when I heard he has a '32 Lincoln Roadster."

"He's got a whole garage full of cars that'll knock you out."

"I hear he's also got a dual cowl phaeton."

Sonnie looked blank.

"A Cadillac. 1930. They're incredible."

"How did you know that?"

"He told the police the night of the murder."

He looked at her with admiration. "How'd you get so interested in antique cars?"

"I know, it's a strange hobby for a girl."

"Raising pythons is a strange hobby."

"And I'll bet you've known a few chicks who did that, huh?"

He laughed but didn't answer.

"I got it from my dad," she said. "He used to tell me about those beauties. In the sixties he started racing."

"Your father was a race car driver?"

"Not pro level, but he maintained several cars for other drivers, and worked on his own on the side. He was always around the cars, so I was always around the cars."

"Sounds like you were close to your dad."

"Yeah. I miss him a lot. Wish he was here to see me become a little more successful. He was really behind my decision to be a musician."

"Your mother wasn't?"

"Not really. She says marriage and kids will make me happy."

"So she doesn't put career first. Nothing wrong with that."

"It should be a personal choice."

Liz rose and took her car keys off the bar. "By the way, do you have the VIP tickets ready for the first concert? I'd like to give some to Paige."

"Sure." He slipped off the bar stool and pulled a stack of tickets out of a drawer. "Give her as many as she wants."

Liz started for the back door.

"Next time, bring a crowd," he said.

On her way out, she remembered she hadn't checked her messages and stopped at the phone in the corner. She dropped a quarter into the slot, dialed, then punched her replay code.

A rapid chill slithered through her as the first message played:

"This call is from American Airlines. A package addressed to an Elizabeth Hanlon was left aboard flight eight-seventeen, non-stop from Los Angeles to Boston. Please contact the Lost and Found department of American Airlines to arrange for its return."

She hung up, not bothering about the other messages.

●

Lt. Wahlberg's face was devoid of expression as she listened.

"It was him," Liz insisted, her voice tight with anxiety. "He was on that plane—following me to Boston! How could he have known?"

Wahlberg rose from her desk and shut the door leading to the chaotic squad room. "It was who, Ms. Hanlon?"

"This damn stalker! He's following me everywhere now."

"Tell me again about the call."

"It was the airline calling," Liz said, "not him."

"Do you remember exactly what this caller said?"

"Yes. That someone had left a package on the flight I was going to take. "

Wahlberg consulted her notebook. "That was seat number--"

"Sixteen-A. A window seat."

"Was the package found on that seat?"

"I don't know, but he knew I was supposed to be on that plane!"

"We'll check it out," Lt. Wahlberg said, flatly.

"Lieutenant," Liz pressed, I want to be able to carry a gun. Not just for my apartment. I want a permit so I can carry it with me."

"Let's find out if this person actually purchased a ticket and traveled to Boston, proving that he knew your destination, therefore indicating that he may have tapped your phone lines to get these facts."

"How else could the package have gotten there?"

"He could have simply asked someone to carry it onboard."

Frustrated, Liz sat back in the chair.

"How long ago did this call come in?" Wahlberg asked.

"I just picked up the message fifteen minutes ago."

"By remote? The machine hasn't been erased?"

"No."

"We'll have officers pick up your machine. We'll also arrange to have the package retrieved."

Lt. Wahlberg picked up the phone and punched in a number. "Have the bomb squad go in," she said into the phone, "but don't begin evacuation plans until I get clearance from the chief. If there's an all-clear, call me immediately." She hung up.

"Ms. Hanlon, if you want to go back to your apartment, you can meet the officers who will take that phone tape. We'll be in touch about the package. I suggest you make yourself available in case we need to speak with you this evening."

"I'll either be at Suzanne's or my brother's. Depends on the traffic. Carl lives out in Thousand Oaks."

"Do that. Don't stay alone."

"Lieutenant, I can't live in a bubble, especially in my line of work. What are you going to do?"

Lt. Wahlberg's reply was crisp. "We can't baby-sit you. Stay with friends. I can put a squad car in your neighborhood, but we're understaffed."

"What about the gun permit?"

"You can have a registered gun in your home. A permit to carry is not possible."

"Why, because technically I'm still a suspect? You can't be serious!"

"No violent crime has been committed against you," Wahlberg said. "It's not within my power."

Liz began to leave, then stopped in the doorway, snarling loudly enough for everyone in the squad room to hear. "If someone takes a shot at me, you think it would be within your power to bring the bastard in!"

Thirteen

When Liz pulled open the door to Brogino's at eight-thirty that night, the smell of grease assaulted her. The lounge was full, Corky was spinning tales at his usual spot at the bar. His pants were pushed several inches below his waist to give his belly "working room". Liz knew that from her angle at the piano, she'd soon be seeing the elastic band of his underwear, and maybe the colossal cheeks concealed beneath. Corky would tell her the best time in town could be had with him, she'd tell him she'd rather sleep with a slug, and his cronies would laugh. She wanted to turn around and walk out.

She clicked on the sound system, smiling at the same faces she'd seen week after week, but she felt no connection to them. Instead, she kept wondering who might have followed her to Boston.

Someone dropped a dollar bill into the tip jar. "Play Willie Nelson, honey. *On The Road Again*."

When she took this job, Sam had made it clear he wanted "regular music", and nothing else. The Willie Nelson classic qualified. She began the catchy introduction.

Song after song, she played the titles they wanted. Thirty minutes into the first set she glanced up and noticed a white envelope mixed with the handful of dollar bills in her tip jar. She brought the song to an end, pulled out the note, and ripped open the envelope.

Trying to appear casual, she looked up and scanned each individual in the crowd.

One couple on the dance floor stared back at her. "Hey, read your mail later. We came here to dance!"

She was tempted to toss the card away, to let its arrogant sender see she would not be intimidated.

She pulled out the card.

Again, a black grand piano was on the cover, along with several black music notes, and the words, "By Special Request."

Her heart raced. She opened the cover.

Sheet music covered the entire card. The outdated style of chord symbols reminded her of the early days of publishing. On most sheet music, the composer's name was printed in the upper right corner. This one was blank. The song title centered across the card: *United In Death*

Liz gasped. The card fell onto the keys.

"You gonna play or read?" a woman bawled.

Liz's hands trembled. She ignored the woman, and peeked inside the card again, scanning the lyrics:

No ordinary love for an angel like you
This ravenous craving as mortals we do
Play me the tune of our ultimate song
Till I'm united in death forever--with you.

She felt lightheaded. She grabbed the card and pushed her way to Corky's end of the bar.

"Corky! This card! Did you see who put it in my tip jar?"

His rosy cheeks pulled back into a playful smile. "Why, honey, you cheatin' on me?"

"I'm serious! Did you see anyone?"

The bartender moved closer. "Rocky! This card—someone left it for me. Did you see anyone at the piano?"

"What kind of card?"

"A sick one! Who's been near the piano?" she rushed, peering at the customers.

Rocky shrugged. "Everyone."

"Don't be a wiseass. Who?"

Corky played along as if it were a game. "So, there is someone else cutting in on my territory!"

Voices murmured over the noticeable quiet.

Rocky nodded toward the eager crowd gathering on the dance floor. "You got antsy folks there, Liz."

Suddenly they were all the enemy. Any one of them could dance till the night's end, then wait for her in the shadows of the darkened parking lot. A grisly image of being attacked raced through her mind.

Sam Brogino appeared from the kitchen.

"You think I'm payin' you to stand around and flirt?" His head tilted toward the dance floor. "You wanna keep this job, you keep the action goin' around here."

Her anger mingled with rising panic.

"Well? You gonna play or not?" he demanded.

"Not." She grabbed her purse, stuffed the card inside, and made for the front door.

●

Liz jammed out of Brogino's parking lot, eased her Impala wagon into the flow of traffic, snatched her cell phone from the glove box, and dialed Lt. Wahlberg.

"It a murder-suicide thing!" Liz blurted. She described the card. "There's no doubt any more!"

"Alright," Lt. Wahlberg said, "I'll need to see the card."

"What about the package on the plane? Did you find it?"

"Yes. It contained a music box."

"You mean like a wind-up thing?"

"Right. It's shaped like a piano. You wind it up, it plays a song."

"What song? Is the name printed on the bottom?"

Liz heard papers rustling.

"Two Hearts."

She slammed the brake; horns honked around her.

"Ms. Hanlon? Are you there?"

Liz eased into the right lane. "I'm here," she murmured. Her eyes darted to her rear view mirror. "I'll bring you the card in the morning," she said.

"I'm here for the night. Bring it in now."

"Right now I want to get the hell off the road!"

"Where are you headed? I'll have my officer pick it up."

"Suzanne Becklin's house. You've got the address."

She hung up and dialed Carl's number.

"What's up, Liz?" Carl said. "You're interrupting the game."

"Screw the game. I got another card. A really twisted one." She described it. "I'm scared, Carl. This guy wants to die—and he wants to take me with him!"

"Did anyone follow you out of the club? Look behind you, see if you can identify anyone."

She checked her mirrors. "It's all a sea of lights. Listen, I just called Wallpaper. She's sending an officer to meet me at Suzanne's. I'll call you from there."

●

Liz shivered as she sat on the bed in Suzanne's guest room. She pulled a section of the comforter around her shoulders and leaned back. "I can't stop shaking," she said. "I feel like it's ten below zero."

"You can relax here," Suzanne said. "Rob had an alarm system put on the house right after we got married. Nobody can get to you." She emptied the contents of another drawer. "So you just left Brogino's?"

"Yup. Left old Sammy with a room full of charged up boozers, and no entertainment." She shook her head. "This card, Suz, it was beyond sick. Who would write a song called *United in Death*? This SOB must have gone to one of those special printing places and had it made up. Hallmark doesn't print crap like that."

"*United in Death*? Isn't that from one of those dark musical dramas years ago? Back in the '20s, I think."

"That sounds like a pleasant night at the theater," Liz said.

"It was very controversial. I'll see if I can find it on the Internet."

"Thanks, Suz."

Liz hoisted the suitcase onto the bed. "It's a pretty sad state of affairs when you can't even stay in your own apartment." She emptied the suitcase and flopped down on the bed, feeling drained. "That damn Wallpaper."

Suzanne shot a glance at the wall.

"Oh, not your wallpaper," Liz said. "That's what Carl calls Lieutenant Wahlberg. A real ice cube. I've been asking her about a gun permit. She keeps me hanging, and now she says no. I might get one anyway."

"Yeah? You still think it's Sherice's brain-dead older brother doing this?"

"Did I say brain-dead?"

"I'm embellishing," Suzanne said. "But he scares you?"

"There's an understatement. He has dark, beady eyes that glare with pressure, you know what I mean?" She rubbed the palm of her hand up and down her arm. "When he looks at me I feel like there's a disease crawling over my skin."

"You tell the cops?"

"Hell, yes. I'm going to talk to Walter in the morning, too. Carefully, so he doesn't throw Jeffrey against the wall and flatten his face."

"If he's the guy, that wouldn't be a bad thing."

"If he's the guy, I'll do it myself."

"Well, you can relax tonight, and you know you can stay next week when I'm gone, too."

"Where are you off to now?"

"Amy's opening for Tony Bennett next week in New Zealand, then a couple of days in Australia. Great exposure. Our conga player thinks she's going to get him in the sack."

"Bennett? Never happen."

"Don't tell her. I'm sure that's why she signed on."

"I'm glad Marty isn't finding traveling work for us right now. It's going to be awhile before I can set foot on an airplane."

Suzanne went to her computer while Liz called Carl.

"I'm settled in here at Suz's," she told him. "A patrol cop came by and I gave him the card. He said he'd drive by periodically, check on the house."

"Liz," Carl said, "I don't like the way this is shaping up."

"Then you're gonna love this: Wallpaper said the package on the plane was a music box. Shaped like an antique grand piano with a jade top. Very classy," she said. "Something you'd display over the fireplace."

"There's a clue," he said, sarcastically. "Jerk doesn't know you don't have a fireplace."

"The song it plays is called *Two Hearts*."

"Am I supposed to recognize that?"

"Remember my lessons with Sister Angelica? I played it in fifth grade. It's a waltz, a piano classic. It's in all the method books."

"You think this garbage heap is someone from the past?"

She eased down on the edge of the bed. "I don't know. I haven't played it in years until the other day. I'm helping Sherice learn it for Walter's recital."

"Jeezus, it's looking more and more like that odd ball brother," Carl said. "He's probably got a thing for you. He hears his little sister playing a piece you're teaching her, and in his warped mind he figures you chose it as a personal message to him."

"Maybe. The card in the tip jar tonight had the music to a weird song about death. Suz thinks it's from a theatrical tragedy fifty years ago."

"Liz, we're getting you a gun. The hell with Wallpaper."

"I've been thinking about that. What would you think about a bodyguard instead? Don't say it's expensive; I already know that. I'll pay you back somehow."

"Even better!"

"I'm really scared, Carl."

"I'll make some calls. You can pay me back when you get rich and famous."

"I'm not sure I want to be famous anymore."

Fourteen

Brawny, barrel-chested Nuke McPhearson was a tree
stump in human form. His short blonde hair was crew
cut. Liz found him friendly enough, but she sensed a
fierce power beneath the surface. Nuke was in the right line of
work.

He arrived punctually at Suzanne's door in a white sedan

displaying the green and black logo of the McPhearson Private Security Company. Liz had trouble keeping her gaze from wandering over his powerful physique. Even his hands looked iron-hard as they wrapped around the coffee mug she handed him.

They sat in Suzanne's sunny kitchen.

"You'll have to tell me how this works, Nuke," she said. "This is a first for me."

"Simple. I go where you go, do everything you do. I stick around until the situation is secure. Your brother filled me in about your cousin's murder, and this person stalking you. Not what I'd call a secure situation."

"When you say 'go everywhere with me'," she hedged, "you mean, say, to rehearsals, gigs, shopping—"

"Everywhere," he said. "Our company usually works in twelve hour shifts, but your brother thought it would be more comfortable for you to have the same person with you for a few days at a time. After a week, we'll decide whether or not to bring in a replacement."

"I see. Well, good," she replied, thinking about privacy, then quickly dismissing it. Staying alive was the key here. "You know Karate, Nuke?"

He nodded.

"You carry a gun?"

"I do, yes."

"Are you a crack shot?"

"I am."

Another 'one-shot-Erskine.' Mentally, she toyed with names to call him, settling on Nuke-the-Knee-Breaker. Crippling a specialty.

She checked the wall clock. "We better be going. I've got to catch Walter before he opens."

●

Nuke parked under a sign with the words McCAIN'S MUSICLAND in bright red, and several music notes splashed around its border. Walter's car was the only one in the lot. The CLOSED sign still hung against the glass on the front door. Liz got out and knocked on the splintered wood.

Squealing tires whined behind them. Startled, she spun around, but it was only an irate driver squeezing around a slower car at the light. She blew out a big breath, and knocked again.

Inside MusicLand, the overhead lights were on, but Walter didn't answer, and he was nowhere in sight.

"He's probably in the back organizing instruments," she said to Nuke. "He'll never admit it, but his hearing isn't very good anymore." She made a fist and pounded till the door rattled.

Walter stuck his head around the corner of the storage room. She waved through the glass. He jogged toward her, the keys on his belt jangling with each step.

"I'm coming, hold your horses."

Walter McCain was six-foot-four. His curly, dark brown hair was flecked with gray. He had a long, lean face with big, round, brown eyes which sagged from fatigue by the end of the day. But his quick smile gave him an easy, commanding presence. He got his way without raising his voice, and children loved him.

The tumbler clicked in the door. "Sorry, I was in the back."

Liz and Nuke entered. Liz slid the bolt back into its locked position.

"Jesus, what happened to you?" Walter asked, scrutinizing her face. "You look awful. Here, sit down."

"I'm okay. Walter, this is Nuke McPhearson, my new shadow."

Walter pumped Nuke's hand enthusiastically. "Well, it's about time, that's all I can say. I'm certainly glad to meet you, Nuke."

"My pleasure," Nuke said. "Liz told me about your studio on the way over. Maybe when things settle down, I'll sign up for some guitar lessons." He took a seat facing the door.

The silence inside the store was a contrast to the usual cacophony of competing pitches and frequencies during business hours. "I didn't think this place could be so quiet," Liz said.

"Sometimes I stay here late at night just to listen to the peace."

"You mean the overtones aren't still vibrating in the walls?"

He smiled.

"Did the new student model clarinets come in yet?" she asked.

He arched one eyebrow. "You're kidding, right?"

"Sorry. Momentary insanity. Not that I'm in any hurry to hear the honks and squeaks of beginning clarinet players when I'm teaching."

"I started out on clarinet."

"You had talent."

"You didn't come here to talk about clarinets. You said there's some punk leaving cards for you in my piano room. You're pretty sure it's Jeffrey Williams?"

"I'm not sure of anything! I'm not even sure it's a guy."

"How many times has he—or she—done this?"

"Seven."

"Tell me."

"The first was in the piano room downstairs. Since other teachers use that room too, I blew it off. The second was at Brogino's, and the third was stuck inside the new songbook you ordered for me. There were snapshots inside another, taken right after I'd had my hair cut."

"That's four."

She filled him in about the package on the plane, the card on her windshield, and the latest with the sheet music printed inside. "I didn't see Jeffrey in Brogino's, but I freaked out anyway."

"You get fired?"

"No. I think Sam would rather keep me around so he can harass me. That's when we hired Nuke."

Walter pulled another stool from behind the counter, and sat in silence, rubbing his hand over his chin. Finally, he said, "That package on the plane—who knew you were going to Boston?"

"Everybody. I had to make arrangements to cover my gigs as well as my students here."

He looked down at his gnarled hands. "I never liked this Jeffrey kid. I'll take care of him."

"What'd 'ya mean, 'take care of'?"

"I mean you don't have to worry about him. I'll take care of him."

"There'll be plenty of turmoil if you ban him from coming onto the property, or even worse if you stop Sherice's lessons."

He looked shocked. "Who said anything about stopping her lessons? She isn't doing anything. And I never said I was gonna ban him from the studio."

"Then ... what?"

"I cut my teeth getting rid of sleaze balls who bothered the girl singers in the bands, and I did it for darn near fifty years. I know how to handle those types."

"You think Jeffrey is one of those types?"

His gaze was fiery, and she got an image of him as a young man picking up the town drunk by the arm pits and slinging him, head first, out the stage door.

He gave her another direct look. "I think I'm a pretty good judge of character."

"I wasn't questioning that," she said. "But for now, can you just watch him, Walt? Use that good judgment to see what he's up to?"

"I intend to watch him," he said, "closely."

"Good, because if it's him, I don't want him to know we're onto him yet."

"Are you saying you want to take care of him yourself?"

She faced him. "You got a problem with that?"

A glimmer of merriment showed in his expression. "Now I've got to watch the two of you rolling around the floor, fightin' and kickin' like wild animals?"

She put on her jacket. "You don't have to watch."

●

Paige's two-story building was brightly lit, the sidewalk was cleared, the property once again looked inviting.

Nuke parked under a street light, pulled a leather bag from the back, and tucked a body building magazine under his arm. They headed for the front door.

"Some clients are uncomfortable having another person around all the time," Nuke said, "especially someone they don't know. So I usually curl up across the room and read. You just forget I'm there. Nothing I hear will ever be repeated."

"That's good to know," she said, touching the doorbell.

Paige answered in silk lounging pajamas with a matching

robe. "My day off," she said, opening the door wider. "I decided to relax." They stepped inside. "Do you have some news?"

"I wish I did," Liz said. "I do have tickets though," she said, holding up the VIP tickets.

"You mean the show's back on?" Paige said, her face brightening.

"It's on, and you're front row, center." She handed her an envelope with the tickets. "Paige, this is Nuke."

"Hi, Nuke." Paige shot her a questioning look.

"My bodyguard," Liz explained. "With all that's happened, I just thought it best."

"You don't have to convince me," Paige said. Television voices mumbled softly in the background as she led them into the living room.

At the edge of the room, Liz stopped short. The room had been completely redecorated. A deep rose-colored couch was the central theme, accented with large cushions in a printed fabric. New end tables and tall, gold-trimmed lamps added warmth. A dark wood entertainment unit filled one complete wall, its shelves empty except for the television.

Nuke found a corner spot and settled in.

"I have to replace all the stereo equipment tomorrow," Paige said. "Amazingly, they didn't trash the TV."

"Paige, this is beautiful!" Liz said.

"Actually, Gina did it. All I did was finish her plans. She'd started the whole design, had the furniture ordered and the new paint. After the place was torn up, I had to finish just so I could live here."

Liz took a stool at the counter that separated the kitchen from the living room.

"I was about to make some tea," Paige said. "Join me?"

"Sure." It seemed rude to mention she hated tea.

"Not for me," Nuke said.

Paige dropped two tea bags into cups and filled them. "This is great news about the shows. I can't wait to hear you sing. Thanks for the tickets."

"Sonnie wanted you to have them."

"I wish—"

"I know," Liz said, "I wish Gina could be there, too."

Liz glanced around the kitchen. "So Gina really had a decorator's eye, huh? It's so inviting, the way the colors blend together."

"Gina had a lot of talents. I think she managed to put most of them to good use."

"Tell me about other things she liked to do. You said she had an 'act' for her customers. Did it extend to other areas, too?"

Paige's words came carefully, as if handling the memory was like handling a piece of fine china. "When you live with someone, you learn a lot about them. Gina was the sweetest person. She cared deeply about the environment." She pointed to the corner of the kitchen. "Those recycle bins were her idea. And she insisted. Matter of fact, she insisted about a lot of things like detergent and dryer sheets without perfume, soap without chemicals, stuff like that."

Liz took tiny sips of her tea, discovering that with a little lemon and plenty of sugar, it wasn't too bad. "I never knew that."

"Oh yeah. She could get worked up pretty good about people who didn't protect the environment. Of course nothing got her worked up like a conversation with her mother. She'd never tell me what they talked about, but I got the impression her mother had some pretty fiery passions herself."

"Aunt Irene? Fiery? I wouldn't have thought that," Liz said.

"It's good they were close, though."

"I never saw them disagree about anything, but for a long time they didn't speak. Then, once they did, it was like they were hooked on something."

"Hooked? Did they argue?"

"Oh, no, but I know her mother drinks quite a bit. She'd call late at night and they'd get really sappy talking about the past. They'd talk for hours. Sometimes it seemed like Gina was the mother taking care of her own child. They were very loving together, don't get me wrong. Just private."

Paige refilled her own cup and topped off Liz's before she could object. "There is one thing, though, that would have set her mother off if she'd known," Paige said. "Gina had started dating this older guy, and she was going nuts trying to decide whether or not to tell her."

"She was sure Aunt Irene wouldn't have approved?"

"I guess your aunt is kind of old school. Gina said it was complicated and I wouldn't understand, but I just figured she wouldn't have wanted Gina to date a guy almost twenty years older than her."

"Twenty years isn't that much."

Paige shrugged. "Gina worried about her finding out. Hey, you probably know this guy. He's from your club—"

"Sonnie? He's only forty-four."

"Not him. The guy with the fancy car."

"Tony? Tony Perdusian?"

"That's him. They had a big thing going on."

Liz leaned forward. "Gina and Tony Perdusian were dating?"

Paige's laughter bubbled up. "Yeah, what's so odd about that?"

"You're sure?"

"Yes. She didn't want everyone to know, but I knew about it."

Liz wondered who else knew. "How long had it been going on?"

"Let's see. She was still working at the King's Row when she went into Germaine's one night, and Sonnie introduced them. Gina said Sonnie always had influential people around because of all the big names he booked. So their managers and agents would show up, and Sonnie would schmooze with them. Gina loved meeting those types," Paige said. "Big shots. She called it following the money. One night Tony was there talking to Sonnie about this TV broadcast, and how it could make both of them millionaires."

"So Gina worked herself back in as one of the gang at Germaine's?"

"Uh huh. Sonnie was glad to have her back."

"Have you met Tony?"

"He's been here a few times. I don't blame Gina for falling for him. He's gorgeous. And rich." Paige added, "'Course, it sure took her a long time to make up her mind about him."

"Why was that?" Liz asked.

"Well, Tony's kind of eccentric. I mean, he looks conservative with those proper clothes and all. And he's got incredible dark eyes that make you think he's undressing you. But Gina was right—he is full of himself. Always bragging about his cars, his coin collection, how he'd made all these stars."

Liz stared into her cup, thinking about her last night with Gina. She'd asked about a boyfriend, but Gina had denied it.

"Tony had the hots for Gina in a big way," Paige said. "At first, she blew him off, but then she kind of gave in. I think he genuinely loved her. In fact, I know he did, because he worked so hard to impress her."

"How so?"

"First, he dropped the names of famous people that he knew she liked. Then, he showed up here one night with a scrapbook filled with newspaper articles all about himself. Can you imagine? Instead of giving her flowers or jewelry, he gives her a book about himself."

"Did the scrapbook make her fall for him?"

"Well, Gina was good at stirring the pot, turning the tables on people she thought deserved it. At first, she thought he was a real dick, being so arrogant and all. She said she was going to show him by taking him for all he had," Paige said, apologetically. "So when she changed her mind about him, it surprised me."

Liz looked confused. "I don't follow."

"The scrapbook. It made her cry for days. Then it made her mad. Real mad. I'd never seen her like that, but she wouldn't talk about it."

"What did she do?"

"A complete turnaround! She started dating him."

"Would it be alright if I looked at that scrapbook?"

"It's not here. Brad took it, and who knows where he is now."

"Brad?"

"Brad was her real boyfriend."

"*Real* boyfriend?"

"Gina and Brad have been together forever. I figured you knew."

"No! Who is he?"

"Just some guy she was crazy about. I don't even know his last name. I don't want to speak ill of the dead," she said, "but even though Gina and Brad were always together, sometimes Gina dated old guys on the side for their money."

"Brad went along with this?"

"He was part of it! But this time, everything was different. She and Brad poured over that scrapbook for hours. Brad said the guy was obviously loaded and they could get millions. But when Gina got so upset over the scrapbook, Brad took it."

"How can I reach Brad?"

"I don't know. For awhile, he was around here so much I thought he was part of the furniture."

Liz set down her cup. "I should be going."

"You won't tell her mother what I told you, will you? It was just one small part of Gina that was kind of ... questionable, and there was so much good in her. It would only hurt her."

"Not a word, Paige. Thanks for the tea."

Liz spun her stool toward the living room, and was suddenly taken back. Against the wall, Nuke was perched upside down in a full handstand, palms spread evenly, legs straight up in the air. His face was a dark shade of red.

"Nuke?"

His feet glided to the floor. He stood erect, picked up his things. "All set?"

"You've got to be kidding," she mumbled.

Nuke didn't respond. He was already out the front door, surveying the walkway to the car.

Fifteen

Why the hell didn't you tell me?" Liz demanded, pull
ing her chair up close to Sonnie. He was hunched
over a cup of dark coffee. His hair was disheveled,
his chin heavy with a twenty-four-hour beard. He looked as
though he'd slept in his clothes.

Sonnie glanced over at a far table where Nuke was working
his hands weights. "Hold it down, okay?" he said to her. "I

haven't slept, and I'm nursing a big hangover."

She softened her tone. "You haven't been home since yesterday, have you?"

He shook his head. "Marilyn and I had another fight."

She wanted to say something soothing, but domestic bliss had never been her strong suit. "Where did you spend the night?"

"Here. It didn't seem worth it to go to a hotel. It was after two o'clock, and I had to be back here at seven for deliveries."

"Hey, if you need a place to crash, my apartment isn't far from here."

"Thanks, but I curled up right over there," he said, pointing to the booths along the back wall. "It's not so bad."

Compassion tugged at her.

"We've been splitting up and getting back together our whole marriage," he said. "I think I'll be moving out." He drained his cup and lifted his chin in a stoic effort to start a fresh conversation. "What was it you wanted to know about Tony?"

"About his affair with Gina. Why didn't you tell me?"

"I'm surprised you didn't pick up on it that first night we were all together. Their flirting was beginning to get embarrassing."

"Gina flirted with everyone. Tony knew she was my cousin, but he never mentioned it. I find that to be kind of odd. "What's he trying to hide?"

"Softly," he said, holding up one hand like a traffic cop.

"Sorry, but this could be important."

"If you're so worried about it, ask him tomorrow night at his party. Come on, Liz, he's a lonely workaholic. What could it hurt if he spent a few nights with a sexy young woman?"

"It doesn't hurt. But there's a murder investigation going

on. When you go around hiding something like that it, makes it look like you've got something to hide."

"Well said, but consider it the other way. He had a brief fling with a woman who then gets killed. If nobody knows about the affair, his association with her stops right there. But spread it around and now everyone's got their nose into it. His tiny flirtation draws hundreds of finger to him. Hell, the fact that he slept with her will make him look guilty of murder to some people!"

"Yes, that could complicate things."

"So let's keep it quiet."

"But what if the police find out? Then it turns back on him. Hiding it makes him look guilty. It makes you look guilty, too."

He looked at her sharply. "Why me? I'm not responsible for filling in every piece of information the cops don't ask for."

"No, but when it comes out—-and you know it will—it'll make you look like you had something to hide."

"I didn't. The cops can snoop all they want, they won't find anything. Besides," he said, "keeping the affair private wasn't my idea anyway. Gina's the one who insisted."

"Didn't that send up a red alert?"

"I never thought about it. I stay out of things that aren't my business." He looked squarely at her. "And so should you."

His eyelids started to droop again.

"It was probably because of Brad."

"Who's Brad?"

"Gina's real boyfriend."

His face screwed up with genuine confusion. "What?"

"Paige said she'd been with him a long time. She sure didn't hide that affair."

Sonnie's fingers made a steeple in front of his lips. After a thoughtful silence, he said, "Who is this guy?"

"I have no idea. I've asked Enos to check him out. Enos Kaperstein, the world's greatest researcher."

She walked behind the bar to pick up the coffee pot. "We need to get our stories straight, don't we? I mean, once you announce the broadcast date at the press party, won't reporters bombard us with questions about the murder, about our private lives, and especially about Gina?"

He nodded, resigned to it. "It'll be a nightmare."

"Unless, of course, the murderer is caught by then. So are there things I should know?"

"About what?"

"About the club, the concerts, Tony, Gina. Anything they might ask."

"The money for the concerts comes from investors; you know that. And if it was even slightly tainted, we'd have heard by now. Tony furnished complete records to the cops."

"Right. What about the club? They might ask me about you and the business."

"You're not expected to know how the place is run. You're fishing," he said. Spit it out."

"It's Tony. I know so little about him, and I'd hate to blurt out the wrong thing in front of the camera. Those years you two lost contact—do you know much about what he was doing?"

Exhausted, Sonnie's hand flopped down on the bar top. "Oh, Liz, what're you doing, playing Nancy Drew? Okay, you want to know about Perdusian?" he said, sitting up straight. "In the beginning, he didn't have a dime. My Uncle Booker gave him a key to this place, but not just so he could come and go as he pleased. So he'd have a place to sleep." Sonnie pointed to the booths in the back of the lounge. "That booth

I slept in last night was probably the same booth Tony crashed in for months. Uncle Booker would find him here in the morning and have coffee with him."

"Because he was drinking so heavily then?"

"No, because right out of college he'd gone into partnership with someone who took him for every penny he had. He was dead broke. Uncle Booker put him in touch with some people he knew, and in less than a year, Tony was building himself a little music empire. I mean, the guy had, and still has, phenomenal ears. He can tell a hit song before the first eight bars are through. He may have had to borrow the start-up capital, but it wasn't long before Tony was riding on top of the world. 'Cause he's smart."

"I wasn't trying to—"

"I know you weren't, but I've known Tony my whole life. He's a stand-up guy. I'd trust him with my life." His hands flew upwards, "I am trusting him with my life. What I'm saying is that you can, too.

"Here's a guy who's had to pull himself up by his own boot straps more than once," he said. "The guy has paid his dues. So, if he wants to have the company of a pretty girl, I'm not going to tell him he can't. Let's leave him alone, okay? Can you do that with me?"

"Of course," she muttered.

He pushed himself away from the bar with the palms of his hands. "Anyway, forget the past. It's the present that needs my attention."

"Okay. How did it go around here last night? Is business picking up?"

"A few of the regulars stopped in."

"You said it yourself; you give people a chance to be on TV, and they'll line up down the street to get in. We're all spreading it around, letting people know it's the same old Germaine's."

He stared into his coffee. "I appreciate it. Speaking of getting the word out—"

"Uh-oh."

"Nothing kinky. I just want to make sure you and the guys are ready. The press party's Tuesday, remember?"

"We'll be here."

"I'm counting on it. This is going to be a good old fashioned party. I'll schmooze a little with the reporters, give a few supportive words about the law enforcement in this city, then your band will play during cocktail hour. Get 'em relaxed and receptive. I'll announce that Germaine's is very much in business, that we are going ahead with our broadcasts, and give the starting date."

"Are you sure you want to do that?"

"This is essential, Liz. Anything I can do to keep my name in a good light is necessary."

Sixteen

Crystal chandeliers sent flecks of light shimmering across high ceilings. Below, busy white-gloved waiters balanced trays of champagne as they glided through the crowd. Clinking glasses, and soft chamber music filled the ballroom of Tony Perdusian's estate.

The festive mood gave Liz a temporary haven from her fears. That, and the presence of her bodyguard, Nuke, who had not left her side since they'd arrived at Tony's mansion.

"I'm going to circulate a little, Nuke," she said, starting to move away.

He walked with her. "I'll tag along."

So it is come to this, she thought. Liz Hanlon followed around by a security guard. But since his arrival, she'd finally been able to relax enough to sleep through the night.

She glanced around at the lavish furnishings and the expensively-clad crowd. "I don't think there'll be any problem here." She headed into the crowd; Nuke stayed a short distance away.

Across the room, Tony, charismatic in an exquisitely tailored silk-mohair dinner jacket, a silk handkerchief in the breast pocket, beamed smiles and greetings for each guest.

Danny came up behind Liz. "I see Sonnie isn't the only one who likes to play host," he whispered.

"I would, too, if I lived in a palace like this," she said, giving him a hug. "Of course, I'd need a staff of two hundred to keep it up."

"Who are all these other people?" he asked. "I thought tonight was for the Germaine's crowd."

"I guess after the murder Tony decided he'd better invite a few cheerier faces." She watched him welcoming his guests. "He's working hard to keep the mood high. I heard him say several guests are involved in other concerts he's promoting early next year."

Through the crowd she saw a stringy pony tail swing around, a thin hand snatch a champagne glass off a quickly-moving tray. "There's Miles," she said. "Where's Elliot?"

"Boy, I'd hate to pay the taxes on this joint."

She spun around at the sound of Elliot's voice. "We were just talking about how hard it must be to keep it running smoothly."

Elliot took a champagne-filled glass from a tray, and leaned closer to her. "Don't look now, Liz, but this side 'a beef behind me is eyeballin' you like you're his next virgin sacrifice."

"What?" She whirled. "Oh, that's Nuke." She led them over to him. "Nuke, I want you to meet the guys in my band so you don't tackle them when they approach me. This is Elliot Reinberg, our bass player, and Danny Amata, our drummer."

She pointed to the far corner. "The guy over there who's trying to get lucky is our keyboard player, Miles Aulander."

"A bodyguard, huh?" Elliot said, shaking Nuke's hand. His eyes rolled back to Liz's black satin dress as he said, "It must be a challenge to guard a bod like that."

"Elliot!" she cried.

"It's a compliment."

"Why is it always so hard to tell with you?"

Danny nodded toward the balcony. "Sonnie certainly finds it complimentary."

"What?" She turned. Sonnie was standing in the arched doorway, looking beyond the balcony to the tranquil ocean.

"Guys have radar about these things," Danny said. "Sonnie's been stealing glances in this direction all night."

"Earth to Amata," she countered. "I'm not the only female in here." She nodded at four young women in bare-shouldered, clingy-knit summer dresses. "They're blonde, they're tan, Sonnie's a guy. Need I say more?"

"Uh-huh," Danny said, switching his attention to the girls.

"Funny that Sonnie never brings his wife to these events," Elliot said.

"They've been married a long time, and I think Marilyn probably isn't the outgoing type," Liz said.

Danny turned back. "My point exactly."

"Look, let's settle this right now," she said. "Number one, I'm not interested in Sonnie. He is absolutely the wrong type. He's a wonderful man and a great friend, but he's just too flashy, too mouthy, too ... much."

"Okay."

"And number two, he's not interested in me that way. Believe me, I'd know. And number three, I don't fool around with married men."

Danny held up a hand. "Truce. How 'bout them Bears?"

"Moron," she teased, and moved off into the crowd. At the edge of the room, a long row of photos lined a hallway. Soon she found herself absorbed in the faces of famous musical acts she'd followed growing up. With each picture she stepped further down the hall, away from the party.

"See anyone interesting?"

She spun around.

"Oh, Tony, I don't mean to snoop, but these pictures are wonderful. One famous face and I was hooked."

"Like potato chips. Don't worry, I'm glad to have a guest who knows who they are."

"You mean there's someone on the planet who doesn't know Fleetwood Mac? Or Big Rockin' Martha?"

Tony smiled. "Not everybody is impressed," he said.

"If I had a wall like this, I'd be impressed. You've had such an incredible career. Managing so many stars, producing the music we all grew up with. Did you ever imagine you'd be so successful back in the beginning?"

"Funny, the beginning was really my dad's idea. He got me started."

"Really? Was he in the music business?"

"He was a booking agent. I learned a lot from him."

"He must have been very proud," she said. "Making a mark

in the history of pop music. Pretty exciting stuff."

"It has its ups and downs. I love the frenetic chase of getting a new act launched, but the parties and the late nights don't mean much if you're alone."

She nodded toward the crowd of young, attractive, trendsetters. "You seem to have been blessed in that department too."

"Merely business acquaintances. Some of them are here to meet the musicians who're going to be making news in the next few months."

Danny was introducing himself to a girl who seemed to be molded to perfection. Even Elliot was whisking a glass off a waiter's tray, and offering it to a knockout next to him.

"That's why I wanted you all to come tonight," Tony continued. "Your crowd at Germaine's seems to have a special friendship, and you've made me feel very welcome. I'll admit I'd like to whittle my way into your group. This is a way to say thank you, and to show you a little of my own world."

"That's very sweet, Tony. Very … sweet," she said, laughing. "There I go again, my all-thumbs version of communication."

"I think you have a way of cutting right to the heart of the matter. I admire the way you've handled things since the murder. Finding your cousin's body must have been terrible."

She nodded. "How well did you know Gina?"

"Oh, not well."

"No?"

"No, but even so, her death slammed me into a blue funk."

"Sonnie remembers her crackly sense of humor," she said, searching his face. "Did she strike you that way?"

"A sense of humor? Oh, yes."

"That first night we all met at Germaine's, I got the impression you and Gina had known each other quite awhile."

"Those little come on's, they didn't mean anything. Our relationship was just business."

As Tony's eyes left her face and glided over the crowd she wondered why he was lying.

"Even so, a terrible thing like that, it hit me hard," Tony said. "I'm afraid I haven't been very supportive of Sonnie these last few days."

"Well, aren't you juggling several projects at one time?"

"Sure. But getting ready for this party helped pull me out of it. Starting tomorrow, I'm back in the swing of things."

"Speaking of Sonnie," she said, "he keeps telling me about this antique car collection of yours. Any way I could take a peek?"

His face lit up. "That's right, you're a lover of the classics." They strolled back toward the main room. "I probably shouldn't leave the party right now. Why don't you come for lunch? Spend the afternoon. I'll show you around the entire grounds."

Entire grounds?

They moved back into the main room, and strolled onto the deck where Danny was now keeping two girls in rapt attention, with Miles and Elliot goading him on.

"So Gina signs up for this decorating course, see," Danny was saying, "and I'm going to give her a ride to class. Only she says she needs to stop and pick up some materials on the way. I'm thinking paper, pens. Half an hour later, she's in this upholstery store snapping her fingers and flinging her charge cards around. She's ordering fancy silk from China, and this shiny stuff she said would make classy drapes. 'Course, all this fabric comes on nine-foot bolts, you know," he said, his hands swinging wide to demonstrate, "and here I am doing a balancing act with these babies on the way out of the store. I've got all these rolls on my shoulders, and I'm not two feet out the door when I lose my balance, and one end goes smashing through the big window. Glass shatters everywhere, the alarm goes off, I start stumbling, sidestepping—all the time I'm trying to hold onto these heavy rolls on my shoulder."

The girl in red spandex leaned forward. "Then what happened?"

"It looked like Laurel and Hardy out there. My feet went out from under me, the bolts landed on top of the glass, and I collapsed on top of the whole mess. Took a few stitches after that one," he said.

Miles said, "Tell them the ironic part."

"The what?" Stretchy Red asked.

"Oh yeah," Danny said. "When we finally got to my car, we realized how stupid it was to have taken those big bolts out of the store at all. I was driving an Audi!"

Miles and Elliot broke up. The girls' smiles froze in place.

Tony stepped up. "You must be talking about Gina."

Danny turned. "Hey, Tony, this is an awesome party." He pulled up another chair. "You're right; we're telling Gina stories. That's all anyone wants to talk about tonight."

"Terrible thing to lose a friend," Tony said. "Sounds like you knew her well."

"Oh, yeah. Me and Gina," Danny said.

Tony sat down with them.

Liz strolled through the room still wondering about Tony's lies. She decided to tell Sonnie about it, and began searching the crowd for him when she heard his voice.

"There you are." Liz turned to see Sonnie waving at her from the edge of the deck. She joined him as he looked out at the shimmering Pacific. An August moon was low in the sky, painting shades of orange and gold across the horizon.

"I didn't think you should miss this view," he said.

"Fabulous. If I lived here, I'd never leave."

"Look at all the sailboats coming back from a day on the water," he said. "You like boats?"

"I like to watch them, kind of fantasize about sailing off into the sunset. But everything I like to do is on land."

"Music and old cars."

She chuckled. "Is that how my life looks in a nutshell? Just music and old cars?"

Sonnie turned serious, his green eyes searching her face. "No. I see a whole lot more for you than that." He took her hand. "I find myself hoping that I'll be standing next to you when all those things unfold."

She pulled back her hand. "Sonnie—!"

Had she misunderstood, or was Danny right all along? What was wrong with the old Hanlon radar system that she hadn't sensed this coming?

Sonnie made a quick glance over his shoulder. "Don't worry," he said, "I won't let anyone hear. It's just that my feelings keep getting stronger, and there's never a good time to tell you."

She stared at him, a million thoughts conflicting in her mind. She cared deeply for Sonnie, but romance? She'd never seriously considered it. "You just drop this on me out of the blue? Maybe you're not firing on all cylinders, but have you forgotten you're married?"

"No," he whispered softly, "I haven't forgotten. I certainly don't expect you to ... I don't know what I was thinking. I saw you walking toward me, looking so beautiful, and the words just came out."

Did he think his being married shouldn't matter to her? That she would allow herself to be compromised? That he could entice her with the sweet prospect of success, then dangle it in front of her until she slept with him?

"Is *that* why you offered me the concerts? Sex?"

He looked pained. "Oh, God, no! How could you think that?"

Of course he would deny it, she thought. But Sonnie was not devious or underhanded. He put his cards on the table. In fact, that was one of the things she respected most about him. A sudden thought jolted her as she realized that once she let her suspicions go, she rather liked the idea of the attraction.

"Liz, don't think that for a minute. What I feel for you has been growing for a long time."

"You said it just slipped out," she said. "You saw me standing there and the words came out. The champagne, the romantic view—"

"That's not what I meant." He took her hand and looked directly at her. "It's not the booze, it's not the moonlight. I feel what I feel. I know there's a thousand reasons I shouldn't be saying this. But whether I say it now or later, my feelings are real. I wanted you to know."

"I'm flattered," she said, "but working together, that would be awkward."

"It doesn't have to be."

Her voice pinched with anxiety. "Sonnie, I'm lousy mistress material! I can't be sneaking around in dark places, lying about who I'm with, content to be in second place—"

"I'd never ask you to do that."

"Then what the hell are you talking about?" she blurted, turning her face away. He was married. What else was there to say?

He let out an exasperated sigh. "I ... I don't know. I just wanted to tell you how I felt."

Seventeen

Dammit! It was only nine in the morning and already her pulse was thumping double time. As Nuke hit the on-ramp of the Santa Monica Freeway, all Liz could think about was what Sonnie had said last night.

"Traffic's light," Nuke said. "We'll be there in no time."

She glanced through the windshield, hardly noticing her surroundings. "Where? Oh, right." They were on their way to rehearsal. Yesterday it had seemed important. Today her thoughts were all about Sonnie Tucks.

She'd spent the night considering his words from every angle, replaying every inflection of his voice. Was he being straight with her about the concerts? Only an idiot would stick his neck out that far just to get a woman in the sack! If Sonnie made a wrong move and blew this business opportunity he'd be flipping burgers by Christmas. No, he'd separate his personal life from his business.

Which meant he was sincere.

But she felt overwhelmed. Gina's murder, a pervert tracking her, preparation for the concerts. Adding a love affair to all that was too much. Sonnie's timing was lousy.

Traffic bottle-necked ahead. She tightened the lid on her coffee cup, inhaling to calm her nerves. Two weeks ago she'd been a struggling musician with little to look forward to. Then she'd been offered a fabulously prestigious gig, a day later, her cousin was killed, and she's being lied to by one of the people who controlled that gig—and hit on by the other!

"You like hanging out at the library, Nuke?"

"Love it. Why?"

"After rehearsal, let's head over there. There're a few things I need to look up."

"No problem."

She looked out at the glittering orange sun as Nuke pulled into the parking lot of Germaine's.

"You probably think I'm nuts rehearsing on a beautiful Saturday like today," she said.

"Not really. You've got a lot at stake right now."

"That's for sure," she said. "You have a family, Nuke?"

"Not yet. Have to find a wife first."

"It would help. What about hobbies? Sports?"

He withdrew the same leather bag from the back seat. Two body building magazines stuck out of the half-open zipper, along with a set of ankle weights.

"I'm taping the Lakers game for later. Long range, I'm training for the next Ironman competition."

"So that's what this is all for." On the back seat she noticed a gym bag stuffed with weights. An exercise mat was rolled up on the floor, two barbells lay next to it. "You carry a portable gym with you! Very impressive."

"With the hours I keep, I have to fit in the workout whenever I can."

"I run a little, but nothing like this."

"If we get a chance, I'll show you some upper body revs that really produce results."

She packed the music in her arms. "While you're at it, how 'bout telling me your real name?" she asked. "Nuke must be short for something. Newley? Noland? Noel?"

"Can you keep a secret?

"Of course."

"So can I," he laughed. He gestured toward the vehicles in the lot. "You recognize these cars?"

She looked around. "That's Danny's van, Elliot's Jeep, Miles' brown whatever. The Caddie must be Tony's, and I don't see Sonnie's."

Nuke was looking at the bushes.

"Story has it that someone lives back in there," she said, "but I don't know."

●

The band was setting up in the lounge.

"Hey, guys, you remember Nuke, don't you?"

They waved hello as Nuke found a table nearby.

Liz set the stack of charts on the stage.

Danny made a face. "You don't think we're going to get through all those today, do you?"

"This is a music show, remember?" she said. "There'll be a couple of short interviews between performances, but basically this show is an hour of music. If it goes into a monthly broadcast, we're going to need a steady supply of sharp tunes."

Miles grinned at her. "It's a music show, Liz, but have you forgotten there are three other bands playing? We're only doing four songs!"

"I know, but we've got to have extras in the can in case changes come up."

Elliot leaned his bass on its stand. "You mean more than the ten thousand we already do? At the rate you're going, you're going to be so over-prepared, you'll mess things up."

"Jeez, what a wet blanket you are! Only you could see preparation as a character flaw. You guys ready to start?"

Miles began playing softly in the background. The unfamiliar melody drew her to the piano.

"This is beautiful, Miles. You write it?"

He nodded as he played the festive reggae rhythm with chords that led her ear to unexpected places.

Her feet started moving to the beat. "This is great! Keep going. Repeat that part—"

He repeated the four-bar phrase. "It's so catchy," she said. "Makes you want to sing along. You have lyrics yet?"

"I was hoping you'd write some."

Elliot strapped his electric bass over his shoulder, and picked up the bass line from Miles' left hand, giving "bottom" to the sound. Danny jumped behind his drums and added percussive highlights, then broke into steady rhythm on the full set.

Liz moved to the beat. The nuances of the song spilled

around her, giving her hints for the lyrics. "This song has such a joyous feel. Like a fresh, new beginning, or the start of a new love affair."

They were working up a strong ending, when two beefy movers burst through the doors pushing handcarts stacked with huge boxes. They stopped at the foot of the stage. One mover with a clipboard called out, "You the guys who ordered the copy machine?"

The music drizzled to a standstill.

He produced a receipt. "A copy machine, three filing cabinets, one double-sized desk, and one executive chair. Where do you want them?"

Tony Perdusian appeared at the office doorway. "Finally," he called out, irritated. "This way." He motioned them toward the office.

"So much for musical dream land," Liz cracked. "Let's start from the coda. See if we can build some excitement on that ending."

They began again but the mood was splintered by the racket of crates being unpacked.

She sighed, "Let's break till they're done. I want to get your two cents about a few things, anyway." They headed for Nuke's table.

Nuke was sitting upright on the edge of a chair, his hands behind him for support. Weights were wrapped around his ankles, as he raised and lowered each leg in steady, controlled movements, never allowing either foot to touch the ground.

Danny pulled up a chair. "You're makin' us look like weenie's, Nuke."

"Sorry." He started to pull off the weights. "I don't get a lot of time in the gym, so I take advantage when I can."

"Don't stop," Liz said. "Nuke's shooting for the Ironman

contest next year," she told the others. "Can you imagine?"

Elliot stretched his long legs across another chair. "What did you want to talk about, Liz?"

"Gina. I heard she used to put on a real act to make bigger tips. You guys know anything about that?"

"She liked to mess with people, that's for sure," Danny said. "But I never noticed a planned kind of thing. There really wasn't that much scholarly activity going on in her head."

"Like you were looking at her head."

"Contrary to popular opinion, I do have relationships with girls that aren't just sex."

"Name one. And don't say your mother."

"You got me. Actually, I was going to say Gina. We hung out a lot 'cause Gina was into it, but we never ... well, when we played that gig here last summer we almost did, but nothing really happened."

"I remember now," Liz said. "I walked out to the parking lot after our last night. You and Gina were sitting in your car, making goo goo's with the music blasting."

"That's what I'm saying," Danny said. "Me and Gina almost, but we never did. We were just friends. It's not like I rip the pants off every girl that walks. Besides, I think Gina got off more on the idea of hanging out with Elvin than she did with me."

"Who's Elvin?" she asked.

"The guy who lives behind the club."

"There you have it, Nuke," she said. "Someone really does live in those bushes."

"Good to know," Nuke said.

Danny nodded. "He's there getting sauced every night—you must have seen him. Gina loved slummin', you know? At first she was a little afraid to be alone with Elvin. That's why she asked me along. Although Elvin's very cool. He'd never hurt a soul."

"Elvin's a pussy cat," Miles said.

"He's usually got a bottle of rot gut whiskey. The three of us sat around that night shooting the bull," Danny said.

"A regular garden party," she said.

"Don't go turning up your nose," Danny said. "Elvin's a decent dude. Just going through a hard time. He doesn't really want to be part of society right now. His choice. But he'd never hurt anyone."

"I'm not being judgmental," she said. "The reality is that with a different set of circumstances, any of us could be in his position. It's scary."

"Not for Elvin," Danny said. "Believe me, he's got a handle on it."

"You're saying Gina liked the idea of hanging with a drop-out, but she took you along as a bodyguard?" she said.

"I'm saying me and Gina never did what you were thinking."

Tony strode out of the office with two workmen hurrying behind him. He pulled out a tape measure and began measuring the wall space near the edge of the stage.

Liz turned back to Danny. "Okay, so you and Gina were friends. What else have I missed?"

"She had an outrageous music collection," Danny said. "You knew about that, right?"

"Lots of CD's, tapes?"

"Yeah, and boxes full of music. Handwritten charts, yellowed around the edges."

"Uncle Victor's music! He wrote most of his own material. Gee, I can't believe Gina had his music all this time."

"So songwriting talent runs in the family," Miles said.

Tony squeezed behind Danny and stretched a tape measure behind the table. "'Scuse us," he said.

Danny pulled his chair forward to make room. "Yeah, Gina had boxes of his music," he said. "It was a legacy thing with her. I was teaching her how to read it. She was starting to catch on, too."

"Boy, I'd love to see some of those old charts," Liz said.

"Ask your aunt," Danny said, pushing his chair back after Tony squeezed back. "She'd probably know where they are."

"I will. Gina was just a kid when her father died in some kind of accident," Liz said. "Not long afterward, Aunt Irene remarried and they moved to Chicago. It was hard to stay close after that."

The workmen returned to the office while Tony measured the walkway near the bar. The lounge was quiet.

Liz pushed back her chair. "C'mon. We've got a broadcast to prepare for."

No one moved.

"If there ever are any broadcasts," Miles said.

"What the hell are you talking about?" she said. "It's Sunday. Tony's not paying this crew double time for nothing. Besides, I've grilled Sonnie a thousand different ways. He says the last step is to dismantle the brick wall, and we're in business."

"Okay," Miles said, "maybe I'm so jaded from working with producers who never come through, I can't tell a good one when I see one."

"I think we're finally on to something here," Danny said. "Maybe someday our pictures will be on Tony's wall of famous faces."

"Let's hope we don't go out like some of them, though," Elliot quipped.

"What does that mean?" Liz asked.

"Look at how some of them ended up," he said. "Big Rockin' Martha was damn near as big as Elvis for awhile, and she died dead-ass broke. Makes you wonder."

"Big Martha," Danny said, "now there was some down home Blues. My dad had a million of her old records. Nobody grooves better than Big Martha."

"Back then, lawyers didn't write the kind of air-tight contracts they write today," Liz said.

"If they wrote any at all," Miles said. "I know this isn't much of a consolation, Liz, but at least your uncle probably left your aunt with a comfortable income. Victor was a prolific writer. Even if he ended up with only half the publishing royalties he'd get today, there'd be a sizeable nest egg."

Aunt Irene had not mentioned her finances and Liz hadn't asked. Other than the small condo, Liz had no idea about her aunt's income.

The pounding started again in the office.

"Let's wrap it up," Liz said. "I've got something else to do before the gig tonight."

Eighteen

The afternoon was still bright when Liz and Nuke packed her charts into the McPhearson sedan.

"You still want to hit the library?" he asked.

"Definitely."

Nuke pulled out of the lot and headed for the freeway. "What are you looking for?" he asked.

"I want to get the feel of what the business had been like

for my Uncle Victor. The years he was managed by Tony Perdusian."

Tony had lied to her about the early years of his career. They were the beginning years of Sonnie's career too, and she wanted to know more about them. "The scrapbook contained articles chronicling Tony's whole career," Liz said, "but they'd upset Gina. I'm wondering what it was about that time period that made her fly into a rage, then break down into sobs?"

"Paige didn't know?"

"No."

Had Tony enraged Gina, or did something trigger a significant memory? Tony Perdusian had been in the forefront of pop music back then. A young man who rose to fame in his early twenties, then lost it all. "There were probably hundreds of articles about him," Liz said, "but he selected the ones he thought would impress Gina. Makes me wonder about the ones he didn't chose. I'll bet they're a whole lot more enlightening."

●

"The information you're requesting is quite old," the librarian told her, letting her glasses swing freely against the front of her multi-colored blouse. "Its all on microfiche. You search by subject or author, then narrow it down by headings until you find the actual placement of the article. Follow the instructions. It's very simple."

Expecting a long struggle to master the equipment, Liz was surprised to find the librarian was right. In a few minutes she was staring at dozens of newspaper and magazine articles about Tony Perdusian, producer, manager, a figure of prominence in the music business. The articles detailed the early development of many well-known pop artists, and she knew she could not remember all the facts.

Nuke was leaning on a filing cabinet a few feet away, his eyes sweeping the room.

"You have any change, Nuke?" she asked.

He pulled a wad of bills, two quarters, a dime, and a penny out of his pocket.

"That'll never do." She went to the front desk and changed several dollar bills, then began dropping quarters into a nearby copy machine. Two hours later she was still making copies.

As the pages piled up, she grew more fascinated with them. She did not notice when the room emptied out, or when the librarian in the bright-colored blouse left for the day. In her place, a man in his early twenties pushed a cart stacked with books, and began replacing them on the shelves. He worked his way to the copy machine where Liz copied the articles.

"You'll find a lot more material downstairs," he said to her.

"Even more than this?" she said, astonished. "Where would I look?"

He pointed to an elevator around the corner. "Turn right after you get off the elevator. You'll see the rest of the periodicals."

A ring of keys dangled from his belt. Singling out one key, he started toward the elevator. "This one's supposed to be for employees only, but I'll bring it up for you," he said. "Save you a trip to the stairs on the other side of the building."

"Thanks." She followed him.

Nuke was scanning a card file close by. She set the stack of copies next to him.

"I'm going to check the rest of the periodicals downstairs, Nuke," she said.

He pushed the cards back into place. "Wait for me," he said, struggling with the drawer that had stuck in an open position.

The young man turned the key, then left, pushing his book cart. Liz waited for the beep to announce the elevator's arrival.

The light came on, the doors started to open.

"You coming?" Liz said, glancing back at him.

Nuke looked up, instantly horrified. Behind her, the elevator doors opened, revealing a view of thick cables suspended in darkness. She started to move forward.

"No!" He charged toward her.

She turned back when she heard him scream, but her step had shifted her forward. She was teetering on the edge of the empty shaft when Nuke raced for her. He dropped to the carpet at the elevator's door. Arms thrust over the edge, he grabbed for her waist, but she dropped, slipping through his grasp. He squeezed harder, and caught her by one arm.

Her feet dangled. Pain ripped through her shoulders. Her other hand opened in a desperate attempt to clutch a solid object. She caught the edge of the door, but her palm glided down the slick-coated material.

"Christ!" Nuke grunted. "Grab my arm with the other hand!"

"I can't!"

His hands tightened around her wrist. "You've got to! Do it, Liz! Don't look down, just grab on as tight as you can."

Involuntarily, her gaze slipped. Below, a mass of cables and metal. Beyond it, the deep, black abyss of death. She focused on Nuke's thick hands wrapped tightly around one wrist. With a swift move she locked the other hand over his, her life now in his control.

Grunting with effort, Nuke began to pull her higher. When she was even with the floor, she folded a knee onto it, and pulled herself the rest of the way. She crawled onto the carpet and collapsed.

Nuke lay nearby, sweating, and breathing hard.

"That kid," she gasped, "he tried to kill me!"

Nuke pulled himself to his knees and leaned on the sofa. He scanned the huge room. "I don't see him." He knelt next to her and began messaging her shoulders. "You okay?"

"I think so. But I'm not imagining it. That kid told me to take this elevator!"

"I know. We'll find him."

He applied pressure below her neck, and she winced. "Ugh! Right there. That hurts."

"You're going to be sore for awhile."

Jangling keys and footsteps echoed in the empty room. Two men in maintenance uniforms ran toward them with two-way radios in their hands. The first to reach them was short, with slick, curly hair. His badge said his name was Oscar.

"You alright?" Oscar cried. "We saw the cables working from the floor below, but this car's been on the fritz for a long time."

"Then why the hell is it still in use?" Liz barked.

They looked at each other. "It isn't," Oscar said. "This one's been off limits for weeks."

The second worker's arm was bandaged from elbow to wrist.

"Where'd you get a key to this baby?" he said. "We collected the employees' keys two weeks ago. Right after I had my accident."

"Well, you missed one!" she said.

Oscar shook his head. "Six employees. Six keys. We got 'em all back. They're in the office."

An icy flutter went through her. "Where can I call the police?"

"We'll call them for you," Oscar said.

"Ask for Lieutenant Wahlberg, Hollywood Division. We'll be waiting right here," she said, easing onto the long sofa near the copy machine.

The workers took off, and Nuke began working her neck muscles again. "Like I was saying," he said, "your shoulders weren't made for that kind of strain."

"I'm sure glad yours were, Nuke. A simple thank you hardly seems enough."

"Part of the gig."

"Playing a song you don't like is part of the gig. Saving someone's life elevates you to hero status."

"You ever see that kid before?"

"Never."

"The cops'll find out if he really works here."

"You know damn well he doesn't.

●

No evidence of tampering was found in, or around, the elevator. The head librarian gave Detectives Milleski and Robbins the names of all employees. Two were young men in their early twenties, but neither fit Liz's description, and neither had been working at the time.

All six keys to the elevator were found hanging in the maintenance office.

●

The articles were bunched together in Liz's lap.

"How're the shoulders?" Nuke asked, pulling the car away from the library.

"Not bad, considering. I've been thinking. Maybe it's so obvious we're missing it," she said.

"How's that?"

"What if he's just a deranged killer who wants everyone dead? There could have been others before Gina. Now it's my turn."

She glanced sideways to see Nuke's reaction.

He shook his head. "Never happen. Put it out of your mind, Liz. I'm very good at my job."

Fighting to push the elevator scene from her mind, she said, "No argument there."

She glanced at the headlines in the articles. Nearly every one mentioned Tony Perdusian. The heart and soul of the pop music business had been controlled by only a few people, and he was one of them. Now she wanted to know everything about him, about HotRock Music, and about his relationship with Uncle Victor.

"C'mon, Nuke, it's the big pedal on the right."

He laughed. "I'm not driving fast enough for you? Is that because you're shoulders hurt, or because you can't read in the car?"

"Both. I had this stuff in order by date, but now it's a mess. I need to spread out."

Nuke checked his mirror, and sped around slower drivers.

●

Nuke had barely pulled into Carl's driveway when Liz bolted from the car and charged inside. She spread the papers across the dining room table and onto the floor. "I've got so much, it doesn't matter that I don't have the real scrapbook. This is better," she said as Nuke came through the door. "How about some coffee? I'm going to be awhile."

"Sure." He moved to a far corner of the living room and set a pair of hand weights on the floor. "I've got plenty to do."

She swallowed two aspirins, put on the coffee, and turned

her attention to the articles.

It was easy to guess which ones Tony might have included in his scrapbook. They'd be the ones that made him look like the 'Golden Boy.' She marked them with a yellow highlighter.

But others she found more interesting; she marked them in red. Seen through the prism of modern-day business practices, these articles were not so flattering. One in particular caught her attention. When Carl came through the door, she yelled, "Grab a beer. You've got to see this stuff."

He peered around at the papers spread on the table.

"There's some very curious info here," she said. "The things Sonnie told me about Tony being down and out just don't add up. At least, not in the time frame that he remembers. I mean, Tony had to be absolutely loaded back in '77. We're talking major wealth, and if these articles are true, his wealth is one of those continuing things."

"You mean like syphilis?"

"I'm serious. Listen to this," she hurried on, reading the parts in red. "It says that he was responsible for creating the careers of guys like Pepper Marvin and The Love Knots, Janey Sylvestri, The Big Toppers, Big Rockin' Martha, Victor Markham—"

"What years did he manage Uncle Victor?"

"From the end of 1975, right up till the fall of 1978," she said, stressing, "when he seems to have disappeared off the earth!"

"Who disappeared?"

"Tony! From 1978 to 1980. Two whole years when the name Tony Perdusian is mysteriously dropped from sight. Now think about Sonnie's story."

Carl was blank.

"Sonnie told me that in the early 70's, his Uncle Booker

put Tony in touch with some guys who could lend him the cash to start his production company. He did extremely well, and by the time Victor went to him, he'd already built several careers. He was well-known, well-respected."

"Okay. So?"

"I asked Tony about that, and he said his father got him started!"

"Maybe Sonnie didn't really know how Tony got started. That's an easy mistake, and it was a long time ago."

"They grew up together. He'd know. Anyway, Tony climbed to fame fast and hard, but after awhile there was a serious down period that worked something like a black hole. Supposedly, he lost everything. No one would go near him after that. Sonnie credits him with reinventing himself out of nothing, but frankly, in this business, I don't see how. Music is a business of contacts and connections. If he came back when everyone was against him, he must have had a fairy princess tucked under his arm."

Carl pursed his lips. "Or a whole lot of money."

"Bingo. And why not? He was loaded up till then. But what was he doing during those two years? How did he get back on his feet if nobody would help him?"

"Why'd they turn against him in the first place?"

"Another good question," Liz said, easing into a chair. "It's so strange. Up till '78, the name Perdusian is in every news article printed. He did everything but have tea with the Queen. At the very least, his name is used to enhance other stories about the business. Then, suddenly, in the middle of 1978, he disappears from print. Like he never existed."

"Maybe it's nothing more than someone else dominating the favor of the press for awhile."

She shook her head. "I don't think so. Sonnie's story makes

me think something big happened. I'm going to see if Enos can find out what."

Carl looked down at the printouts. "When does Tony's name reappear in the papers?"

She shuffled pages around. "The fall of 1980."

"Doesn't that year ring a bell with you?"

"No. Should it?"

"You were only a kid," he said, "maybe not. That's the year Uncle Victor died."

"That's right! He manages Victor's career, disappears for two years. When he comes back—bigger than ever—he avoids telling us that he ever managed our uncle. What the hell is going on here?"

"Our last names are different," Carl said. "He probably didn't know."

"He dated our cousin and lied about it."

"Didn't Paige say Gina dated him because he was rich?"

"Yes. She called it 'following the money.' Why?"

"Maybe Gina knew something we don't."

"I'll have Enos start with the black hole years."

Nineteen

My old chug-wagon would be groaning in low gear if I drove down a hill this steep," Liz said, as Nuke descended the curved driveway off Pacific Coast Highway leading to Tony's Malibu estate.

"What kind of car do you have?" Nuke said.

"An old one."

"C'mon, what do you have?"

"An '86 Chevy Impala wagon. Big enough to hold my equipment and house a family of four."

"Did I hear you say you love the classic cars?"

"I do. Kind of ironic, isn't it? I'm one of the few people around who really knows about old cars, and I'm driving a buggy that's overdue for the junk yard."

Nuke laughed. "If it runs, and it's got brakes, what else do you need?"

"I'd feel safer in one that was built in this decade." Failing brakes was one thing she wouldn't have to worry about with Nuke and his Herculean brawn around. He'd catch the car with one hand before it crashed into the sea.

"You seem a little anxious today," Nuke said.

"I'm thinking about Tony," she said. "He lied about his start in the business, and about his affair with Gina."

"A lot of guys would do that."

"And then there's Gina's "real" boyfriend, Brad. I wonder if Tony knew about him."

"Ask him."

"I intend to."

The paved driveway twisted sharply. As they got closer, she could smell the sweet scent of salt water. Nuke passed a row of trees that obscured the estate from the road. The stone pavement appeared, and they rolled to a stop in front of the house.

Though Liz had been there at night, she was struck by the exquisite beauty of the landscape in daylight. Lush, perfectly manicured trees and flowers, a luxuriant lawn went straight to the expanse of ocean. Nice to know there were some people making fortunes in the music business.

She wondered if Gina had ever come here.

Instead of hurrying to the door, she lingered, watching a

gardener diligently tending the flower beds. He patted the soil around several new flats of flowers, then returned to an old white pickup streaked with road dust, and crammed with gardening tools. He withdrew a pair of mid-calf rubber boots, pulled them on, and stepped gingerly through the areas of wet mud, giving the new plants an extra sprinkle with the soft spray of a hose. An artist at work.

At the front entrance, hand-crafted clay pots brimmed with bright-colored pansies, impatiens, and camellias. It was impossible not to notice the perfection of each leaf, each flower petal. Even the soil was freshly churned as if the flowers had been planted ten minutes ago.

She touched the door bell, but before the last notes of the melody chimed, Tony was in front of her, one arm outstretched to welcome them.

"You made it. Come in, come in."

"Tony, you remember Nuke from your party?"

"Sure," he said, shaking Nuke's hand.

"What an incredible palace this is," Liz said, stepping inside.

"You've seen it before."

"It was dark the night of the party. In daylight, it's even more sensational."

One step down led to the spacious room with a huge picture window large enough, and close enough, to the blue-green of the sea to give her a feeling of infinite space.

"I've been here so long I suppose I take it in stride," Tony said, "though I know I shouldn't."

"No," she said softly, "you shouldn't. It must take an enormous staff to keep this place up."

"There's a head grounds keeper, three gardeners, and, of course, the housekeeping staff."

"I imagine you have quite a security staff," Nuke said, nodding at a camera placed in the corner near the ceiling.

"State-of-the-art," Tony said, stepping behind the bar. "What can I get for you, Nuke?"

"Iced tea, please."

Tony filled a tall glass from a pitcher, then poured a glass of Chardonnay and handed it to Liz. Tapping the label, he looked at Liz. "I heard this was a favorite of yours. I'm a Scotch drinker myself."

"Scotch leaves holes in my memory."

"Wine doesn't do that?"

"Not that I can remember," she said, taking the glass.

"Let me show you around."

They followed him through the living room, past a display of rare coins in a glass case, and down the hallway lined with photos that had intrigued Liz before. To her, these famous faces represented the richness of Perdusian's life. She stopped to examine them again. "It still blows me away that you know all these people, Tony."

"I didn't handle all these acts. Some were just acquaintances."

"Didn't you manage Cat 'Blue' Casey? I don't see her picture here."

"Cat! Boy, that was a long time ago. I almost forgot," he said. "It was early in her career."

"Who else did you manage?"

"Oh, nobody you'd recognize."

"Try me."

"Let's see, there was John Wellington, Keith Starr and Freeway—"

"Keith Starr, the actor?" Nuke asked. "I remember him in a western series when I was a kid."

"That's him," Tony said. "He started out as a singer. He wasn't much good, but I brought him to some of my friends at the studios, and his looks took him from there."

"There have been stories about Keith Starr for years," Liz said, "but give me the real version. I heard he was such a bad singer, the engineers had to punch in one note at a time! That can't be true, right? I mean, if he can't sing a decent line, why is he even there?"

Tony laughed. "It's true! They'd have him sing the same line over and over, then punch in one note at a time, keeping the one that sounded best."

Liz was astonished. "You mean like 'cut and paste' on a computer? No way!"

Tony raised a hand as if being sworn in. "The whole truth."

Nuke broke up. "Maybe there's hope for my musical career after all."

They passed more photos, stopping at one of Pepper Marvin & the Love Knots. "I'm embarrassed to admit this," she said, "but I can remember being eight years old and standing in front of a mirror, pretending to be one of Pepper Marvin's back-up singers. I had all their moves down, and I proudly announced to the family that my life's ambition was to become a 'Knot.' They were not impressed."

"Sometimes kids' dreams aren't so far off. Now you're fulfilling yours from the front of the stage."

"The family's still not impressed," she said, making him chuckle.

At the end of the hallway Liz noticed one picture showcased by itself. It had no signature, and the man's face was not familiar to her.

"Who's this, Tony?"

"That was my partner, Archie. We started the management

business together."

The small, wiry man smiled with the enthusiasm of a door-to-door salesman.

"Was he a friend of your father?"

"Dad? I don't think so. Why?"

"At the party you said your father got you started in business. I thought maybe Archie was a friend." She watched his face as he paused, uncertain. When he didn't answer, she said, "He looks like he might have been a lot of fun."

"Oh, yeah, me and Arch, we had some laughs. Let me show you something really special."

They passed through another wing of the house. The sitting rooms looked unused, as did the library. Liz and Nuke followed Tony onto a wooden deck lined with the same nursery-perfect flowers, down some steps, and across the plush grassy lawn toward a stable.

"Horses! I didn't know you had horses, Tony."

"Lots of people in Malibu do. But that's not what you're most interested in. Come this way." He led them toward a large garage with a metal door. "This is my real pride and joy."

He pressed a hand-held opener, and a door the width of eight single-car garages began to rise.

The cars. Not waiting for the door to completely open, Liz crouched underneath and went inside.

At the edge of the garage was a 1932 dual cowl phaeton with the original dark blue paint job, buffed to a deep gloss finish.

"My God! I've only seen these in pictures." She moved around the vehicle, reaching to touch it, then pulling back with reverence.

Tony enjoyed her enthusiasm. "These cars represent a remarkable achievement in U.S. history," he said. "I'm thrilled to find someone who knows about them. When Sonnie first told me you were a classic car nut, I thought he was pulling my leg."

"Why?"

"Some people are curious, some are turned on by the cars. Others just know they're worth a lot of money so they like to parade around in them. But I've rarely met a woman who knows about the vehicle itself."

"My family's always been into antique cars."

"Yours is more than a spectator's knowledge" Nuke said.

"You grow up in the Hanlon family, you learn about old cars. How long have you had this one, Tony?" she asked, looking at the Lincoln Roadster she'd heard him mention to Lt. Wahlberg.

"Got my hands on this baby in 1980. Had it ever since."

"You drive it much?"

"On occasion."

She gave him a devilish grin. "I think you should drive it the night of the first broadcast. Show off a little."

With a hand under her elbow, he lead her to another vehicle. "It might be more fun if you drove it that night. Cars are made to be driven."

"My old dump wagon was made to be driven. A Lincoln Roadster is a work of art."

"I've been thinking about your car problems," he said. "I may have come up with a simple way to make them go away."

"You got the power to fix the lottery?" she asked, staring intently at the Roadster.

"A person like you who understands the artistry and craftsmanship of a car should drive a nice one."

She raised her hands in mock defense. "Please, the guys in the band have teased me about my choke-mobile for years. I can't take any more!"

"Then it's time you did something about it. You've paid your dues in this crazy business, you shouldn't have to put up with that old car, too. Why don't you let me advance you the capital? A simple business loan. In a short time you'll be earning so much you can easily pay it off."

"A car loan?" she said, astonished. "Oh no, Tony, that's very, *very* sweet, but I couldn't."

"Think it over," he said. "If you change your mind, the offer stands."

"Don't you know loaning money to a musician is begging for trouble?"

"I know where to find you."

"Ooh, good one," she laughed.

His deep brown eyes were on her.

"It's a very nice offer, and I will think about it," she said. "Thanks."

They moved slowly down the line of cars till they came to a 1957 Lincoln Continental Mark II. "This Lincoln cost ten thousand dollars new, so you can see how special it was, even back then."

"Beautiful," she murmured, but her eyes had shifted to the car next to it, her father's dream car, a 1936 Auburn boattail speedster. He'd longed for it all his life. Now she understood why. She could imagine him gently wiping away an imperceptible smudge on the fender. For an instant, he was in the garage with her, sharing the connection they'd built during his life.

Tony's voice pulled her back. "I've got a trivia quiz question for you," he said, leading her a few yards away. "Ever seen one of these?" Parked behind the famous Auburn was one of the first vehicles ever produced.

"A Stanley Steamer!" she cried.

"Damn, you really do know cars," Nuke said.

"I've only seen these at car shows. This one is, what? About 1905?"

"1903," Tony said. "It's called a Model B. Today they go for anywhere between forty and sixty thousand, but I got this baby a long time ago for a song."

She gave him a wry look. "Are you saying songs aren't worth much?"

Tony laughed, but she was absorbed in the old vehicle, renewing her appreciation for the invention that had led civilization out of the horse and buggy days, and into the age of motion.

"This collection is really something to be proud of, Tony." They lowered the metal door and left the garage. "It says something about the person who owns it."

As they walked back to the deck for lunch, he spoke eloquently about the high points of his life, confirming Liz's impression that Tony Perdusian had indeed lived a charmed life.

A large round table was set for lunch under a pin-striped umbrella. They started toward it when Nuke's pager sounded. He checked the number. "Excuse me," he said. "I should return this call." He dialed his cell phone, and spoke as he strolled slowly across the grass.

Tony led Liz to the table and they sat facing the ocean.

"This is beautiful, Tony, but what about a personal life? There has to be more than work."

"I've been so busy—"

She blurted, "I know about you and Gina."

For an instant, his features became rigid, then just as quickly, he recovered his composure.

"I'm not trying to intrude," she said, "but keeping something like that secret when reporters and police investigators are searching for clues to the murder—it's not really possible."

"Is that how you found out? The police?"

"No, they'd never release that information."

"Sonnie?"

"Never Sonnie. He told me to butt out!"

Tony forced a smile. "But you didn't."

"Gina was my cousin, Tony. My childhood pal. I'm struggling to make sense of her murder. Is it so bad that I know you were in love with her? Other people knew. Her roommate assumed I did. My knowing—what does it hurt?"

His expression relaxed. "It was only the media focus I was trying to avoid."

"Of course. Once they know, all hell breaks loose. But talking to me about Gina isn't going to do that. I certainly won't tell anyone."

"I should have realized that. You're right, trust is everything."

"I was hoping you could tell me about Gina's state of mind before she was killed. Some reason she might have bought a gun. Was she frightened of someone?"

"She never mentioned anything to me."

"What about her previous lovers? Did she talk about anyone with a suspicious past?"

"Really, Gina and I knew each other so briefly—"

A butler arrived with salads and a platter of baked breads, fruits, and cheeses. When he'd gone, Tony said, "Actually, more than the media circus stopped me from telling you about Gina and me. I thought if you added the affair on top of Sonnie's gambling problem, you'd consider the broadcasts nothing more than a pipe dream, and back out."

"Wait a minute. Sonnie's gambling? What's this all about?"

"Purely recreational on his part. I assure you, the broadcasts are not going to fall through. It's just that people like to talk."

"You're saying Germaine's financial problems stem from Sonnie's gambling?" she said, working to keep the surprise out of her voice.

"It's probably my fault," Tony said. "I dragged him to Vegas on his twenty-first birthday, and introduced him to the art of making a fast buck. He's never really given it up. Anyway, I planned to tell you about Gina, but when I overheard you and your band expressing doubts that the shows would ever happen, well, I chickened out."

"Oh, dammit, Tony! You see why we have to be honest with each other? All this doubt and distrust could have been avoided. Whatever you overheard, you got the wrong idea. We're totally dedicated to this project—all of us," she said. "If I'm going to pour myself into these shows, I need to know the truth. All of it, all the time. From now on, straight-forward, up-front, on-the-table, okay? We can't be walking on egg shells with each other!"

"You're right," he said. "I apologize. It's a relief to have this all out in the open."

"I mean it, Tony. Cards on the table."

"Absolutely. From now on, I'll be more up-front than you've ever thought possible."

"Okay. Deal. Tell me about Vegas."

"Twenty years ago," he said, munching his salad. "I introduced him to the gambling bug, but I also saved him from a disastrous marriage."

"Marriage? Sonnie and Marilyn?"

"No, this was years before he met Marilyn. We were drunk most of the weekend. Having a ball. Sonnie ran into an old girlfriend. She claimed she was pregnant, that Sonnie was the father, and he should 'do the right thing'. He was about to marry her, until I had a little heart to heart with our lady-in-waiting. The next morning she was gone."

"You mean she was never pregnant after all?"

"I doubt it. I think she got the idea when she saw all that cash flying around the blackjack table."

"So he started to gamble, and never stopped?"

He put his fork down. "Believe me, it's not serious, certainly not a habit. Simply recreational."

Recreation or habit? Either way, gambling as the cause of Germaine's financial troubles was something she had never considered.

Tony gave her a penetrating look. "Liz, I assure you, if there are ever any cash flow problems, I will see to it that your band is paid first, and in full. You've got my word."

"Okay. Thanks."

"And about Sonnie's gambling—I probably shouldn't have said anything. He likes to keep it discrete. I'd appreciate it if you forgot where you heard it."

"Heard what?"

Twenty

As they drove away from the estate, Liz felt she was leaving Treasure Island. But an uneasiness also rode with her. She had asked Tony to name some of his previous clients, and he had failed to mention Victor Markham. Then she'd asked about his start in the business, and he'd lied again. She'd promised Sonnie she'd respect Tony's privacy where Gina was concerned, but how far was that respect supposed to go?

"Mind if I use your phone, Nuke?" she asked, reaching for the phone on the console. She punched in the number of Germaine's.

"Help yourself," he said.

"Is Sonnie there?" she said into the phone. "Did he say when he'd be back? Okay, I'll try him at home."

She dialed his home number, and sighed when the machine came on. "Sonnie, it's Liz. I really need to talk to you. Call me at Carl's tonight. It's important."

She hung up.

"You told him to call you at Carl's," Nuke said. "I thought we were on our way to the rehearsal for the kids' recital?"

"We are. That won't take long. "Tell you what," she said, "how about staying on the coast highway? Take Santa Monica. Let's see what's happening at The Stop. Maybe I can get one decent answer today."

●

Tiffany's blonde hair bounced on her shoulders as she flitted from customer to customer. Liz sat on a bar stool nursing a diet soda that had come out of the gun flat as rain water. Tiffany hadn't noticed, and Liz didn't intend to be there long enough to send it back.

Nuke sat next to her, surreptitiously observing the room.

Tiffany set another dripping beer mug on a napkin in front of a customer, then came back to Liz. "Yeah, so, like I told you, Gina used to come in here with her boyfriend, but he wasn't that old."

"Around forty, or forty-five, real sexy looking?" Liz asked. "Big, round eyes, dark brown, thick, wavy hair?"

Tiffany thought. "I'm sure this guy wasn't old. I mean, his hair was dark and everything, but I wouldn't call him sexy. I mean, not like Danny or anything."

"No, huh?"

"This guy didn't talk much, either. He hardly ever smiled. Just kind of brooded, even when Gina was laughing with everybody."

"Thanks, Tiffany," she said, dropping a few bills on the bar.

●

Nuke cruised through the narrow lanes of MusicLand's parking lot. Every space was filled, drivers had squeezed in near the edge of the sidewalk and parked.

"Over there," Liz said, pointing to a tiny spot on the street corner.

They rode in the McPhearson security van. "I can't fit this beast in that space," he said. They continued down the street.

"I'm glad to see the kids' families are here for the rehearsal. Walter had wanted to hold it at the high school so the kids could get used to playing in front of a crowd, but they had an event booked in the auditorium tonight. This seems to have worked out just as well."

Nuke slowed and backed into a spot at the end of the block. "At last," he said, locking the doors. They walked together up the sidewalk.

Inside MusicLand, students, teachers, family members all crammed into the Band Room. Those who hadn't arrived in time to nab a folding chair stood in the aisles. Liz and Nuke squeezed in.

"You sure you don't need to find Sherice before she plays? Maybe calm her down a little?" Nuke asked.

"She told me she wants to handle it herself." Liz scanned the warm-up area behind the stage floor and spotted her. "There she is," she said, pointing to the girl in the crisply ironed white blouse and navy pleated skirt. Her tight-curled black hair was pulled back in pig tails and tied with red ribbons. Next to her, two boys giggled, their trumpets held loosely in their hands. One boy took a mouthful of water from the fountain and spit it into the air rainbow style, bringing laughter from others nearby.

Liz shook her head. "How does Walter do it?"

Walter McCain brought the room to order with a few short claps of his hands. "Let's go, people. Woodwinds first. The rest of you are the audience," he said, stressing the last word as if it carried massive importance. "Don't disappoint me."

A group of ten grade-school kids took seats in a semi-circle, ready to perform under the direction of an eighty-two-year old retired woodwind player, who conducted with a fond and painstaking attentiveness. Liz was sure he was another old friend of Walter's, probably from their Tommy Dorsey Band days.

When a couple in the third row vacated their seats, Liz nudged Nuke. "Up there. Hurry." They made for the chairs.

Liz glanced at Nuke. "Fast work. Hey, you don't look so good, Nuke," she said. "You're pale. You feel okay?"

"Something I ate. It'll pass."

"It's all that raw fish you eat." She looked more closely at his face. "Maybe you'd better go home. Is there someone I can call?"

He shook his head. "All our security people are tied up on other jobs. I'll be alright, but I need to find a men's room." He pushed himself to his feet. "You'll be okay for a minute?"

She scoped the room. Sherice's brother, Jeffrey, was nowhere in sight. "I'm fine. I'll stay right here."

Nuke slipped out a nearby exit. Liz sat back and was soon

engrossed in the music. At the song's end, the woodwinds held their last chord for a big finale. The conductor gave the cut off, and chaos broke out as all ten bolted for the stage exit with clarinets in hand. At the same time, the brass players took their seats. Liz chuckled to herself, grateful that stage direction was not part of her job. She thought of her first recital when she and Carl had played a piano duet together. The minute the song ended, Carl gave her a swift shove with his hip, and knocked her off the piano bench. She'd landed with a thump on the floor, her lacy petticoat fluttering. He was ten and had scored big with his pals.

She lost herself in the brass ensemble arrangement, until the back of her neck suddenly started to burn, as if someone was holding a flame to her. She spun around. Faces of family members stared back at her.

The song drew to a climax. Enthusiastic parents were still applauding when Sherice walked on stage. Barely more than four feet tall, she paused by the piano and announced that she had decided to make a slight change in the program. "I had planned to play a classical piece called *Two Hearts*," she said, "but I've changed my mind. "I'm going to improvise over a song everybody will recognize." Not announcing the name of the song, she added, "I hope you enjoy it."

She smoothed her skirt beneath herself on the bench, and began the familiar piano introduction to *Satin Doll*. Smiles broke out among the parents. Liz was apprehensive at first, but after a few bars, she relaxed. Sherice Williams had mastered a sense of control in her playing, and she had done it completely on her own.

Halfway through the song, Liz's neck was on fire. She twisted around. Directly behind her, eighteen-year-old Jeffrey Williams stared straight into her eyes. He had dark, scraggly hair that reached his shoulders, and wore a wrinkled tee-shirt and jeans. His most striking feature was a silver tongue-pierce. Liz could not take her eyes from the gleaming metal embedded in his tongue. Her stomach twisted.

She spun back around, chest pounding. She jumped to her feet, slipped out to the aisle, and dashed into the crowd that gathered behind the makeshift stage.

Jeffrey stood up, starting to side-step to the aisle. Walter McCain came from behind and blocked his exit. Jeffrey froze.

Walter's eyes locked onto Jeffrey's. "Don't be moving around while someone's playing, Jeffrey. It's not polite."

He applied a slight pressure to Jeffrey's shoulder. Jeffrey eased back into his seat. Walter took the one next to him.

Sherice's song built to its grand finale. Walter beamed, applauding proudly. Overhead lights clicked on, parents began filling the aisles.

Jeffrey fidgeted. He wiped his slick palms on the legs of his jeans and started to rise, but Walter's hand landed on his shoulder.

"Relax, Jeffrey. Don't run off. Tell me what you thought of the show. Especially that sister of yours. She's something, huh?"

Twenty-One

Germaine's lounge was quiet on Sunday morning, a good time for the band to rehearse new music."We can probably work through lunch time," Liz said. "There's not much of a crowd today."

"Not me, Liz," Danny said, tightening his snare drum head. "Got a session at two."

From the stage, Liz looked over the empty room. Nuke sat alone at a corner table, sipping a soda water, absorbed in a Muscle Magazine.

The band had arrived at nine. They'd worked out introductions, endings, and rhythmic feels for all the new songs Liz had slotted for the day.

"Wow, we're ahead of schedule," she said. "Let's run through Miles' new song. I finished the lyrics." She withdrew a sheet from a folder and started to count off.

"Hold on," Miles called out. He bent down and hit the "record" button on a large boom box on the floor. "I want to tape it for later. Go ahead."

Liz counted off the high-energy reggae beat, and led the song up to its abrupt ending:

Part of me is breaking, but this I know
Your kind of love—
You can take it all back!

"Great ending!" Danny cried, as he grabbed his cymbals to stop the ringing in an instant.

"I love the lyrics," Miles said, grinning. "They've got your usual tongue-in-cheek kick. Listeners are going to identify with these lyrics, Liz. They're perfect."

Danny looked at his watch. "We're done, aren't we?" he asked, starting to tear down.

"Guess so," Liz said. She reached for the boom box to play back the song they'd recorded, but touched the radio button by mistake. A rock guitar wailed furiously, bringing a song to its climax. A heavy gong rang out, and a deep male voice announced, "It's time for another *Moment of Truth* from the all-knowing Professor Prodigy! Separating fact from fiction!"

"What the hell is that?" Liz said, reaching to shut it off.

"Wait!" Miles cried. "The Professor's cool. Leave him on."

"Another factual actual!" the Professor announced. "A legitimate literal, the unfabricated, unadulterated word in musical history!"

"You've got to be kidding," Liz scoffed. "I'll bet most of his brilliance comes right out of the tabloids."

"Shhhh!" Miles said. The group gathered around the radio.

"On this day in history, exactly twenty-five years ago, this vocalist made her first appearance on The Tonight Show, giving her career the proverbial *boot* it needed to climb the ladder of fame! Let's hear the very song she sang on that show, *Just A Shadow of Love*. Be the first caller to name the correct singer, and win two tickets to tonight's concert at the Greek."

The music started as the Professor made his final announcement. "Remember, you heard this moment of musical truth from Professor Prodigy. The first, the foremost, the sage of real music!"

"Oh, please," Liz said. "It's Janey Sylvestri, and if he's such a sage, ask him what ever happened to her, or to so many of the other artists who were big at that time."

"Hey, you're right," Elliot cried, "it is Janey Sylvestri! You going to call in?"

She shook her head. "They've had ten calls already."

"Do it!" Elliot cried, and pulled a cell phone out of his jacket. "Here. Call 'em." He punched in the number. "I'd like to see those tickets go to one of us." He handed her the phone.

"You mean you, don't you?"

Before she could say more, the Professor was on the line. "Hello, you're caller number three, and you're on the air with Professor Prodigy! Our first two callers could not identify our mystery singer. Caller number three, we need the artist who sang *Just A Shadow Of Love*. Can you name her!?"

"Janey Sylvestri."

"Cor-r-r-rect! We've got a winner, folks! Your name is—?"

"Liz Hanlon."

"Well, Liz, you've just won two tickets to the Greek, plus an opportunity to quiz Professor Prodigy on virtually anything in pop music history! Liz, what slice of musical wisdom do you request from the sage of all musical knowledge?"

She rolled her eyes, as if to say, "cut the crap."

"Careful," Miles whispered, "you're on the air."

"Yeah, yeah." Into the phone, she said, "I'd like to know about a singer named Victor Markham. His career was climbing in the seventies, then suddenly it was over. What ever became of him?"

"Victor Markham! A tragic flash from the past," the professor said. "It seems Markham got mixed up with what one might call the wrong types—if you know what I mean. One of those career choices gone bad. And now, folks—"

"Wait! That's ludicrous! How can you say a thing like that with nothing to back it up? Victor Markham wasn't mixed up with any wrong people!"

"Ah, but history never lies. And there you have it, folks. Another factual actual—"

"Newspapers lie all the time!" she cried. "Factual, my ass!"

The line went dead.

"He hung up!" she said. "That son of a bitch accused my uncle of making a deal with gangsters, and then hung up on me!"

"You didn't get the tickets?" Elliot asked.

"Screw your tickets. I want to know how he can get away with lies like that on the air!"

"Maybe there's something to it, Liz," Miles said, gently. "I mean, there's a lot you don't know about those years."

"My uncle wasn't like that. I've searched every article the library had, and there wasn't even a hint of unscrupulous behavior on his part. This is such crap! I'm going to try the Internet tonight. Maybe I can find some essays written recently that look at those years in retrospect."

"That was back when the tones of the instruments were pure," Miles said, "not sampled, synthesized, and altered by computers."

"*Just A Shadow of Love* was recorded in the mid-seventies," she said. "I guess everything in the business was different then."

"I started out in the sixties," Miles said. "Before drum machines came along, before Fender Rhodes electric pianos were all the rage, or string basses had pickups. I assure you, it was a great time to make music."

They packed the last of their equipment.

"Thanks for getting up early, guys," she said, waving as they left.

Nuke walked to the foot of the stage and helped her gather her charts. "While you were rehearsing, I firmed up the plans for security at the press party. Sonnie's got his own team who'll work the room, and handle the crowd, but I'm bringing in three extra operatives from my office. Their focus will be entirely on you. I'm placing them around the room with radios, and, of course, I'll be with you."

"Good," she said, but she was thinking of what the professor had said about Uncle Victor. Was the music business really as different a short twenty-five years ago as Miles believed? It was rumored that many famous artists had faded into obscurity, and even poverty because they'd failed to sign proper, or binding contracts at the start of their careers, or because their management had simply swindled them. Perhaps it had been that way decades ago, when the recording business was just developing, but the artists Miles remembered had gotten their start in more recent years. The same years that Tony rose to fame.

●

Reggie filled a lazy susan with shrimp and stuffed mushrooms, and swirled it around in front of Liz and Nuke. "Don't wait for Carl," she said. "He's got the Lab on the phone trying to find out if there were any prints on that music box or on the plane."

"I was hoping I could borrow your computer later, and do some searching on the Internet—if he ever gets off the phone in there," Liz said, stabbing a mushroom. "Thanks for letting us both crash here, Reg. It won't be like this forever."

"It's not a problem. I made up the bed in the extra room."

"This is royal treatment," Nuke said. "On a lot of my jobs, I end up on a short couch with cat hairs."

"I'd like to hear about some of those jobs," Reggie said.

"Forget it," Liz said, pushing back her chair. "He won't even tell me his real name. Grab your bag, Nuke. I'll show you where everything is while we wait for Windy to get off the phone."

She led him into a guest room at the end of the hall. There was an eight-foot sofa with two recliners built into each side, the center section pulled out into a double bed. Reggie had opened it and made the bed.

"All the comforts of home," he said, "only fancier."

"Let me know if you need anything. I'm going to see what's up with Carl."

She returned to the kitchen as Carl walked in. "The lab

didn't find any prints on the music box or the packaging from our zoned-out friend," he said. "So our boy is crafty enough to cover his tracks. They're still trying to trace the box in other ways, but don't hold your breath."

"What do they know about him so far?" Reggie asked.

"Well, he hand-wrote those cards. No typewriter with idiosyncrasies to match so we're out of luck there."

"Don't forget about the new nutcase, too," Liz said.

"You mean Brad? Gina's *real* boyfriend?" he asked.

"Right. When Gina got caught running that scam, wasn't her partner's name Brad? That's an awfully big coincidence."

Carl flopped back in her chair. "Man, I forgot that. She told us she was dumpin' him, starting over."

"Looks like she raided the trash again," Liz said. "Do you still have the old files so you can find his last name?"

"Sure. I'll look it up," he said.

"If Brad's the same jerk Gina was involved up with before, and he's got the scrapbook about Tony, do you think Tony's in danger?"

"I hadn't thought about it before, but—"

"Let's see what Wallpaper think," Liz said, reaching for the phone.

"Ask her if the results of the crime scene investigation are in yet," he said. "I'm getting the great run around when I ask."

Liz stretched the phone cord into the living room as she spoke to Lieutenant Wahlberg.

"A first name isn't much to go on, and my detectives are swamped right now," Wahlberg said.

"I know, but my brother will find his last name in his files. I'll call you with it," she said. "Lieutenant, why are we getting the snow job whenever we ask about the investigation?"

"Germaine's is a public place, Ms. Hanlon. There were hundreds of prints to check, and that process is still going on. As for physical evidence, I've just now gotten those results myself."

"Great. What did you find?"

"There were marks in the white powdery debris."

"I told you that!" Liz said. "The drag marks I saw."

"There were two distinct sets of marks. Only one set is consistent with the placement of the powder residue on Gina's shoes."

Liz was stunned. "What about the other? You mean the killer dragged two people?"

"Perhaps."

"What else could it mean?" Liz asked.

"It proves only that there was another person present."

"Couldn't the killer have made those marks himself to throw you off the track?"

"Possibly."

"Unless there was another killer there," Liz said."

●

Liz woke before sunrise. In the bedroom darkness, she slipped into a robe, tip-toed down the hall to Carl's den, and closed the door.

Ever since Miles had mentioned Uncle Victor's prolific songwriting, she'd been thinking about little else. She remembered him playing with her in the backyard, but her uncle traveled frequently with his work, and was not always present at family gatherings. What had his career really been like? How did he feel to be right on the edge of national fame? What was it like on the bandstand during those years before instruments were amplified? Before synthesizers sampled other sounds, and played them back authentically enough to fool even the trained ear? How did he feel to be part of the creative world when music was played by people instead of computers? Or was she glorifying it in hindsight?

She connected to the Internet and typed in Rock 'n' Roll Music as a subject. After narrowing her search to the mid '70s, a query with Victor's name produced dozens of articles, but the publicity photos drew her in. Soon she was sharing in the life of the uncle she'd hardly known. She wondered if Gina had seen these pictures of her father.

Two top reporters covered Victor Markham's career, and their work appeared in both newspapers and trade magazines. As she read, Liz realized Aunt Irene had been right. Victor was star material and these reporters knew it. His career had reached a plateau in the early '70s, then skyrocketed in 1975 when he signed with a manager who had the clout to get wide airplay and exposure for his acts. The media tagged this manager "the Bullet" because he had a magical ability to shoot artists to nationwide fame. The Bullet's name was Tony Perdusian.

With Tony as his manager, Victor played nationally in "name" venues and concert halls where he sometimes opened for major acts. By 1977, he was close to the top. The next step would have given him top billing.

But then his career faltered, and he went into a downhill slide.

Why?

Aunt Irene would know. Liz checked a clock. Four-forty-five in the morning. Too early to call.

She yawned, knowing she should go back to bed. But her thoughts were firing now. She clicked on the listing of Victor Markham's music.

The songs he'd recorded were listed by title, with the year

recorded, and the statistics of its progression up the charts. The song's recording company was at the end of each listing. Next to it, the legal owner of the copyright of each song. To her surprise, in every case the owner of Victor's songs was HotRock Music—a company owned by Tony Perdusian.

●

Two hours later, Liz sat with Carl at the kitchen table. He filled her coffee cup for the third time.

"You look awful," he said. "Go back to bed."

"I will, but this is important. Uncle Victor's history. Tony's, too. Tony received an award for being one of the top music publishers with over four hundred titles to his name. No one can write that many songs. Well, they can, but they've got to be true writers. And they've got to be hermits. Don't get me wrong, I think the guy is massively talented, but nowhere is there any indication that he's a prolific songwriter. I don't think he even plays an instrument. Yet he's listed as having four hundred song titles to his name."

"A lot of producers hold the publishing rights to songs they produced."

"Doesn't sound right to me. I'd never sign away my publishing rights," she said. "That's where your biggest income is. Sometimes your only income."

"Things were different back then."

"Yeah," she said. "I was hoping to learn something about Tony's black hole years too, but there was nothing."

"All you know is that the papers stopped writing about him."

"No, Sonnie said he was completely wiped out of the business. But I can't figure out why. I thought Enos would have found something by now. I mean, where did Tony's money go?"

she asked. "I suppose he could have hidden it."

"Sure. There are lots of reasons people hide money," he said. "It's usually the IRS, or some kind of spousal or family dispute. Or he could have given it to someone else to hold for him. But who?"

"What am I, Madame LaZorra? But we should be able to connect the dots here. I mean, no one gets into a position of power without having a few questionable moments in the past."

"What are you saying?" Carl asked.

Her eyes began to droop again. "I don't know. But it bothers me that Tony never once mentioned Uncle Victor to us, or the fact that he was sleeping with our cousin. I had to drag that out of him."

"Our last names would have prevented him from connecting us to Uncle Victor in the beginning," Carl said. "After Gina died, didn't you say he asked Sonnie to keep the affair quiet?"

She stared into her cup. "That's what he said."

"Has Tony given you any reason to believe he isn't completely straightforward about these broadcasts?" he asked. "'Cause if you're worried, I can get you out of that contract."

"No, not at all. Ah, maybe Sonnie's right. Maybe I should butt out. I mean, the guy offered to float me a car loan, for godssake! But I want to know more about his relationship with Uncle Victor. Can you imagine what it must have been like to be that successful? Victor was almost there, Carl! Almost close enough to touch that rainbow. Then he died before he could reach it. He died so young."

"Just like his daughter."

"Right. We owe it to Gina and Uncle Victor to find out whatever we can. I'm going to light a fire under Enos."

Carl finished buttering an English muffin and slid the plate toward her.

She glanced at the clock. It was six-forty-five. "There's really only one person who can fill in the blanks from the past, and that's Aunt Irene. I think I'll rest my eyes for an hour, then head over there."

"I've got to get to the office," he said, downing the last of his coffee. He started out of the kitchen, then turned back. "Don't get any slick ideas about driving to Irene's alone. Wake up Nuke. That's what we're paying him for."

She started upstairs. "What's this 'we' stuff?"

Twenty-Two

Deep in a disturbing dream, Liz kicked the covers into the air. They landed on the edge of the bed, then slid down onto the floor. Another kick and her eyes shot open. Instantly, she was aware of another pounding rain storm outside.

The phone rang. She glanced at the clock on the night stand: nine-fifteen. She sat up, pulled the covers around her, and answered in a groggy voice.

"Liz? Rise and shine, blue-eyes. Enos here, already on the job."

"I was going to call you this morning. What's up?"

"I've uncovered something I think you'll find titillating. Are you fully awake?" he said.

"Shoot."

"You wanted details about Tony Perdusian. I've found an interesting twist about a business partner of his."

"Archie something," she said, recalling that Tony had been hesitant to talk about him when she'd asked.

"Archie Winthrop died within a day of Perdusian's disappearance. He was murdered."

Her pulse kicked up. "Tony killed his partner?"

"Didn't say that. I'm saying his partner was murdered at the same time Tony went to prison for bribery."

"*What?*" She jerked up, the fogginess clearing.

"That's where he was from 1978 to 1980."

"Prison! That's why he doesn't talk about it. No wonder Sonnie told me to drop it. He was looking out for his pal."

The phone clicked twice. "Hang on, Enos. There's another call coming in."

"Can't wait," Enos said. "Call me later. I'll have more."

"Will do." She clicked into the other line.

"Liz? You up?" Suzanne said.

"Hey, Suz! You're back. I wish I had more time to talk, but I've got to get to my aunt's."

"Remember those quartet charts I loaned you? I need 'em back today. Amy called another rehearsal, and she insists on doing those songs. If you're headed this way, I'll meet you someplace."

Liz got out of bed, carried the phone to the closet, and

pulled on a pair of jeans. "The charts are at my apartment. Tell you what. I need to pick up some clothes for the press party tomorrow night anyway. Meet me there."

●

Fifteen minutes later, Liz and Nuke were in the security van. White cotton-like clouds glided gently across the sky. Morning sun was peaking, a sweet relief after the series of rainstorms.

Liz's thoughts kept returning to the news about Tony's jail sentence, and the death of his partner. "Jail!" she said. "I can hardly believe it. It's important I get the rest of the facts, and talk to Sonnie today. The press party's tomorrow night! Reporters will be digging for information."

"You're right, there," Nuke said. "No telling how much fact or fiction might be dredged up."

"I know," she said. "We need to be prepared."

Nuke pulled the van to the edge of the curb in front of her apartment. Liz spotted Suzanne's red hair bouncing with each step as she crossed the street toward them. She met her half way and gave her a hug.

"New Zealand was fabulous," Suzanne said. "The name Amy Renoir is growing, and our conga player never even got close enough to Bennett to get an autograph. All in all, a great trip."

"This is Nuke McPhearson," Liz said, "my steady date. He's going to check out the apartment before we go in."

Nuke started to insert Liz's key in the lock, but the door pushed open by itself.

"Wait here," he said, pulling a revolver from a waist holster. He moved through the living room and into the kitchen.

Liz's curiosity got to her. Without waiting for Nuke's okay, she followed him into the living room, and gasped. The cushions on the couch were slashed, stuffing ripped out of them, the large throw pillows on the floor were cut up and tossed haphazardly. Contents of drawers had been dumped and piled up in heaps. Curtains hung askew from their rods, picture frames were broken and thrown on the floor.

Suzanne stood beside her, stupefied. "Liz—?"

"—I have no idea."

"Let's go back outside and let Nuke do the rest."

"Wait. I need to get some clothes from the bedroom."

"This gives me the creeps, Liz. I think we should call the police."

"We will." She pulled a folder from the bookcase as she walked past it. "Here're your charts."

Nuke called from the bedroom, "Liz? Can you come in here?"

At the bedroom door, her jaw dropped. Again, drawer contents were heaped on the floor, clothes from the closet had been handled, and tossed in a pile. Even the bed was upturned, the mattress leaned half off the box spring.

In that brief moment the events of the last few days converged on her. All the threats, all the spooky implications, it all seemed so personal. "This guy better hope I never get my hands on him."

Nuke was hanging up the phone. "We'll meet the cops in front. It'll be just a few minutes."

Liz rummaged through the pile of clothes and pulled out a favorite silk blouse. She tossed the few other items over her arm, and followed Nuke out.

●

They sat on the front steps, the door open behind them. Flowers along the border of the courtyard were in bloom, the grass around the stepping stones neatly trimmed. Liz surrendered to a moment of self-pity. "Typical. I finally find a decent apartment and I can't even live in it. With the number of nights I've spent at other people's houses lately, I ought to get a refund on rent."

She heard voices on the other side of the iron gate and jumped up. "That's probably them."

"Thorry to meet again under thuch bad circumstances," Officer Milleski said, hurrying down the walkway.

Officer Robbins hustled to keep up. "Let's take a look."

Liz took them inside. "They didn't cut the phone cord," she said. "Is that significant? I mean, maybe they weren't trying to harm me at all, but were just looking for something?"

"What might that be?" Milleski asked.

"How should I know?"

"It's premature to say what they were doing," Robbins said.

"Great."

Suzanne nudged her. "Let's wait outside till they're through."

While Nuke showed the detectives what he'd found, Liz and Suzanne sat on the same steps.

"You get any more of those creepy little cards lately?" Suzanne asked.

"Nothing since the musical masterpiece in my tip jar. Walter put the scare of a lifetime into Jeffrey. I hoped that would be the end to all this."

"Ms. Hanlon?" Robbins called out.

She stepped inside where he was poking through cupboards.

"You're not aware of anything missing?" Robbins asked.

She glanced around. "How could I tell in this mess? But--"

"What?"

"Couldn't this be related to the break-in at Gina's and Paige's place?"

The officers exchanged glances. "Probably not," Milleski said.

"Why not?"

He showed her where her door lock had been jimmied. "This lock was broken."

"And Paige's wasn't?"

"The methods of entry were different," Robbins replied.

"But why would anyone break in and not take anything?"

"There could be any number of reasons."

"Like what? They plan to come back?"

"Could be. Which is why you shouldn't be here, even with security. Don't make our job harder by putting yourself in harm's way."

"Believe me, harm's way is not a place I long to be."

Twenty-Three

Aunt Irene's sickly pallor accentuated the dark circles under her sunken eyes. To Liz, she looked beige and bruised. She opened the door, then swerved unsteadily and settled herself into a corner of the couch. Her clothes were wrinkled, her hair uncombed, and matted down on one side. The condo was in disarray. Clothes hung on the back of chairs, papers and mail were piled up.

"You comin' in?" she asked, acknowledging Liz with a hollow look.

Nuke followed Liz inside and closed the door.

"Didn't know you were bringing company," Irene said.

"This is Nuke, a friend of mine. Nuke, this is my aunt, Irene McCurdy."

"It's nice to meet you, Mrs. McCurdy," he said. "I was sorry to hear about your daughter."

Irene made a tiny nod. Liz sat next to her. Nuke took a seat across the room.

"How are you doing, Aunt Irene?" Liz asked.

"Got her buried," she said. "Been signing a lot of papers ever since."

"Carl and I have been worried about you being here alone. You know, he's got that big house. Maybe you'd like to spend some time there. I've been staying there myself lately, and it would be nice to have the family together."

Something flickered behind Irene's sullen gaze. "It's going to be the same no matter where I am. Unless you found some way 'a bringin' her back."

A strong odor of alcohol wafted toward Liz.

Irene finished the contents of a dark green plastic glass and reached for a bottle of V.O. to refill it.

"What'd ya drinking?" Irene said.

"Nothing, thanks. Too early for me. I was hoping we could talk a little."

"On the phone, you said you wanted some ancient history?"

"Yes, if you're up to it."

"What're you drinking?"

"I just finished some coffee."

"Honey, you wanna stroll down memory lane, I'm drinking. And I'm tired of doing it alone."

"Well, I haven't had much sleep, but I ... I could share one with you. Do you have some soda?"

Irene struggled off the sofa and weaved her way to a bar in the corner. "What about you, Nuke? You look like a guy with enough stuff to hold a good drink."

"I'd enjoy that, but we'll have to save it for another time, I'm afraid," he said.

"Why?" Irene said. "Someone at home gonna check your breath?"

Liz interjected, "Nuke's on duty, Aunt Irene. The truth is, he's my bodyguard. Lately ... I haven't felt comfortable being alone."

"A bodyguard," she echoed, shaking her head. "Imagine that." She looked from one to the other, then weaved her way to the kitchen, opened the refrigerator, and drew out a can of soda.

Liz followed. "Can I help?" She noticed a left-over container from a fast food chain, and an ossified cube of partially eaten cheese. There were also two full six-packs of beer and a few cans of generic brand soda.

Irene handed a soda can to Liz, then used one hand to steady herself as she tossed ice into two glasses, filled one with bourbon, and set the other in front of Liz.

"Thanks," Liz said. Before she could pour the soda, Irene poured bourbon into her glass, took the soda can from her hand and filled it until the fizz touched the rim of the glass. She handed it to Liz.

"Tastes like dog piss if you don't doctor it up," Irene said.

Bourbon and coke on an empty stomach. Liz swirled the contents and tentatively brought the glass to her lips.

"Aunt Irene, I know you told me to stop saying this, but I

really am deeply sorry for what you're going through."

"Don't be delicate about it. Call it what it is. It's hell. My baby's dead. Anybody thinks they could do better than me, I invite 'em to try. There's no hell after we die, you know," she said. "It's right here. This is hell."

"I know."

"I feel dead," Irene said. "Dead inside. Only my body hasn't gotten the hint yet. Every night I go to bed bound and determined to die. Then damn if I don't wake up again in the morning in this same stinkin' place. Dogs barking outside, kids yelling out on the street. But in here," she touched her hand to her chest, "in here I'm dead."

"I remember my mother saying that the loss is so horrible you'd wish—"

"You wish you could die, too." Irene nodded. "Your mother, she knows. Your daddy never should 'a died in that crash. But this—losing your baby—this is worse."

The bourbon warmed Liz, relaxed her jitters, and she found the taste wasn't too bad. "Could you tell me about Uncle Victor?"

Irene stared at her. "My Victor?"

"Yes."

The story emerged in spurts as Irene's memories rambled backward. By the time she'd come to the 1970s, Liz noticed a cozy feeling spreading through her. She set her empty glass on the table.

Irene began pouring another.

"Oh, no, I can't," she protested. "I don't have much tolerance."

Irene's shoulders sunk visibly. "Jeez, am I so disgusting even my family won't drink with me?"

"I get sick," she said, apologetically. Her hands stressed

her point, but Irene had already risen and was teetering against the counter, filling Liz's glass half full of ice cubes, the rest with bourbon.

"Not so much!"

With barely enough room in the glass for soda, Liz poured in a few drops of soda each time she took a sip to cut the alcohol.

"You never met my old man, Jerry, did you?" Irene asked, taking her place on the sofa again. "You're not missing much."

Liz sipped slowly.

"But Victor, he was a talent. God, he was good. We'd sit up half the night and he'd sing me a new song he'd just finished. Wrote a couple about me, you know? And some about his baby girl he wanted so bad. Gina wasn't even born yet, but Victor adored her already."

"That's wonderful. Do you know what became of his music?"

"He wrote it all down. When I was packing up to move to Chicago with Jerry, I found boxes and boxes of the stuff."

"So you still have it?"

Irene shrugged, "Not all of it. Jerry would have called me a sentimental old fool. I saved some, though. Hid it away in the basement."

"I'd love to see it someday."

Irene waved a hand. "All that stuff probably should 'a gone to you, anyway. You're the musician in the family. Funny, though, Gina insisted on carting a lot of it out here when she moved. Said it helped her remember him."

"That's understandable."

Irene smirked. "Yeah, lot 'a good it does her where she is. Well, at least maybe they've met up by now. Floating around together in heaven."

Liz smiled, suddenly noticing her cheeks felt stuffed with cotton. "It's a good thought, isn't it?" she said. "Gina being reunited with her father."

"Wish I was with them. You ever get the feeling you want to chase after your father?" Irene asked.

She had not identified it as that before, but that's exactly what she'd wanted to do. "Yes. Especially right after he died. I couldn't stand the truth. Every night I'd go to bed and imagine myself running down a dark hall after him. Anything to get close, see that he was okay. He was just ... gone."

Irene nodded. "I hope you never have to find this out, but there's an even deeper level down there. You find it when it's your own kid."

Irene's mournful words touched her, sparking a moment of intimacy between them. If Gina and Aunt Irene had talked like this, Gina had been a lucky child.

"Uncle Victor had such an exciting career. Did he have a manager, or an agent helping him?

"A manager! Ha! Some manager. Twenty years later, and I still can't get that bastard out of my life."

"What bastard?"

"The great Tony Perdusian. Victor thought his troubles were over when he took him on. Him, and that wimpy little partner of his. Archie," Irene snorted.

The photo on Tony's wall rushed back to Liz. The guy who looked like an eager salesman.

"Some managers they were!" Irene said. "Oh, they were great in the beginning, while they were getting Victor's name built up. That's when the cash was rollin' in, so naturally they were on their toes. They got Victor into every big club on the coast. Got him right to the edge of stardom. Even got him booked on the Johnny Carson show! And then—shit!" She waved a hand through the air in disgust.

"I heard Archie was murdered. Is that true?"

"Hell, yes, he was murdered. Tony sold him out! The same day he sold out Victor!"

"Sold out?" She tried to connect Enos's information to Irene's.

"To the mob! Those two were connected to the mob back then. Either in cahoots with 'em, or they did something to piss 'em off. 'Cause these bums wanted Tony and Archie, and it wasn't too hard to figure out who they were."

Professor Prodigy's words haunted her. "You mean like gangsters, killers?"

"There's only one Mafia, honey. They controlled a lot of the business anyway, but we never thought we'd have to get mixed up with them. One night three slant noses show up at our door wantin' to know where their money was. As if we'd know!"

Irene had shifted forward on the sofa now, stirred up by her memory and unleashed anger. "They got there just as me and Victor were getting ready for bed. They'd been ripped off, they said, and they wanted their money back!"

"Why did they come to Victor?"

"Victor and Tony were real tight then. They thought Victor was in on it, too."

"Do you remember when this was?" Liz asked, fumbling in her purse for a pen and pad of paper.

"Way back. Must 'a been around the summer of '78." Her eyes narrowed when she looked at Liz. "You wouldn't think I'd remember the exact year, but I do. There are some things that're planted in your brain like tombstones. That year's one of 'em. Everything changed. After that, he was gone, and Victor was never the same."

"Who was gone?"

"Tony Perdusian. Then those sick, lyin' bastards showed up again later that night!"

Tears slipped into the crevices of Irene's cheeks. She grabbed her stomach and arched forward as if she was going to vomit. Softly, she added, "I remember, 'cause that's the night they worked Victor over."

"Victor was beaten?" Liz moved onto the couch, sliding an arm around her.

Irene nodded. "So bad we thought it best not to let you kids know. These three pieces of garbage busted in, threw Victor up against the wall, yelling for him to tell 'em where the money was! When he couldn't tell them, they smashed his hands. Broke every bone in his hands and fingers so he couldn't play his guitar."

As a child, Liz had heard stories about Uncle Victor's "accident." She'd always assumed it was a car accident. Now the truth sent her mind reeling. Her tongue felt like dry flannel. She wanted to get some water, but Irene's grasp of events was too sharp to interrupt.

"Sweet Jesus, it was horrible," Irene went on. "I had to sit there and watch while they held him down and kicked him, punched him. After that," she murmured, "they took a hammer to his hands."

Irene's shoulders made jerky movements. Liz held her. "Maybe you should stop, Aunt Irene. I'm sorry. I never knew."

"Wouldn't have told you now, 'cept you asked."

After a long silence, Irene leaned back on the couch. "That's all past now. Going back over it won't help bring my baby girl back."

The past wouldn't bring Gina back, but it seemed to have a direct link to the present.

Irene picked up the bottle and refilled both glasses. Liz sipped the bourbon and soda only because it was wet. She wanted water but Irene was going on, purging her memories, freeing them.

"It's all a blur of hospitals and surgeries after that. My Victor—trying to force his hands to move across the guitar strings, denying how much it hurt."

"His faith in his music is probably what helped him heal."

"He had faith alright," Irene snorted, "in the wrong thing. Victor's faith was in that lyin' son of a bitch manager of his. Just before those slugs burst in, it was all over the news that Tony Perdusian was going to do time on some stupid bribery charge! They claimed he was bribin' radio jocks!"

"He wasn't?"

Irene shrieked as if the idea was ludicrous. "No one had to bribe DJs to play Victor's music. Kids were buying up his records like candy. He was right on the edge of makin' it when this happened; he wasn't gonna let go. So he put himself through all that recovery pain and waited for his manager to get out of jail. He believed with all his heart and soul that Tony would come back. That they'd be a team again."

"You didn't believe this?"

"Lord no," she sneered. "He had to be hiding something for them to be after him in the first place. Besides, anybody who would allow those monsters to do what they did to Victor, and let his own partner get killed—"

"Tony *allowed* Archie to be killed?"

Irene's face tightened with the vivid memory. "A grisly thing, that murder. Twisted. It was Perdusian these animals wanted, but when they couldn't find him, they took his partner, Archie. Took him down to an old cellar and pounded on him for awhile, then asked him again where the money was.

Archie didn't talk. I don't think he knew. And you know how they tortured him?" Irene said. "I know, 'cause they described the whole thing for us later. They revved up a chain saw right in front of Archie's eyes, telling him what part they were gonna cut up next. Let him sweat it out, screaming, praying for help. Then they did it. They cut him up while he was alive."

Liz was nauseous.

"Poor guy finally couldn't take any more, and he just up and had a heart attack right there on the concrete floor. When they found him, his legs were cut off at the knees, his arms sawed off at the elbow. But you know what the coroner called the cause of death? A heart attack. The pain. It was the pain that gave him a heart attack. And the fear."

The graphic details sucked the energy from Liz's limbs. Her head whirled. Maneuvering to the bathroom was an impossibility right now. The bourbon alone would have sent her head spinning, but the butchery Irene described made her want to throw up. She turned to ask Nuke for help, but he was leaning on the arm of the chair, his eyes covered by his hands.

"I never knew any of this," she muttered, starting to pull herself off the couch.

"Victor recovered, can you imagine?" Irene said, her voice low and flat. "They thought they'd break him, but he was strong back then. Doctors had him swallowin' pain pills, but even before they operated on him, he kept telling me, 'Call Tony. Call Tony.' I called him, alright. That bastard never returned my calls. He was nowhere to be found. And believe me, I looked. On Victor's behalf, mind you."

Liz was confused. "But Tony did come back—"

"Sure! After two long years! And then what he did hurt Victor worse than anything. He blew him off! After Victor had been hanging onto the dream that they'd be partners again,

Perdusian shows up in town, but doesn't call us. Victor races off to see him, and the great Tony Perdusian barely speaks to him! Tells him the markets have changed. There's nothing he can do for him now!"

Irene pulled a Kleenex out of her pocket and dabbed her eyes. "Victor was crushed. I could have killed that bastard," Irene said. "Nearly did. But then I could see that Victor was going to need some help getting over this one," she said, shaking her head. "I suggested we split town. Forget this music crap. But Victor couldn't even talk, the hurt was so deep."

Irene looked down at her hands. "Long as I've gone this far, I might as well tell you how your uncle died."

"It wasn't a heart attack?" Liz asked.

"That's the story I told the family," Irene said. "Once I realized the kind of pricks we were dealing with, I knew I better be careful what I said. No telling what they might do." She paused, then said, "I've never spoken of how he died before."

Irene took another long sip. "One night," she said, "they came back. Two grunts. One was even the same guy who smashed Victor two years before. Here we are just a few hours after Tony dumps him, and these two gorillas are *back*."

"My God! Did they hurt you and Gina?"

"Didn't lay a hand on us. They had Victor's contracts in their hands. Told Victor they'd just acquired him from HotRock Music. They owned him now. From then on he worked for them!"

Liz gasped. "You mean these guys just marched in and took over Victor's contract?"

"And there wasn't jackshit we could do." Irene took a long breath. "That's what broke him. Not the struggle to get known, or the years of being broke. Not even the loneliness of being on the road. It was those murdering bastards who broke him."

Liz forced herself to her feet. The room spun around. She grabbed the edge of the counter. "I'm going to get some water." She filled a glass and raised it to her lips, looking up and seeing Irene's sorrowful expression.

She gulped the water.

"Cutthroats is all they are," Irene rasped. "Victor couldn't work for them. He left his guitar collecting dust. Started drinking heavy. He made it through Christmas. By spring he was dead."

Liz sat down, trying to place the facts into the context of her own family, her own memory. But when she started to get up again, her legs wobbled, buckling beneath her. Her body felt ten times its normal weight. The glass Irene had refilled too many times rested on the coffee table in front of her. Logic told her there was only one glass, but she saw three. She eased back down and hugged the arm of the sofa.

"Oh honey, you're history," Irene said. "You better lay down awhile."

"I'll be okay," Liz said, clutching her forehead as she tried to get up again. It felt as if someone was banging her skull with a baseball bat.

"Just lay back," Irene said, gently. "I've lived with this stuff a long time. It's news to you."

"Nuke and I have to get back," she said, glancing up and noticing how pale he'd become.

"A few minutes would be okay," Nuke said. "I'll get us back in time to talk to Sonnie."

She leaned back. "I'm supposed to be making you feel better, Aunt Irene. I'll just rest my eyes here for a minute." The thought of riding in the car made her sick. "Just a few minutes."

"I'm glad for the company." Irene placed one of the couch cushions behind her head.

Twenty-Four

The press party began at six o'clock the next night. Sonnie had instructed the band to arrive before 3:00 to unload their equipment because the lot and the surrounding streets would be jammed. Liz could see from the freeway congestion that he hadn't exaggerated.

"How's the headache?" Nuke asked, as they crept along the Hollywood freeway.

"It was a full-fledged hangover."

"I know. I saw you debating whether or not to down that coffee. You going to be alright?"

"I took aspirin. I'll live. Can't you get around these idiots? The whole thing'll be over before we get there."

Nuke inched along with the crowd. At Camden Street, he swung into Germaine's back parking lot. It, too, was clogged with camera crews.

"Look at this crowd!" she cried. "I can't believe it. Sonnie said to park against the building near the door." She pointed. "Over there."

"When we get out, I'll be making myself into a shield between you and everyone else, so stay with me," Nuke said.

"Sounds like the voice of experience. How many times have you done this?"

"A few hundred."

"Come clean, then. Tell me some of the famous stars you've wrapped your arms around."

"Would you believe Nancy Reagan?"

"No. C'mon, who?"

"I traveled with Bonnie Raitt for awhile."

"Why, you devil! I used to date a sax player in her band," she said. "I know all about the action on those band buses. I'd like to hear some of your stories. By the way, you still haven't told me your real name."

"I haven't, have I?"

They squeezed through the crowded entrance. Nuke's six-two height and stocky build dwarfed Liz. They got inside without being recognized. When they reached the door of the lounge, the room had the luminous glow of a fireworks display. Kliegs flashed, camera shutters snapped. Exhilarated voices intensified the excitement.

"Let's head for the stage," Nuke shouted over the noise.

"I've got to find Sonnie first."

"Are you kidding?"

"No, it's important," she said, her gaze skimming the crowd. She spotted him waving to her over the heads of his guests. He was wedged into a far corner. She started toward him. Nuke caught her under the arm.

"I can't let you do that," he said. "Let's go backstage. I'll bring Sonnie to you."

"You'll never get that far in this crowd."

"I've got the radio. Another guard will get a message to him." He started to lead her away.

"No, wait. He's right there—" Sonnie was weaving through the crowd in their direction.

She'd stepped toward him when a woman's voice called her name. Instinctively, she turned. A silver microphone appeared beneath her lips.

"Are you going to tell us who the killer is tonight, Ms. Hanlon?"

"What makes you think I know?" she said.

"You were there. There's a lot of talk circulating."

She faced a woman with long, bright orange fingernails that curled around, and beneath her fingers. Each nail had a sparkling stone set into it. Wrapped around the microphone, they resembled heavy, chunky jewelry.

"I wasn't there during the murder," Liz stressed, "I found the body. There is quite a difference."

Nuke had pushed his way through and stood next to her. "This event was supposed to promote good will for Sonnie and the club," she said to him, "not be a damned interrogation." They started to move forward, but were surrounded again.

"What can you tell us about the relationship between the

victim and the owners of this club, Ms. Hanlon?" another voice shouted.

"Gina worked here. We were all good friends," Liz said.

"Rumor has it there was more than friendship going on."

"Yeah, there was also some great music," Liz shot back.

The woman with the exotic nails stepped in close. "The police investigation revealed that Mr. Tucks, the owner of Germaine's, was very friendly with the victim," she said. "Do you know if he was with her that night?"

"Did you follow the two of them here?" another voice shouted.

Liz drew back. "Go to hell." She headed toward Sonnie with Nuke's hand under her arm. One last squeeze through a pair of tuxedos, and they reached him at the bar.

"You made it!" Sonnie cried, beaming. "Fantastic night, isn't it?" His hand encircled the room. "Smartest move I've ever made."

"Sonnie, there's a story circulating you need to know about. I've been trying to reach you since yesterday."

"I've been going non-stop. Look at this place!" he said, enjoying the chatter and the exhilaration. "The night's a success. We might make it after all!"

"Sonnie, listen!" She leaned close to his ear. "Reporters are implying that you were with Gina that night."

"Don't listen to these vultures. It's their job to stir up trouble. Sells news."

"Listen, we have to talk tonight. It's important."

"Sure." Sonnie's gaze slid down Liz's form, taking in her floor-length, clingy, blue velvet gown.

She saw his eyes trace the slit that ran from her left ankle to mid-thigh, and felt a flutter of electricity.

"Whew! You look hot," he said. He motioned to the bartender, and held up two fingers.

The bartender placed two glasses of wine in front of her. Sonnie handed one to Nuke, one to Liz. "The band ready to start?"

Standing on tip toes she could see the stage. Danny's drums were set up, Elliot's base leaned against the wall. "Looks like it. We'll talk later."

"Sure," he said, sliding off his bar stool. "Right now I'm going to see if I can charm some reporters. You're on in fifteen."

Sonnie was instantly swamped by reporters and well-wishers. "The murder was an unspeakable tragedy," he said to the camera. "The worst thing to happen at Germaine's since my uncle opened this place back in the '40s."

As Liz forged a path to the stage, she spotted another group of eager reporters swarming around Tony. He held a drink in one hand, and dabbed beads of sweat on his forehead with the other. His face was flushed, but, as usual, he was impeccably dressed.

A cameraman zoomed in on him. "What was your relationship with the victim?" a reporter demanded.

"She was a waitress. It's like a big family around here."

"But you two had more than just a business relationship?" the reporter asked.

Liz saw the reaction in Tony's face, then the quick recovery. These pointed questions were the reason Sonnie had not wanted to let the word out about the affair. She wondered if the reporter knew his facts, or was fishing. She headed backstage.

"How does it feel to perform in the same club where your cousin was murdered?" a voice called out.

"Are you still a suspect, Ms. Hanlon?"

She kept a smile on her face and her sights on the stage as she bounced up the steps, through the backstage curtain, and into the dressing room.

Miles, in a tuxedo, was pacing the cramped room.

"Hey, you make a pretty sharp-looking penguin," she said.

"Amazing what we'll go through for success, isn't it?" He lifted a champagne bottle from the standing ice bucket and examined the label. "Although there are certain perks. You want some?"

"No, thanks. Sonnie just handed me this wine I really shouldn't finish."

"That depends on how much fun you want to have tonight."

"I'd like to be able to stand on my own power at the end of the first set. Where are Danny and Elliot?"

"Danny's on the phone calling the bimbett of the week and Elliot's in—"

The curtain flew up, Elliot came in from the stage. "Man! It's total chaos out there." He helped himself to the champagne. "How did we rate this?"

"Marty sent it. What's taking Danny so long?" She peered out at the hive of activity.

"A little nervous are we?" Elliot said.

"Sonnie wants us to start. Maybe we should walk out on the stage—"

As if on cue, Danny breezed in.

"Great time to be settin' up a date, Amata," she said. "Okay, we walk out together. Everybody ready?"

"Wait," Danny said, and hurried to pour a mouthful of champagne into a glass. He held it up in a salute. The others joined him. "To Liz Hanlon," he said, "and to tonight. May it take you where you deserve to go."

●

The applause roared when they stepped onto the stage. It built to a crescendo, and diminished only as Liz began the verse of *The Child In You*, an original song that had become her favorite. Only the band heard the quivering of her voice. This was no "regular" gig. This was not a drinking crowd that had come to zone out. This show was all about good press. Tonight mattered.

Concentrate only on what you're doing. Not the results, not the future. Just make music.

Miles counted off the next song, shifting her out of her anxiety groove, and instantly into the tune. The mood relaxed, Liz responded, letting herself float on the cushion of sound.

She was in concert. The quivering eased, her intonation was perfect.

> "It's THE CHILD IN YOU,
>   That I miss most of all—"

On the bridge, the meter remained the same, but the rhythm slipped into a slow rock beat. Guests began to move to the beat. One cameraman put his camera on a table and pulled a partner onto the floor.

Liz closed her eyes to visualize as she sang:

> "Funny, tho, I've always known it to be so,
>   The things you loved become the things
>   That make you go—"

When the song ended, a hush filled the room.
A split second of discomfort.

Until applause rang out, reaching a level that seemed like thunder. Liz shouted, "Go to number three. *This Was Meant To Be*."

Miles counted off. Elliot started a syncopated Latin beat on the bass. Miles played a montuno against it, a rhythm pattern of two chords repeated over and over. Danny picked it up, his hi-hat keeping the underneath steady while he added spice by tapping out a pattern on a cowbell. The mood turned into a full-blown party atmosphere.

From the stage, Liz saw Tony speaking to a small group of women whose high heels tapped in rhythm to the sounds. A woman in green satin pulled him onto the dance floor.

●

By midnight, the stage was dark, the party wound down in the lounge.

Danny packed the last of his equipment into the car and joined Liz at the bar. Next to her, Nuke was engrossed in a conversation with another security guard.

"Let me buy you a drink, Liz." Danny said.

"Big-spender, it's open bar tonight."

"That's why I'm buying. Besides, I want to talk to you," he said, gesturing to the bartender.

"Can it wait till morning? I've got to find Sonnie."

His tone was serious. "It really can't."

"What's wrong? You're not leaving the band?"

"Hell, no." He took a long swig of beer, keeping her waiting. "Don't let this go to your head, but I think tonight is the best I've ever heard you sound. You're really stretching."

"Hey, thanks."

"I'm serious, Liz. Some people strive all their lives just to feel that they're there. You know, that they achieved a special level. I think whether you get famous or not, you're there."

"Danny, that's—it's the biggest compliment coming from you."

"Now don't wreck it by talking through it," he said. "But it's important to know where you're at. You've never been one of those pain-in-the-ass singers, and it's a pleasure working with you. We all feel that way."

"That's so sweet. What an honor."

"And now I've gotta go."

"Go? Ah! The Tif awaits."

"As a matter of fact." He flashed a devilish grin and set his empty beer bottle on the bar. "Talk to you tomorrow."

"Danny ... thanks."

She watched him go, thinking of what he'd said. Maybe just for one night she could let herself feel satisfied, and not poke holes in it.

In the office, Sonnie was flopped in his chair, legs draped over the arms, shoes off, tie loosened, tux jacket open. A powerful scent of men's cologne hung in the air. Her nose began to tickle, and she sliced her hand through the air.

"Whew! What did you do, spray the whole bottle on yourself?" she said.

He laughed without answering.

She started for a nearby chair but stumbled over his black patent leather shoes, kicking one a few feet away. She bent to retrieve it. "Nice shiny new shoes for the big occasion, I see."

"I didn't think my running shoes would be appropriate."

She examined the bright printing on the inner label. "Size Eleven E. Chubby little tootsies you got there for someone so thin."

"Wise guy. As good as you were tonight, you can call me names from here to eternity," he said. "Reporters fired a few accusations at you, but you were calm and cool. Then you blew them away with your singing." His eyes twinkled. "Not to mention that you look hot."

"You're pretty good in front of the cameras yourself. You've got 'em eating out of your hand now."

"They can eat off the floor for all I care, as long as they come back! Hey, here's something you'll like," he said. "I overheard a couple of entertainment writers actually trying to outdo each other with descriptive words about you for tomorrow's paper."

"No!"

"You know, Liz, being able to rise to whatever comes your way, that's an important characteristic to have. Necessary, if you're going to make it in this nutty business. I think you're going to do just fine."

She felt herself turn pink. "Wow, this night is turning out pretty good."

Sonnie leaned back. "Mission accomplished," he said with a yawn.

"No, no, don't go to sleep," she said, pulling a chair up close. "I've learned some things from my aunt that involve Tony."

One eye opened. "We can't talk in the morning? I'm dead."

"No."

He sighed and rested his head on the top of his chair. "Okay. What?"

"You told me that Tony had gone into some kind of partnership with guys your Uncle Booker knew. Do you think these guys could be, uh, you know—did Booker ever say anything about them being—mob guys," she blurted, bracing herself for an explosion.

He sat up.

"There are some very important inconsistencies in the things you remember, and the things my aunt remembers."

"Like what?"

Quickly, she gave him the high points of Victor Markham's tragic "accident," and Irene's version of how Victor lost his contract. "They didn't buy him out, Sonnie, they took him! If Tony had to run from these guys once, he'll be running forever. You're in business with him now. That puts you in danger, too."

His face tightened into a scowl. "You're sure Irene's got the whole story?"

"She was there. She says going to jail saved Tony's ass—" She saw him look away. "Yes, I know about prison. I won't tell anyone, but look at it this way. Since Tony went to jail within a day of Archie's murder, it's no wonder he had trouble getting back into the business. His reputation was shot when he received the conviction, and the word would have gotten out about who killed Archie! Innocent or not, everyone in the music business would have been afraid to be connected with Tony. It makes sense, don't you think?"

He began to object.

"It does, Sonnie. The two of you lost contact for a long time. You have no idea what he's been doing since."

He frowned. "He's been working himself into a strong enough position to put on these concerts."

Liz eased up on her tone. "I'm just saying there's too much we don't know."

He sighed. "What do you want me to ask him?"

"Not him. I want you to ask your father what he remembers."

His feet hit the floor with a thud.

"He took over when Booker died," she said, "and ran the place till 1985, didn't he? I'll bet he knows who Tony's partners were, and probably a whole lot more."

Twenty-Five

Liz sank into the cool sheets, tired, but exhilarated from the successful night's performance. The numbers on the alarm clock glowed: 4:18. She wondered if she would ever get on an earlier schedule. She drifted off to sleep with the sound of the night's music replaying in her head.

An hour later, she jerked awake, wired, alert. She glanced around in the murky light, expecting to see moving shadows.

After several moments, she realized the noise she'd heard had been a newspaper hitting the front door.

The time was 5:22. The house was quiet. She slipped out of bed and cracked open the front door. One glance at the porch, and she broke into a grin. Newspapers and trade magazines were scattered across the steps. Sonnie must have sent them. What a buddy.

She spread them on the kitchen table.

The entertainment pages offered more than she'd hoped. Her name was mentioned in the headlines, attached to words like "provocative," "stirring," and "alluring."

She sighed deeply and sat in the quiet kitchen for a long time, letting Danny's advice sink in, aware of a change coming over her, a newfound confidence.

●

A half hour passed before she could calm her lively thoughts. When she next awoke, the phone on the night stand was ringing. She groped for it, knocking the clock on the floor, setting off the high-pitched chime.

"Hello. Just a minute." Still groggy, she touched the button, then pulled herself back under the covers.

"Liz?"

"Um-hmm."

"Are you awake?"

"Depends. Who is this?"

"It's me. This is important, Liz. Wake up."

With effort, she forced her eyes open but they slid down again.

"Carl? What time is it?" The clock was face up on the floor. "Seven o'clock! What's the matter with you? You know we had the press party last night. I just got to sleep."

"I know, and I'm sorry. But you're going to have to sleep later. There's some terrible news."

She bolted up. "Mom? Is she alright? Aunt Irene?"

"They're fine. Listen. Oh God, I hate this. It's Danny," he uttered softly."

Before he finished, cold shock shot through her like an electric current.

"Liz? Are you there?"

"What's happened?"

"He's been strangled. Late last night, at his home. Looks like he returned from the party, went inside briefly, then came out again. That's when he was attacked."

Young, strong, talented, compassionate Danny? "By who? He had a date with Tiffany." She pictured him going inside to change, then racing out again, bathed in a new cologne.

"Liz, listen to me. I want you to wake Nuke, and get down here as fast as you can. Right now."

"Down where?"

"I'm at the office. The cops are going to want to talk to you. I want to be with you when they do."

●

Liz sat in front of Carl's eight-foot mahogany desk, rubbing her tired eyes, aware of an eerie silence in the whole suite of offices. In the corner, Nuke's eyes drooped as he tried to concentrate on the morning paper. Carl was absorbed in the papers spread in front of him.

"Norma will be in soon," Carl said. "She makes the best coffee. I just got this fax; give me five minutes." He returned to the pages he was reading.

Liz stared straight ahead. Grief and shock made it impossible to move. Why would anyone kill Danny?

"You're sure about this?" she asked Carl for the second time. "There couldn't be a mistake?"

"We're sure, Liz," he said, softly. "Cops found the body a couple of hours ago. They'll be here soon."

"But why? I mean, this is senseless! Danny Amata couldn't threaten a spider!" She dragged herself up and stood by the window, watching the city slowly brighten.

"I know he was a good friend," Carl said. "I'm sorry. Apparently, the killer used a scanner on his garage door. It's easy to get the three-digit code when the driver pulls in to park. This guy must have waited, maybe watched the lights go on in the condo, then opened the garage and hid inside."

"Waiting for him. Poor Danny."

"His house was ransacked too."

She shuddered, and turned away from the window. Her eyes watered, partly from tears, partly from an allergy attack beginning to come on. She inhaled deeply, hoping to stop it before it took hold, but she could muster little resistance.

The reality of losing Danny hit her with force. She crumpled into a chair. "My God, what are we going to do without him?" she murmured. "It'll never be the same."

"No. It won't. But you'll replace him, and in time—"

"Are you crazy? We'll never replace Danny. Even if we tried, we'd never do it in time. It's over."

Carl's gaze went over the top of his glasses. "Don't make any decisions right now, Liz. You can pull things together later."

"Yeah," she said, not meaning it.

"Here, read these," he said, waving his hand over the printouts he'd just taken from his fax machine. "Some pretty interesting facts."

"About Danny?" she asked. Her sinuses began to throb. The odor of industrial bathroom cleaner wafted through the air. Through the partially opened door she saw a maintenance engineer wheeling his cart down the hallway.

"No. About Gina." He pushed several pages toward her. "Criminal records, both of them. Gina McCurdy, and that slimeball she was hanging with named Brad Gerrick."

"Gina had a criminal record? But I thought you worked it out with the D.A. so she wouldn't have one."

Carl shrugged. "She did it again. Read it yourself."

Liz squinted at the pages. "'Brad Gerrick, twenty-eight. One conviction for theft in 1995. Another for shoplifting.' Mr. Dreamboat. How could she bother with this slug?"

"Read Gina's. Last year they were caught together running vacation scams on elderly couples."

She scanned the fax. "Looks like she was going out of her way to ruin her life."

"Brad started dating Gina two and a half years ago. He already had a record. Some of us go to restaurants or movies for entertainment, but they planned ways to rip off unsuspecting victims for fun and profit."

"This hard-core stealing " she said.

"She was on probation when she was murdered." He tapped the printouts on the desk in front of him. "This guy, Gerrick, was quite an influence."

"You think he killed her?"

"Could be."

"But he didn't have a reason to kill Danny, unless he was insanely jealous. Danny and Gina were pretty close."

"What kind of 'close'?" he asked.

"They liked to party together. It started with a little flirtation, and ended in a good friendship."

"You sure about that?"

"Yes. Gina took Danny along when she wanted to drink

with Elvin, the man who lives in the bushes behind Germaine's."

"I suppose Gerrick could have had a motive there," he said.

"What about Tiffany? An old jealous boyfriend?"

"They're all possibilities at this point."

"*Why?*" she moaned, flopping into a chair. "Two murders, both senseless."

Carl came around the desk and put his arms around her.

"I loved Gina when we were kids," she said. "It doesn't just go away."

Her chest heaved, her breathing grew more difficult. She sat up and put her head back to relieve the pressure on her sinuses. With difficulty, she inhaled a big breath and held it.

"Wouldn't it be better to let it all out?"

"It's not that. I can't ... breathe."

"Oh no. Allergies?" he asked. "You need some water? Ice?"

He closed the office door, snapped the lock on a window and pushed it open. Fresh air filled the room.

"That's better," she said. "I'll be okay. Damn cleaning solvents make my nose feel like someone's pricking it with a sharp knife. Happens every time."

A door closed in the outer office. Footsteps echoed through the reception area. The suite would soon be filled with lawyers, secretaries, and anxious clients.

"That's Norma," Carl said. "You'll have some coffee in a minute. Will that help?"

"The steam will."

Keys were jangling, water running.

"No one really knew her, you know?" Liz said.

Carl made a sarcastic smirk. "Guess old Brad knew her pretty well. And maybe Tony."

"Certainly Tony, but he won't talk. He only admitted knowing her when I told him I already knew about their affair. He says he didn't know about Brad."

"Did you press him? See what he did know?"

She sighed. "No. I was trying to tread lightly. But now, with Danny dead," she said, "everything's changed. We've got to piece every detail together before someone else gets killed!"

She stood up. "Is there anything that ties these murders together? We know a little more about Gina now," she said, gesturing toward the fax pages, "but still so little about Tony. Twenty years ago he made a fortune, then went to jail. When he got out, he was broke, and no one would go near him. Of course, we still don't know why he was broke, do we?"

"I think his money was eaten up by attorney fees. I'll get the name of his law firm."

"Enos is working on bank records, IRS statements, passports," she said. "See, the thing that bothers me, is that he must have had money coming in constantly. Over four hundred songs copyrighted in his name, remember? So why was he broke when he came back?"

The aroma of fresh ground coffee drifted into the room. A short woman in her late twenties appeared, carrying a tray with three mugs. A sugar bowl and creamer were tucked into the side.

"'Morning Norma. Thanks. Your timing couldn't be better."

Carl's fax machine beeped as Norma set the tray down.

"Want me to get that?" she asked.

He shook his head. "I've got it." Norma vanished. Carl withdrew the fax and began to read.

Liz stirred her coffee, raised the cup to her lips, and let the steam encircle her face. Smelling coffee was a ritual that reminded her of lazy Sunday mornings with time to read the paper. As she relaxed, other images emerged.

The sweet smell of fresh brewed coffee.

The murder scene.

"Carl?"

No answer.

"Carl, I just remembered something. Gina's murder—"

He looked up, a frown etched into his forehead. "I'm working on something here—"

"The cologne, remember? That awful perfumy stuff—"

"What cologne?"

"Just now, the smell of coffee was such a pleasure because it disguised that cleaner your janitor's using. That's what happened at the murder scene! The coffee aroma covered up someone's heavy perfume. When I walked into Germaine's, the place smelled different. Too sweet. When Sonnie made the coffee, I was glad to have something to cut the perfume smell."

"So?"

"I assumed the perfume was Gina's. And that when she died, you know, maybe it turned kind of—"

"Stronger?"

"No. Sour."

"There was nothing in the police or autopsy reports about it." He shuffled through a large folder. "Nothing about perfume here."

"I don't know how they could miss it. It was stronger than that stuff you wear. What's in the new fax?" she asked, gesturing toward the pages he'd just received.

"It's about the muddy footprints they found inside Germaine's. They were made by rubber boots, the kind that go over street shoes. So the size is close, but not exact."

"That's no help."

"The lab says they're about size eleven. Someone slightly smaller could have worn them, too."

She looked down at Carl's feet. "What's your size?"

"Ten and a half."

"They'd fit half the guys in L.A!"

"Cops're trying to match them."

She strolled back to the window. "The only connection I can see between both murders is the break-ins," she said, thoughtfully. "First Gina's place, then mine. Danny's is the third."

"They're not necessarily connected," he said. "Danny's killer entered the garage by knowing the code, and it's easy to get."

"How did the others happen?"

"Someone had a key to Gina's and Paige's."

"That's why the cops asked me if I had a key to their place. I wonder if Danny had one."

"Someone did."

"Brad," she asked, thinking out loud. "I'll bet he did have one."

"If Brad and Gina were in on a scheme to steal from Tony, but Gina changed her mind, that could be why Brad killed her. They could have argued, maybe it developed into a big fight..."

"At Germaine's?"

"Okay, maybe Brad didn't know. Maybe it was all Gina's idea, but Brad found out. He flew into a rage—"

Carl's phone interrupted. He touched a button.

Norma's voice came through the speaker. "It's Lieutenant Wahlberg, Mr. Hanlon."

"I figured she'd be calling soon," he said, tapping another button. "Morning, Lieutenant. If you're looking for my sister, she's here."

"You said you'd call as soon as you heard from her," Wahlberg said, dryly.

"She just got here," he said.

"Keep her there. My detectives will be at your office in

fifteen minutes."

"Wait," he said. He cupped his hand over the mouthpiece and looked at Liz, then at Nuke. "Why don't we go to the station now and get this over with?"

Liz nodded. "Fine with me," Nuke said.

"Lieutenant," Carl said into the phone, "we'll save your detectives the trip. We're coming in."

He hung up. "Let's go," he said to Liz and Nuke. "This place will be crawling with clients in half an hour. The last thing I need is a bunch of cops showing up."

Twenty-Six

In the squad room, Detective Robbins squeezed his large belly between two desks to reach the fax machine. He'd been drumming stubby fingers on a desktop while he waited for it to print. Now he tore the paper from the machine and charged across the noisy room, gesturing for his partner, Milleski, to follow him. They burst into Lt. Wahlberg's office as Liz was telling the Lieutenant about the press party the night before.

"Lieutenant—" Robbins interrupted.

Wahlberg held up her hand to hold him back, then said to Liz, "You're sure the last time you saw the victim was around midnight?"

She remembered Danny's complimentary words. "Yes. I'll never forget our last conversation."

"Why's that?"

Robbins pushed in closer. "Lieutenant, I found—"

"Robbins, I'm in a conference here," Wahlberg snapped.

"You'll want to see this, Lieutenant," he said.

"The prints from the McCurdy murder scene?" she asked him.

Robbins looked sheepish. "Uh, not yet on those, Lieutenant. With so many fingerprints around the bar, it's going to be awhile. The lab's working on prints from the bathrooms now."

"I didn't think there were that many people in the city who aren't in our system," Wahlberg said, dryly.

"Right," Robbins said, not sure whether it was a joke or not. He began to read his fax. "We found---"

"Any word of prints at the Amata murder scene yet?" Wahlberg asked.

"Not yet. This is something on that kid. Except I don't think it's current."

"Which kid? I do have other cases."

Robbins read from the print-outs. "'Brad Gerrick, twenty-eight. Last known address 645 Linden Way, Los Angeles.' But this is damn near two years old."

"Great. What about that other kid you were checking out?"

"Jeffrey Williams?"

Liz looked up.

Robbins turned to Milleski, who consulted a small notebook in his shirt pocket.

"Williams," Milleski said, "yeah, this kid's strange, Lieutenant, but that's all. No priors. No indication that he prowls around, peeping in windows or anything."

"Just because he isn't in your system yet, doesn't mean he's a lily-white," Liz interjected.

Wahlberg ignored her comment and spoke to Milleski. "Is he smart enough to have tapped Ms. Hanlon's phone, or gotten her travel plans some other way?"

Milleski considered this, then shook his head. "I don't thee how. We've been checking him out. He's not exactly a high beam, and I don't thee him as harmful."

He turned to Robbins for corroboration.

"Me neither, Lieutenant." Robbins flicked his finger on the papers he was holding. "I think Gerrick's a better lead. We're going through every database now."

"Gerrick's your man, Lieutenant!" Carl said. "Has to be. He must have killed Gina when something went wrong with the scam they were running, then killed Danny because he was jealous of Gina's close friendship with him."

"How the hell do you know that?" Wahlberg asked.

Carl motioned toward Liz. "Liz was trying to tell you about their friendship—"

"If you'll let me finish, Lieutenant," Liz said.

Wahlberg held up a hand. "In a moment." She turned back to Robbins. "Who's doing the research on Gerrick?" she asked.

"Lorenzo," Robbins said.

Lt. Wahlberg sighed. "Put some heat under him. No one's that hard to find. Anything else that can't wait?"

"Yes," Robbins said, reading from the fax. "Store owner on the corner of Melrose and Gramercy Place—across the street from Germaine's West—"

"Hold it," the Lieutenant said, turning to Liz and the others. "Excuse us." She gestured for her detectives to follow her out to the hallway.

Liz watched through the glass as they gathered outside the door.

"What's that all about?" Carl said.

"Something they don't want us to know," Liz said, as she leaned on a filing cabinet close to the doorway, turning her head sideways to eavesdrop.

Out of earshot, Lt. Wahlberg said to Robbins, "Okay, the store owner across from Germaine's, what about him?"

"He called in a vehicle that had been parked facing north on Gramercy for about a week. It got tagged by the street sweepers on Friday. Still there this morning. We towed it to impound."

"And?"

Robbins lowered his voice. "It's registered to Irene McCurdy, mother of the dead girl. You want us to notify her?"

Lt. Wahlberg paused, then said, "Not yet. Let me see that sheet."

Robbins and Milleski returned to their desks. Wahlberg remained in the hallway reading the fax.

In the Lieutenant's office, Carl whispered to Liz. "What did they say?"

She shook her head. "Couldn't hear. Just that someone's car was parked near Germaine's."

●

In the police parking lot, Carl walked to the security van with Nuke and Liz.

"Go to my house, Liz," he said. "I'll call Reggie and tell her you're both coming. You can crash there and catch up on some sleep."

"I like that," Nuke said, unlocking the van.

"Okay," Liz said. "Make sure you let her know, though. I don't want to barge in unannounced."

Carl waved goodbye and headed for his car. "See you this evening."

Nuke drove out of the lot, and headed for the freeway. In less than a mile, the freeway split, one way toward Carl and Reggie's, the other the cut-off to Pacific Coast Highway, and Tony's Malibu estate.

As he approached the fork, Liz said, "Go left, Nuke. Toward Malibu."

He eased to the left. "I thought we were going to your brother's."

"We are. Eventually."

●

Twenty minutes later they were descending the hill to Tony's estate. Tall, lush pepper trees rolled by on both sides, sunlight streaming through their delicate branches. At the bottom of the hill, Nuke cruised to a stop on the stone driveway.

The place looked abandoned. The landscaping seemed unattended, a newspaper lay on the front steps, two more were strewn nearby. The shallow-rooted flowers had wilted in dry, cracked soil. The gardener's rusty white truck was nowhere in sight. As Liz walked across the driveway she saw the grass had not been watered.

They went to the front door. At the archway, large circular patterns of ground-in potting soil were all that remained of the gigantic clay pots and healthy ficus plants. She rang the doorbell.

No answer. Three more rings. Not a sound came from the

house.

"Let's look around," she said.

"Wait here," Nuke said. He went toward the stable.

Liz watched from the driveway, expecting to hear a few sounds from inside.

Hearing nothing, she started toward Nuke. As he pulled open the wooden door, they peered inside. Each stall was empty. "No horses, no riders, no trainers," she said.

Liz went to the garage where Tony stored his cars. The metal door was down, and locked.

"It's a ghost town," she said. "We drove out here to ask pointed questions, get some solid answers, but that isn't going to happen."

●

Liz slumped in a chair behind the glass counter at McCain's MusicLand and waited for Walter to finish explaining to an eight-year-old boy why he should keep practicing his clarinet instead of running with the gangs in the neighborhood. The second wind she'd had an hour ago was slipping away. Right after Gina's murder, she had believed she could keep up her teaching schedule; but now with Danny's murder, an ugly exhaustion was creeping through her entire body. She needed time alone.

She glanced at Nuke paging through a booklet on beginning harmony. She wondered why she was so drained when he seemed to be rejuvenated.

Walter's large hands were expressive. "I know," he told the boy, "hanging with them street guys, it feels real good—for awhile. But you're a smart kid. And you ain't no baby anymore; it's time you thought about your mama's feelings. Now wouldn't she be mighty proud to watch her son up there on that stage playing music? Ain't none of her friend's sons up there. They aren't smart enough. They're all in juvie. See how special that would make your mama feel?"

The boy nodded. It was hard to argue with Walter.

"You wouldn't leave me cold by cutting out on the recital, would you, Sly?" Walter asked, calling him by his street name.

"No."

"You're my best player. I can count on you to be there? I don't have to come looking for you?"

The child's eyes darted at the thought that Walter might come looking for him. "I'll be there."

Walter beamed and backed off. "Thank you." He held out a hand for a handshake. "I appreciate your help."

Sly stood a little taller, having been addressed as a grown-up.

Liz waited till Sly was gone. "Walt, you blow me away. You can get anyone to do anything."

"I wish." He began counting the morning's receipts. "I heard about your drummer. Horrible. How're you doing?"

"That's what I wanted to talk to you about."

"If you want my opinion, I think you ought'a get yourself out of this city for awhile. I'll handle the recital.

"I do need a little time to pull myself together."

"Hiring that gorilla over there was the smartest move you've ever made," he said, indicating Nuke.

"Nuke the knee breaker. He's not much on gossip, but that's sort of the point."

The phone rang behind the counter.

Walter picked it up, and frowned when he realized he was not going to be allowed to get a word in. "Just ... just ... hold on. She's here."

"Liz, it's your Monday night." He handed the phone to her.

"Sherice Williams."

Liz could hear sobs before she answered.

"Sherice? What's wrong?" Sherice had never called her at the store before.

The child's voice quivered. "I've been calling you all day. But you never answered."

"I've been away from my apartment for a few days. Tell me what's wrong, Sherice."

"It's too small."

"What is?"

"My dress. It's too small. And Mama," she sobbed, "she doesn't have no more money to buy another one. She says I outgrew it so I ... I tried to make it fit, but the zipper ripped. Now it's ruined and I can't be in the recital," she wailed.

The child's tears tore at Liz.

"Oh honey, listen to me. Are you listening?"

The sobs diminished to a whimper. "Uh huh."

"We can fix this. First, you calm down. Your Mama's right, but that's exactly what you're supposed to do. You're seven years old, and seven-year-old's grow so they can become eight-year-old's, right?"

Sherice was quieting.

"We'll get you another dress and you'll knock'em out when you walk out on that stage."

"But Mama—"

"Don't worry about that, Sherice. We'll go shopping, you and me. We'll hit every store in this city until you find the one you like. Okay?"

Walter was looking at her quizzically. Sherice was drifting back into the child's world she was often denied.

"Will you let me buy you a new dress for your birthday? I've been trying to figure out what to get you anyway, and this will save me a lot of hassle. What'd 'ya say?"

"Could we go tomorrow?"

"Tomorrow? That's a little soon, honey."

Sherice sniffled. "I don't have choir tomorrow, or my extra English class," she said, her voice cracking.

"Tomorrow. Alright, I'll try to work that out. Four o'clock. I'll pick you up."

Sherice's composure had returned. "Liz, you're the best teacher I ever had."

When she hung up, Liz found Walter suppressing a grin. "You got a pretty good way 'a getting people to do what you want too, you know."

"Walt, she was so upset. You should have heard her."

"Uh huh. Those fancy dresses for little girls're pretty expensive." he said. "You know, you'd be saving me the hassle of buying the wrong thing if you'd let me go in on that dress with you. Could be from both of us. I don't have time to shop."

She gestured to Nuke, and they headed toward the door.

"Consider politics in your senior years, Walt."

Twenty-Seven

In the morning, Liz joined Reggie in the kitchen, nearly tripping over a large wooden delivery crate that rested on the floor.

"Just kick that out of your way." Reggie said to Liz. "Carl had some heavy books delivered. It's going out in tomorrow's trash."

Liz took the glass of orange juice Reggie handed her.

"Thanks for letting both of us crash here again. Boy, did I need sleep."

"You feel better?"

She thought about Danny. "No, but at least I'm not as tired."

"Losing a friend takes a long time."

Liz doubted time would be a great healer.

"Coffee's made," Reggie said. "I've got to go, but I'll be back by four. You don't mind being around here by yourself, do you?"

"I'm fine. Besides, Nuke's up. I heard him in the shower."

She sipped coffee, struggling to deal with emotions that seemed to change by the minute. "I keep thinking about Danny. Not having him in my life."

Reggie put on her blazer. "Oh, I almost forgot. Enos called. Said he's working on something crucial, but with Enos everything's crucial."

"He didn't say what it was?"

Reggie picked up her keys just as the phone rang. "That's probably him," she said. "You get it. I've got to go." She waved on her way out the back door.

Liz answered.

"Hey there, baby-blues, I see you finally got your luscious form out of the sack," Enos said.

"Enos—"

"Relax. Got a 'coupla'a things you're gonna want to hear. They concern your friend Tony."

She grabbed a pen and paper. "Shoot."

"For starters, he ain't exactly as flush as he would have us believe. On the one hand, he does own several antique autos. Bought'em back in the '80s just like you said, but he hasn't bought much since. Recently he brought in a lot of elegant furnishings around this Malibu place. Guess he wanted to make an impression. Also a load of high-tech computers and other hardware—all rented."

"Can you rent art work, crystal, china?"

"You can in the circle he travels in. The horses are boarded, none of them are his. Even the newer cars are leased. He had the money once, and that's when he purchased all his collectibles. After that, he's just been living the impressive lifestyle."

"What about the property itself?"

"Nope. That's owned by his company, and I'm sure we'll find out soon that the company is owned by another, and then another."

She sank down onto a chair. "I don't get it, Enos. Why?"

"This guy is the promoter of your concerts, right? Mr. Big Shot? You can't do that without flashing cash."

Liz felt as if she were sinking. "You're saying he's a fraud?"

"Not really. A lot of these high-profile types operate on a financial shoestring. The appearance of big money is what allows him to play the game in the big leagues."

"This is crazy! You mean the concerts are a game to him? A hoax?"

"Didn't say that. His investors and their cash are rock solid. What happens next depends on his particular skill as a promoter. And Perdusian's consistently been one of the best over the years. Only his personal finances seem to be light."

"How did you find this out?"

"I got wind of a labor dispute that was filed about a year ago. It's taken most of this time to get settled, but it looks like our Mr. P. owes some back pay to his employees. They claim his checks were always bouncing."

She thought of the gardener and the wilted flowers she'd

seen yesterday. "He can mastermind a TV show, but he can't write a paycheck?"

"Could be. But before you demand to see a financial statement, I've got something even bigger. Those years he was gone, the ones you call the black hole years—"

"What about 'em?"

"He wasn't in prison."

She lurched forward. "Where the hell was he?"

"Don't know yet. The papers reported on his jail sentence, and because he was gone it was assumed that's where he was, but he never served a day."

"Wait a minute," she said, downing the last of her coffee. "Tony was sentenced to prison but never did the time?"

"Some kind of deal went down. Maybe he didn't counter the story of prison because the truth would have been worse for his career than the lie that he'd done time."

She shook her head. "Does this make any sense to you?"

"Not yet. All I can figure is that he booked during those years."

"Booked—as in vanished? For two years?"

"Yup. Within one day of his partner's murder."

She recalled Aunt Irene's account of Archie's death, and Tony's disappearance. Her pulse began to race. "Are you saying Tony killed his partner and split?"

"Nope. I'm saying that while his partner was being murdered, the papers were announcing that Tony was heading off to prison. But instead, he seems to have gone fishin'."

"The mob guys! Has to be. Aunt Irene said they came looking for Tony," she said, her tone rising. Tony really was running from the mob! What if he still is? "Enos, drop your other jobs!" she cried.

"Now, you know I'd do a lot for you, blue-eyes—"

"Find out about any kind of mob event in the news around 1978. A robbery, a mob-style murder. Anything connected to the music business. Get on it, Enos! Call me back."

"I have other clients, you know."

"You're getting paid, Enos. Just *do it!*"

●

Liz paced the quiet living room, deep in thought. Twenty years ago, Tony had hidden out from the gangsters who'd given him his start in the business. Could he have paid them—or someone—to avoid his jail sentence? That would explain why he was broke when he returned. Was that the "deal" Enos was referring to? If so, how did that affect his situation now? After all, he'd recovered, rebuilt his career, and become a wealthy man.

But Enos said Tony's finances were "light." That seemed incongruous with the image of a successful concert promoter with legitimate investment partners. Unless the high-profile concerts had brought someone from Tony's past out of the woodwork. Perhaps he was being blackmailed.

The answers were connected to the past, she was certain. She thought back and imagined Victor's and Irene's excitement in 1975, when he was offered a recording contract with Tony's company, HotRock Music. A young couple striving to carve out one of the few successful places allotted for the truly creative. Victor had done it. They must have been giddy with happiness. Victor concentrated on his music, paying little attention to the business of contracts, or song rights. After all, he didn't have to worry about those things anymore. He had partnered with the most successful manager on the scene. He could spend his days creating music that would reach the whole world.

Why would Uncle Victor sign away his publishing royalties?

Had he willingly assigned his song rights to HotRock Music? Or had he been duped? A fifty-fifty split between writer and publisher was commonplace during the recent years Liz had been a performer, but what about twenty-five years ago?

Irene had described Victor's overwhelming depression when Tony returned and would hardly speak to him. Had Victor learned something devastating, but failed to tell Irene about it? Irene despised Tony for hurting Victor, but she had never considered that Tony might have been on the run. Or that because he'd led these thugs to Victor once before, he was trying to avoid doing it again. Without Tony around, Victor might not have a strong career, but at least he'd be alive.

Victor's music was the only tangible link now. The songs, and their royalties. The songs were still being played today, and they were her uncle's legacy, a body of work that was meant to be a financial legacy for Irene.

Those publishing rights had made Tony a wealthy man. But the recipient should have been Aunt Irene, not HotRock Music.

But the Tony Perdusian Liz had come to know would not have stolen Victor's royalties. Tony had insisted on proper contracts even before they'd started to rehearse the shows, and her own brother had approved the contracts. Perhaps Irene could recall something significant about the details of Victor's contracts.

To Liz, it seemed the past and present were on a collision course. Something had caused Tony to go into hiding once before, and if he was in trouble again, anyone connected with him could be hurt.

She had to warn Sonnie. She jumped up, heading down the hall to Nuke's room. At his door, she yelled, "I don't care if you're decent or not. Grab your keys."

The door swung open. He grabbed a jacket, pulled car keys out of his pocket, and followed her into the living room.

"What's up?" he asked.

"I've got to talk to Sonnie pronto. Aunt Irene, too."

The phone rang. "Let the machine take it. I'll explain on the way," Liz said, as they started for the door.

She heard Suzanne say, "Liz, got some news about Danny. I'll catch you later."

Liz raced for the phone. "Suz? I'm on my way out. What's the quick version?"

"I just came from Marty's office, and he says that a few days before Danny was killed, he asked for an advance against his upcoming salary from the concerts."

"What? Danny borrowing money from Marty? No! He was one of the few musicians in this town who earned six figures. He wouldn't need to do that."

"He told Marty that he was in the hole for nearly a hundred and fifty thousand bucks—to someone who couldn't wait any longer."

Liz was astounded. Why would Danny owe that much money?

Gambling.

Sonnie.

Twenty-Eight

Had Danny been placing bets through Sonnie? Was it possible that Danny's death was connected to gambling money and not related to Gina's after all? There was a bigger picture involved, one that included Tony and his concerts, and perhaps Sonnie. She needed to know *all* of it. She grabbed her phone, dialed Germaine's, and asked for Sonnie.

"Not there? Dammit! When he gets back, tell him to stay

put! I'll be there in one hour." She slammed the phone down.

Nuke's eyes remained straight ahead. "Where to now?" he asked. "Your aunt's place in Studio City?"

"Yeah, I'll talk to her first, then go into Germaine's and find Sonnie. If he thinks he's going to avoid me—"

"What about Sherice," Nuke said. "Aren't you supposed to pick her up at four o'clock?"

"Oh God! I forgot. I can't take her shopping now! I must have been out of my mind to agree to that."

"If you're worried about her being disappointed, maybe you could ask your sister-in-law to help out."

"Perfect!" she said. "A security guard with smarts. I like that, Nuke. I'll call Reggie, see if she'll do a little baby-sitting," she said, reaching for the phone. Before she could pick it up, it rang.

"Hello? Oh, hi, Enos. What's up?"

"You are a shrewd one, blue-eyes," he said.

"That's what they say. What did you find?"

"There was no actual theft of a large sum at one time, but toward the middle of '78, several versions of the same story were circulating. They concerned dividends from a recording company that were not making their way to the accounts of their parent company."

"English, Enos."

"Record companies run by unscrupulous owners claimed they were being ripped off, bled over a period of two or three years."

"Did they report this?" Liz asked.

"Nah. These guys don't want the government stomping around in their books."

"So what did they do?"

"They handled the problem privately."

"I owe you one, Enos." She hung up and sat staring out the window as the sun dipped lower in the sky, her imagination firing again.

●

Nuke parked the van on Whitsett.

"A beautiful sunny day," Liz said, "and I'm here to talk about murder and rip-offs. After today, you're going to know every secret my family's ever had, Nuke. I'll bet you get tired of hearing people air their dirty laundry."

"In my line of work, you learn to watch for danger, and forget the rest."

A small sandwich shop with white lace curtains faced the corner of Whitsett and Ventura Blvd. Stairs outside the cafe led to the condominiums next door. Liz turned and noticed the traffic whizzing by on Ventura Boulevard. At any time of day or night, this part of Studio City was alive with activity, but her aunt was completely withdrawing. Liz worried about her being alone, hiding in her memories, taking too many tranquilizers.

They hurried up the stairs, and rang Irene's bell.

The door opened. Liz had to stifle a gasp at the sight of Irene's ghostly color and red, swollen eyes. She encircled the thin shoulders with a gentle hug.

"How are you, Aunt Irene?"

Irene's hair was unstyled, flat on one side, and looked grayer than just a few days ago.

She mumbled a greeting to Liz, and shuffled toward the living room.

"You remember Nuke, don't you?"

Irene gestured with a weak hand motion.

"Nice to see you again, Mrs. McCurdy," he said.

The smell of alcohol permeated the room again. When Liz sat next to her on the couch she spotted the green plastic glass filled with V.O. She glanced around the condo. Little had changed since her last visit. Several newspapers were tossed in a pile, still rolled up with rubber bands around them. Mail stacked next to them. On a corner table she saw a white beaded evening purse. She tried to recall where she'd seen it before, then pushed the thought aside.

"Aunt Irene, I need to ask you about Victor. When he was about to record his first songs, do you remember anything about the contracts he signed with the recording company?"

"Just that they'd get his songs on the radio."

"What about how Victor got paid? Do you remember receiving money when the songs were played?

Irene sipped her drink and leaned back. "He got paid when he played his shows. I don't remember anything else."

"You don't still have the contract, do you?"

Irene snorted. "I tore that thing up in a million pieces the day those animals said they owned Victor."

"Have you been receiving royalties from his songs all these years? Many of Victor's songs are still being played today."

"No one remembers who wrote'em now. It was too long ago."

"It doesn't matter if anyone remembers. When a song is used in any way, the person who holds the copyright gets paid."

"Lizzie, it just doesn't matter now."

"The trail of the royalty money could tell us a lot."

"Then the trail leads to Victor's son of a bitch managers."

Or the people he's running from, Liz thought. "You've got

most of the hard copies right here, don't you?" Liz asked.

Irene nodded toward a closet door. "Still in the same boxes Victor kept'em in, but I'm not interested in any legal battles with those bastards."

"It might not tell us everything, but maybe I can prove that you should be the legal holder of the copyrights," Liz said, excitedly. "Those songs are Victor's legacy. Something special he left for you."

"I already lost the special thing Victor left me."

Liz took her hand. "Victor wrote some of these songs for you. With the handwritten music right in our hands, I think we can prove they belong to you."

Irene faced her with a tormented expression that devastated Liz. She drew back, awestruck by the intense magnitude of Irene's pain.

Irene sighed. "I appreciate what you're trying to do, Lizzie, but you have to understand, it's too late for me. Fighting over music. What for? If it would bring Victor and my baby girl back, I'd hunt'em down, and torture'em myself. But the way things are," she said, her voice raspy, "nothing matters anymore."

●

Liz left Irene's condo greatly subdued by Irene's poignant words. She rode in silence as Nuke drove.

"You want to go to Germaine's next, right?" he asked.

"Absolutely." She pulled out her phone and dialed Germaine's.

"He not back *yet*?" she cried. "Where the hell is he? When he gets there, would you tell him to call me on my cell phone right away? Thanks." She hung up.

"Now what?" Nuke asked.

She checked her watch. "Guess we'll pick up Sherice and take her to Reggie's, then go back to Germaine's. If Sonnie's not there, we're going to *wait* for him."

Twenty-Nine

Traffic on the Hollywood freeway was fierce.

"Finally!" Liz cried when Nuke skated down the exit ramp. "Floor it now, will you, Nuke? I'm late. The kid's only seven; she won't understand."

The van's tires squealed against a curb as Nuke went around a car and sped down Vermont Avenue.

Impatient as she was with the other drivers, Liz was more impatient with herself. "I hoped that with the right details from Aunt Irene I'd be able to uncover a motivation for both murders, but now I'm confused again," she said. "Maybe Gina's murder has nothing to do with Danny's. But why had Danny owed Sonnie so much money when he died? It just doesn't add up."

After Tony had told her about Sonnie's gambling, she hadn't looked into it further. What else had she missed?

A taxi slowed in front of them, then eased halfway to the curb, blocking the lane as it stopped to pick up a passenger. Liz shouted out the window, "Come on, you idiot!"

Two blocks from Sherice's building, Nuke turned the corner into a run down neighborhood which had once been a cozy suburb. The trees, planted early in the century, pushed their over-developed roots through the concrete sidewalks. Groups of young kids clustered around the corner market, waiting, watching.

They turned onto Sherice's street. Liz looked for the familiar wooden door centered between two tall, opaque glass panels. As she studied each building, she failed to notice the brown pickup cruising behind them.

The apartment door swung open. Sherice waved goodbye to someone inside, then skipped down the cracked walkway.

Without warning, the brown pickup swerved around Nuke's van and screeched to a halt in front of it. The driver, a young man with dark hair, jumped from the truck, leaving its door ajar, the engine idling. He ran to the sidewalk and swept up Sherice.

Nuke slammed the van into park and threw open his door.

The driver carried Sherice to the driver side and stuffed her inside.

Nuke raced toward the truck.

"*Sherice!*" Liz screamed, running to the passenger side of the truck. She yanked on the door handle, but it was locked.

Nuke reached the truck before the driver got in, and lunged, trying for a choke hold, but the driver whirled on him, thrusting a long-bladed knife into Nuke's gut. Nuke's eyes widened, his grip still on the man's throat.

Liz ran around the front of the truck, coming up behind the driver as he yanked the knife back. She grabbed him around his back and shoulders, but he shoved her hard enough to knock her down, then spun around and thrust the knife into Nuke again. Nuke collapsed on the pavement. The driver jumped behind the wheel, slammed it in gear, and sped away.

Nuke lay in the street. Liz pulled herself up and raced to his side. A puddle of blood quickly formed around him. She knelt next to him on the street, stunned. Her eyes went from Nuke to the brown pickup speeding away. After an indecisive moment, she ran to the security van, jumped behind the wheel, and took off after it.

A woman ran from the apartment building, arms pumping, she chased the truck down the street. Liz slowed and shouted, "Call the police! Get an ambulance!" She floored it, bolting after the pickup.

●

Policewoman Harriet Lang took the call from an agitated woman who peeled off the facts too quickly, as if she thought she might be cut off.

"Ma'am, I need you to calm down," Officer Lang instructed.

"The truck was black, I think," the caller replied. "No, no it was brown. A brown pickup!" she confirmed. "He just whisked her up and away. I got a license plate number. 3-X-S something. I seen the whole thing from inside the building."

"And you're sure it was a man?"

"Yes, it was a man. Young, dark hair. And he was white. Mean looking. And the lady took off right behind him."

"What lady?" Officer Lang asked her.

"The lady who came to pick her up. Liz. She's driving right behind him!"

"Can you describe Liz's car?"

"Wasn't no car. It was a van. White, with green and black writing on the side."

"Do you know what the writing said?"

"No. Didn't see that. Send an ambulance, too. Right away!"

"It's on the way. Did you see what the kidnapper was wearing?"

"A plaid shirt. One of those wintry things. Red plaid."

●

When the light changed, the brown truck turned right, picked up speed and passed by the freeway ramp. Liz stayed with it.

Alone in the van, her thoughts whirled. Sickening images flashed; she'd never allow those things to happen to Sherice.

Nuke's phone. She grabbed it and punched in 9-1-1.

The line kept ringing.

"Come on!"

She worried about Nuke.

She worried about Sherice. The kidnapper had stabbed Nuke; there was no reason to believe he would hold back because Sherice was a child.

She sped up and pushed in close to the pickup's bumper.

Sherice had crawled up on the seat of the truck and turned around, her tiny fingers pressed to the glass. Liz could see her agonized expression glaring back through the window, and it made her heart ache.

Oh God, please keep Sherice safe.

The truck slowed to a steady pace now, paying attention to stop signs and lights.

Who was this twisted creature? Was he the stalker? Why not take me? Why kidnap a child? To hurt, to antagonize, to taunt? For ransom? Was he a sick pedaphile who hung out in dark places looking for easy prey?

Liz cleared the phone line and dialed again. "C'mon, for godssake! Answer!"

Close to the truck's back bumper, she could make out furtive eyes glaring back at her through the rear view mirror.

A voice crackled through the phone. "Emergency 9-1-1."

"I need help!" Liz blurted. "I'm in the McPhearson Security van, following a brown pickup, license number 3-X-S-4-6-7. There's been a kidnapping, a little girl."

At the station, Policewoman Lang logged in the information and sent an urgent signal to Lt. Wahlberg just as she had five minutes earlier. Within seconds, Wahlberg was standing next to her.

"I want to hear," Wahlberg said.

"It's a woman's voice," Lang said to her. "I heard the word kidnapping, and a street location."

Into the phone, Policewoman Lang said, "State your name, please."

"Liz Hanlon," she said. "We just turned off Vermont, onto Lexington."

The pickup made a quick right in front of Liz, then another left.

"We're on Fountain now," she cried, "heading toward the freeway. Jesus, can you send someone or not?"

"We're locking onto your destination," Lang said. "Officers are in the area."

"Wait," Liz said, "he's going under the freeway. We're turning North on Cahuenga Boulevard! Get a patrol car out here!"

She slammed the phone down and moved in closer to the truck. *Who is he?*

The truck shot forward. She floored it to keep up.

Liz watched as the little girl faced her again, and a thought slammed at her: Sherice was not wearing a seat belt. If she could get the truck to stop, she might be able to get Sherice out quickly.

A shrill noise made her jump. The phone was ringing; hesitantly, she picked it up.

"Don't ever do that again!" The voice was harsh. Through the glass she could see the driver holding a phone to his ear. "No calls. Understand?"

"Who are you?" she shrieked.

"I've got your friend here, and we're going to talk about a trade."

"I'll give you anything, but if you hurt her, I'll kill you! Do you hear me? I will kill you!"

Sherice screamed out, "Liz!"

"Touch that phone again and this kid dies," he said.

Liz felt sick. "You stop and let her out, or I'm going to start ramming you with the front end of this van till I knock you off the road."

"Great. Give the kid a concussion. That'll settle her down."

She hated him.

"Now, you do anything stupid again," he said, "and I'll go up to the Hollywood Freeway and dump her right out onto the street below."

"Why are you doing this? Neither of us has any money."

A punishing laugh came back at her. "Not true, Miz Hanlon. You have all the money. And you're going to tell me where it is. Or I'm going to kill your little friend here."

"I'll give you anything you want, but I don't have any money."

"Lyin' bitch! We're coming up on the intersection. Blood and brains splattered across windshields below. Think about it."

She roared at him, "If it's me you want, come at me, you son of a bitch! But don't touch her!"

"We're getting close." He hung up.

●

In the squad room, Lt. Wahlberg arched a finger for Milleski to follow her as she dashed toward her office.

"Get an APB out," she barked. "Get the chopper ready, too. And call Garrison. I want him in on this."

"Detective Garrison's out today, Lieutenant," Milleski said.

"Find him! Tell him to get his ass in gear. I want him flying that chopper."

"You're going up too, Lieutenant?"

An eyebrow arched at his impertinence. "You think women shouldn't fly, Milleski? Might get all those little hormones scrambled and send them into PMS?"

"No thir. Ma'am."

"Lucky you. I'll be coordinating from the ground," she said. "You'll go up with Garrison."

A portly man in a mustard-stained white shirt stuck his head in the door. "We've got a newer address on this Brad Gerrick, Lieutenant. He's right here in town."

"How convenient. Get over there."

Detective Robbins pushed his way past his partner and

stepped in front of her. "Lieutenant! You gotta hear this. That car in the impound that was parked across the street from Germaine's. The one you ordered dusted—"

"Irene McCurdy's car? What about it?"

"Her prints match a set taken from the ladies room at Germaine's West."

Wahlberg sank into her chair. "Get Carl Hanlon on the phone."

Thirty

The brown pickup made a sharp right, then two more quick turns, driving in circles.

Liz's phone jangled. This time the kidnapper's sarcasm started before she got it to her ear.

"Alright," he barked. "What's it gonna be? Money or the kid's life?"

"What money? I told you—"

"*Gina's money.*"

She was silent, her brain whirling.

"I've been through every inch of your apartment," he shouted. "You stashed it somewhere."

"You bastard! You tore three places apart for some money no one even knows about? Who are you?" The name seeped from her lips before she realized it. "Brad—"

"Well, well," he said, with a morbid laugh," our killer has done her detective work."

"Killer?"

"There was no one else there!"

"You're accusing me of killing my own cousin? Gina was dead when I got there. I found her. I tripped over her, for godssake! There was no money around."

"It was *there.*"

"Then someone else has it! How do I know it wasn't you? You could be trying to make the perfect cover-up by acting innocent. Demanding money you already have."

He was silent. She had him.

No. If he was the murderer, he'd have gone underground long ago. He was risking exposure now because he was greedy. But he was not Gina's murderer.

She could hear his breathing intensify, the threat of action and harm quickening his pulse, exhilarating him.

"We're almost there," he said. "Talk, or I splatter the kid."

"I don't know about any money!"

The truck slowed as they reached the freeway overpass and stopped at the edge of the road. She could see Brad reaching in front of Sherice. Opening the passenger door.

"What are you doing!?" she screamed. "No! Stop!" Her hand slammed the horn over and over, arms waved in frantic motions through the windshield.

"Alright! Alright! I'll ... I'll take you to it!"

●

Dodger fans at O'Shay's Pub in Hollywood were wild, toss-ing paper coasters, table tents, and beer cans for their team's final run to win the game. The television over the bar blared. Excitement crackled as patrons speculated on the rest of the season. Chopper pilot Joe Garrison rested a foot on a bar stool, and leaned in to get the bartender's attention. He pushed his mug across several signatures that had been etched into the glossy wooden bar over the years.

The bartender looked uncertain. "You sure?" he asked, implying that Garrison had already consumed plenty.

"My day off."

The bartender drew another beer from the tap. "Dodgers are gonna do it this time, huh?"

Garrison's pager went off. He grabbed it and shut it off. "We can put money on it this year," he said.

"'Course we gotta wait and see what New York does," the bartender countered.

"Screw New York," Garrison grumbled. "Bunch 'a ball-breakin' weenies. No class."

The phone rang behind the bar. The bartender answered, raised his eyes toward Garrison, who shook his head and waved his hand in a cut-off gesture. "I'm not here," he said in a coarse whisper. "I gotta get one day off, for Crissakes.

Thirty-One

At the familiar stop light, Liz sat behind the wheel of Nuke's van, staring at the flashing red sign above Brogino's Bar & Grill. The brown pickup idled behind her.

"What is this place?" Brad snapped through the cell phone.

"Brogino's. I work here. This is where I hid it."

She had taken several wrong turns on the trip to this corner, trying to buy time while she formulated a plan.

Her time was up. The light changed.

"Park in the back," he ordered.

She drove to the back, surprised to find so many cars in the lot. He signaled for her to park in a spot facing north, while he circled to reach a space that faced her. In the moments it took the pickup to make the turn, she cleared the phone line and dialed 9-1-1 again.

Officer Lang picked up. The words gushed from Liz. "I need a squad car. He kidnapped a child. *Please*—"

Her door flew open and his hulking body was over her, arms closing in on her. Liz drew back, but his hand grabbed the phone instead of her. He whirled it across the parking lot, shattering it into pieces that bounced along the pavement.

Stunned, her eyes snapped straight ahead, and she noticed what she had missed before: the passenger door of his pickup was ajar. Sherice's short legs hit the pavement. She hesitated, unsure of where to go. Tentatively, she came toward them.

"No, Sherice—! " Liz shouted. "Run! Go inside. Get help!"

Sherice bolted toward the entrance, but Brad's longer legs were faster. They struggled as they had before. She kicked at him, but his bulky arms held her still.

Liz jumped from her car and began pounding on his back. "Let her go, you son of a bitch!" She kicked at the back of his knees. His legs buckled. He and Sherice dropped to the ground, but he kept a firm grip on her arm. With his other hand, he grabbed Liz's leg, knocking her off balance. She fell onto the ground with them.

"Hold still," he hissed, yanking Liz's arm, twisting it until she could not move. "We're going inside. Just a nice happy couple out for the night, you got that? Nice and normal."

Normal. How many times had she joked that nothing was ever normal at Brogino's?

"Once we get in there, where is it?" he asked.

She did a mental once-over of the restaurant. "I hid it."

Brad twisted Sherice's arm until she wailed. "I said where?"

"In the kitchen, for godssake! The walk-in."

He relaxed his pressure on Sherice. "This place got a problem with a kid in the bar?"

"No. They serve food, so she can be in there with adults."

"Alright. Walk in, sit down and order something," he said, "Drink it and act like nothing's unusual. When everybody's used to you being there, you get up, pretend you're going to the john, and get the money. The kid stays with me till you bring it back. You two stay there while I walk out the door nice and casual."

She knew he was lying about leaving them inside. He intended to kill them both.

●

They entered by the back door and walked through smoke that clung to the air. Across the room, lights from the front foyer cast their brightness in wedges that landed on the piano bar area, leaving the rest of the rectangular room with a cloudy look to it. Liz took Sherice's hand and led her to a table.

"Hey, Liz!" Rocky's voice rang out from behind the bar. "You don't get enough of this place you gotta come in on your night off?"

She turned a strained smile his way. Perhaps looking worried would tip him off.

Others had heard her name. The regulars smiled and waved.

At the front end of the bar, Corky worked his two beer mugs. With any luck he would make a crack about her being with "another man." Something she could develop into a verbal ruckus back and forth, maybe kick a hole in Brad's plan.

Corky called out, "Just can't live without me, eh Liz?"

"It's you, Corky," she shot back. "It'll always be you."

They took a table for four on the other side of the room. Rocky tossed a grimy towel over his shoulder and walked over to them.

"Hi, folks." He nodded to Brad and Sherice. "You're not playing tonight are you, Liz?"

"No. Just out with the, uh, family. Thought we'd stop by and say hello." Everyone knew she wasn't married. In fact, the bar crowd was constantly reminding her how lousy a woman's chances were of snaring a husband after the age of thirty.

Rocky looked at Brad. "So you're the reason she's outta here so fast every night, huh? Nice to meet ya. Name's Rocky." He offered his hand. "I've worked here so long I ought'a own a piece of the joint, but I don't. What does that say about me?" He looked at Sherice. "And who's this pretty lady?"

Liz nudged Sherice's knee under the table. "This is Brad's daughter, Sherice. Sherice, this is Rocky. He's kind of the head guy around here."

With a child's dryness, Sherice replied, "Hi."

"Except for the owner, Sammy. He's the real boss," Rocky said.

"Is Sam here tonight?" Liz asked.

"Just got back from a fishing trip. 'Least he smells like he's been fishing. I think he's back in the kitchen. What can I get you folks?"

"Three cokes," Brad snapped.

"Three cokes it is."

When Rocky returned to the bar, Brad leaned forward. "Where is it?"

"I told you, the kitchen," she said, unsteadily. "I'll go get it." She started to stand up. Brad's hand clamped down on her wrist, twisting it with insistent pressure. She winced and lowered herself back into her seat.

From the bar, Corky had been observing them. He called Rocky over. "Looks like an asshole, don't he?" he said.

"The jerk with Liz?" Rocky said, filling the glasses with ice and coke. "Man, I'll never understand women."

"Look at him. He's twisting her arm. He's hurtin' her, and she ain't arguin'. That ain't like her."

Rocky stretched to look at Liz's table. "You're right. She ought'a be knockin' his teeth out."

Rocky served the cokes. "There you go." Brad dropped several dollar bills on the table. After a few awkward seconds of silence, Rocky walked away.

"Change of plans," Brad hissed, his eyes on Liz. "You and I are walking into the dining room."

Sherice interrupted, "I have to go to the bathroom."

"Hold it. Walk straight into—"

"I can't," she whined, fidgeting in her seat. "I have to *go*."

"For god's sake," Liz pressed, "let me take her to the ladies room."

She started to rise when Brad's hand twisted her wrist again, forcing her back into her seat. He turned a contemptuous look on Sherice. "You wanna go, get going, but you'll have to manage by yourself. And I'll be watching. Don't talk to anybody. You got two minutes."

Her face scrunched up at him. "I can do a lot of things by myself," she shot back and raced out of the lounge.

"Brat," he muttered.

Thirty-Two

L t. Wahlberg stood like an ice statue in the center of the squad room. "Did you get him?"

"No, Lieutenant," Milleski said. "Mrs. Garrison said, and I quote, 'Leave him alone. Doesn't he deserve one day off from you bloodsuckers?'"

Wahlberg huffed. "He's drinking. His pager's off. Call Fetzer."

At that instance the door flew open and Carl Hanlon stormed in.

Barbara Reed

"Your officer called me," he said, hurriedly. "Where the hell is my sister, Lieutenant?"

"We've got units following their vehicles, Mr. Hanlon. You'll have to be patient."

"Patient? My sister's come to you three times in danger. She asked you for police protection, you told her you were understaffed. She asked for permission to carry a weapon, but you were too busy checking her out as a suspect." His volume rose higher with each word. "Now she's been kidnapped, and you're telling me to be patient?"

"Let's go into my office," she said, "I have some news about your aunt, as well."

Halfway to her office, Milleski and Robbins approached.

"We got it, Lieutenant," Robbins announced. "Brad Gerrick. We found his place. Landlady let us in."

Carl stepped back, pretending not to be eavesdropping.

"What did you find?" Wahlberg asked.

"A lot of pictures of the dead girl. And bullets for a twenty-two. No gun."

Milleski chimed, "Don't forget the thcrapbook!"

"Oh yeah. We found that. Loaded with articles about this Perdusian guy."

The phone rang behind them. Lang responded.

"Okay honey, everything's okay," Lang said, waving to the Lieutenant. "Stay calm, and whatever you do, don't hang up. Lieutenant! This is her. The little girl."

"Do you know where you're calling from?" Lang said, into the phone. "That's the name, Brogino's? You're sure? Brogino's Bar?"

Carl stepped forward and yanked the phone from Lang's hand. "Liz? Are you okay?"

Officer Lang yanked the phone back.

298

"Mr. Hanlon!" Lt. Wahlberg growled. "You are interfering with an officer in the line of duty!"

"That's my sister! Brogino's is where she works. Brogino's Bar and Grille. It's a dump up on Lankershim."

Wahlberg held up a hand to hold him back as she listened to Officer Lang, then found a more compassionate voice and said, "We'll find her, Mr. Hanlon."

Lang continued, "Everything's alright, honey, squad cars are on their way. I want you to stay on the line, though. This way we know you're safe."

"I can't," Sherice said. "If I don't go back he'll kill her."

●

Sherice hung up and walked around the corner with the same composure she'd used at rehearsal. She slid into her seat. "So this is where you work, huh, Liz? Kind of dingy. I thought you played big shows and stuff."

Brad leaned in. "Cut the chat, girls. Stand up."

"You said you were on TV," Sherice went on.

"Soon," Liz said.

Sherice's face pinched as she took in the room. "This place is a dump. Oh, I remember!" She pointed toward the piano bar. "That's the piano that's really a fake. It's a junky little spinet under that table, right? Can't the people tell by the sound?"

"Not everyone has ears like yours," she said.

"Or a mouth either," Brad's sneered. "Stand up. Both of you."

He stood with them, unaware that as he rose, the side of his jacket caught on the back of the chair, exposing the .22 tucked into the waist of his jeans.

Sherice blurted, "Can I play it? You said I could play it

someday."

Brad hissed under his breath at Liz, "Shut her up."

"No, she's right," Liz said. "Let her play. The attention will be on her while I'm getting the money." Anything to keep Sherice away from him.

His narrowing eyes fixed hard on Sherice. "Start playing. And don't stop, you got that? You keep playing no matter what. The minute I hear you stop, I blow her head off."

Sherice's gaze was unflinching. Her words spit at him. "You just make sure she comes back unshot or I'll blow yours off."

The child marched to the piano bar and began the introduction to *Satin Doll*. All heads spun around to look at her.

"Hey, isn't that Liz's kid playing?" a customer asked.

"Must be. Sounds better than Liz!"

Brad nudged Liz's forearm. They entered the dining area, the piano music behind them.

Corky waited till they had passed behind his stool, then motioned to Rocky again.

"Did you see it? The asshole's got a gun in his belt! What the hell're they trying to pull, you suppose? They gonna rob this place?"

"Liz? No way."

"Then him maybe. Could be he's got the gun on her. Is Sammy back yet? You better let him know."

"You didn't smell him when he walked in? He's fryin' up some of that trout he caught."

Corky leaned his sizable girth backward on his bar stool, and spied into the dining room. "They're just standing there."

"I can't get to the office if they're standing there," Rocky said. "Wait. I got an idea." At the other end of the bar, an opening led to the kitchen which had been blocked off years ago by boxes of bar supplies and equipment. Rocky began shoving boxes sideways. The light from the kitchen peaked through. He stacked them around his feet and under the bar, increasing the size of the opening. When enough cartons had been removed, he discovered a baseball bat leaning against one wall. He picked it up, getting used to the feel of it again, and smirked, "How 'bout that? There was so much crap piled up, I forgot I had this thing."

●

In the dining room, Liz looked straight ahead, purposely ignoring the people she saw each week, hoping her odd behavior would spark a little confrontation. No one noticed.

Brad nodded toward the parallel doors leading to the kitchen. "Back there?"

"Yes."

●

Behind the piano bar, Sherice scanned the faces of her rapt audience, determined to be able to identify each one if she ever had to. Just like the legal dramas she watched on television. She smiled when they clapped, pretending she lacked a care in the world, while keeping her eyes on the doorway to the dining room, listening for signs of trouble, and wondering why the cops were taking so long.

Thirty-Three

Liz walked through the swinging door to the kitchen with Brad behind her. A waist-high chopping block was positioned in the center of the room with burners, stove tops, and ovens on either side. The kitchen was deserted, but a large cast iron skillet sizzled unattended on one of the burners, a full-size trout sputtering in two inches of oil. Another pot held several quarts of boiling water.

Near the stove, she hesitated. Straight ahead were the stainless steel doors of the refrigerated walk-in, and floor-to-ceiling shelves stocked with cans and cartons on the adjacent wall to the right. On the left was the opening to the liquor pantry that Rocky had begun clearing away. Through it, Liz could make out the faces of customers at the bar, and hear Sherice's piano playing as the crowd urged her on with encouraging applause.

Brad's pistol was low at his side. He went toward the walk-in. "In here?"

"Yes, but it's locked."

Grease splattered from the frying pan. She jumped back, thinking Sam must have turned the fire on high, then gone to the men's room with a magazine. She'd never been so eager for his return.

"Open it," Brad commanded.

"I don't have a key."

He cocked the gun, aimed it at her. "Find one."

Under his malignant gaze, perspiration tinged every pore. She scanned the counter tops, pulled open drawers, hoping to maneuver Brad inside the walk-in, then jam the door handle behind him.

Searching for a ring of keys, she saw motion in the liquor pantry. Rocky's beefy thigh stretched over a tall box. He wedged himself into a narrow space, the baseball bat in hand, arms positioned to swing.

Her eyes flickered. Brad's followed. He spun around and snapped the gun up, aiming at Rocky.

Liz pulled down the hot pads above the stove, grabbed Sam's skillet, and sloshed the hot grease at Brad's feet. He went sliding like a Vaudeville dancer. She tossed the rest around the counter tops, touched a towel to the flames, and lit the cardboard boxes against the wall. Flames ignited around him with a *whoosh*. He hit the floor with a thud.

The gun wavered. Rocky saw it an instant before it fired, and dove behind a cabinet. The bullet whizzed past him, and lodged in the mirrored wall behind the bar. Glass and liquor flew into the air like a shoot-em-up in a western movie.

The shot sent customers rushing to the exits. In the commotion, Sherice ran behind a hostess' desk and huddled for cover. She pulled a telephone off the desk and punched in 9-1-1 again.

In the kitchen, hot embers sparked other objects. The place was ablaze in seconds.

Rocky stood up, feet crunching against broken glass.

Brad leaned on side and tried to aim, but his elbow slipped on the grease. The gun dropped from his hand.

Liz made a dash for it. As she crouched, Brad stretched to pin her to the floor.

"Let her go," Rocky ordered. Instead, Brad grabbed the gun and fixed his aim at Rocky again.

"What the hell is going on in here?" Sam Brogino bellowed from the doorway. His voice was drowned out by the sound of Rocky taking a pulverizing swing. Brad's neck snapped. The full weight of his lifeless body collapsed over Liz.

She struggled free. "Get him off me!" she cried.

Rocky heaved the body over; Liz rolled away and lay on the floor, breathing hard.

"You okay?" he cried. "Liz? Ah, Liz, I wasn't aiming at you." He pulled her to his chest.

"I'm fine, I'm fine," she said, still panting from rushing adrenaline. "Is he—?"

"He's dead."

She fell back against the wall, her pulse returning to normal.

On the other side of the chopping block, Sam pulled the pin on the fire extinguisher. The old canister fizzled, it's pressure gone long ago. He tossed it aside and grabbed the five-gallon pot of water he'd been boiling for pasta. He aimed for the highest flames first.

Liz looked up. "No! It's a grease fire!"

Flames magnified around them, heat soared. The entrance to the lounge was engulfed in flames, the back door now the only exit.

"Let's get out 'a here," Rocky yelled, and pulled Liz to her feet. At the door he stopped, turning back to see that Sam was fixated by the blaze around him. He had not moved. Rocky grabbed his arm. "Sammy! C'mon. We're gettin' outta here!"

"This has been my place for over thirty years."

"Then it's time for a new one," Rocky cried. "C'mon." He got behind Sam and nudged him through the back door.

●

Within minutes fire trucks were slamming to a halt at the front entrance. Shouts from customers and neighbors caused a commotion on the sidewalk. Flames licked high into the sky, sending turbulent clouds of black smoke twisting into the night. Firefighters stretched hoses across the sidewalk, cutting down tree branches and removing bush along the sides of the building as they worked their way toward the back.

Liz squeezed between a thin row of trees and a rusty chain-link fence to search for Sherice in the front of the building.

A crowd gathered on the front sidewalk to watch the destruction of what had been a landmark in their neighborhood. Liz spotted Sherice standing inside a circle of customers looking as if she was holding court. She was describing the complexities of musical harmony, announcing how easy it had been to learn from someone as smart as Liz. Through the crowd, she spotted Liz and raced toward her, collapsing in her arms, her audience forgotten.

"You're okay," Liz repeated, as they huddled beneath a tree at the edge of the sidewalk. She rocked her back and forth. "No one will hurt you now, Sherice. It's all over. What you did in there—you are one brave little girl."

Sherice looked up. "You shot him, didn't you?"

"He's dead now," she said, gently. "He can't hurt you."

Thirty-Four

The flames discharged intense heat, but Liz shivered as she sat on the ground, leaning against a tree with Sherice in her arms.

A customer from Brogino's offered a blanket from his car, and Liz bundled her in it. Red lights flashed around them. Emergency vehicles blocked the exits. While they sat beneath the tree, Liz concentrated on the puzzling pieces of both murders.

She thought about the night of Gina's murder. Brad must have had advance warning that the money would be there. He, and someone else.

Television crews had arrived. Microphones went up onto tripods within seconds.

Sherice peered at the crowd. "How did everybody get here so fast?"

"Disaster brings people together," Liz replied.

Brad Gerrick's body was placed in the coroner's wagon. Liz shifted the blanket to be certain Sherice didn't see. Her own gaze was caught in a long stream of pearl-white brilliance that came from a TV camera and bounced off the chrome of the ambulance. She stared into it, allowing herself to be pulled into deep reflection, transfixed by the white opalescence. A hazy memory was taking shape. The pearliness formed into an image of Gina's white pearl evening purse she'd last seen in Aunt Irene's condo.

A thought flickered; her body shook with a sudden jerk.

"What's wrong?" Sherice asked.

Shocked by the reenactment in her mind, Liz could barely speak. "Just a chill."

Over the shouts and confusion, she heard her name being called. She peeked through the side of the blanket and saw a pair of highly polished brown shoes nearby.

"Liz?" Carl's voice was pinched with anxiety. "*Liz?*"

She tugged at the leg of his trousers. "Hey," she called softly. "Keep it down."

He bent down.

"Don't you know not to wear a suit to occasions like these?" she said.

"My God, Liz, I've been looking all over for you." He threw his arms around her, enclosing Sherice in his embrace too.

"Thank God you're alright. I was so worried."

"How did you know we were here?"

"It's all over the news now, but Wallpaper called me awhile ago. I was at the station when Sherice's call came in." He touched a hand to the child's cheek. "By the way, good going there, maestro. I'm Carl. Liz's brother."

"Figured." Sherice said. "She talks about you a lot."

"Someday you can tell me what she says. For now, let's see if we can find a way to get you out of here without getting swamped, okay?"

He started to rise; Liz caught his arm. "Wait. Is the News flashing our names? Sherice's mother doesn't know."

"The cops have contacted her. She's waiting for them to bring her home," he said. "And you wouldn't believe what my phone lines look like. By the way, Sonnie's left at least a dozen messages for you."

"Sonnie?"

"He told me to tell you not to go anywhere without your bodyguard, but listen, there's something else—"

"Wait! Did anyone get Nuke to the hospital?"

"Squad cars were at the scene right away. We'll be hearing soon. Listen, Liz, there's something important—"

"How could Sonnie have known I was in danger?"

"He said you'd know. Anyway, I need to tell you about Aunt Irene before someone else does."

"I've been thinking about her, too. She's got Gina's purse. Do you know what that means?"

"That's what I've been trying to tell you. It's complicated. Let's see if we can get Sherice out of here, then you and I can sneak through, and I'll explain."

"Look for Rocky in the back," she said. "He'll know a way out."

While they waited, Liz thought of her last conversation with Sonnie, and wondered what he'd learned from his father.

Sherice broke into her thoughts. "Did you have a gun all the time, Liz?"

"No. What made you think that?"

"You shot Brad, didn't you?"

"No, he fired the shot."

Sherice looked confused. Liz explained about Rocky saving her life with a baseball bat.

"Then it was you who set him up so's Rocky could whack him?"

"Well, there was a frying pan smoking on the stove—"

Sherice's mouth dropped with incredulity. "You started the fire?"

"Shhhh. I'd never do such a thing if there had been any other way."

"A fire! Wow," Sherice cried. "That's way cool."

"It's many things," Liz said with a sad chuckle, "but I don't think way cool is one of them. We'll talk about it someday."

She saw Carl's brown loafers approaching. Behind him, black sneakers hurried along the cement.

Carl raised the top of the blanket.

Rocky bent down. "Hey, Liz. We gotta stop meeting like this."

"I'm just glad you're okay, Rocky." She made a friendly jab at him. "That's some arm you got there."

"Yeah, well, I played for the Sox, you know."

"I owe you."

"Yeah, Liz started the fire!" Sherice blurted.

Rocky laughed. "You think you can keep that quiet while we sneak through this crowd? There's a patrol car in the back. Cop says if we can get back there without being surrounded, he'll get you home."

He shifted her weight into his own arms and rose to his feet, using the blanket to hide her face. The cover-up allowed them to get away.

Carl sat down on the sidewalk next to Liz. "You ready to make a break for it?"

"First, tell me what's so important about Aunt Irene. And why does Sonnie think I'm in danger?"

"Irene's car was towed from a spot across from Germaine's. It had been there since the morning of Gina's murder. Prints matched those found in the ladies room at Germaine's."

"So she stopped in to see her daughter the night before. What does that prove?"

"Gina hadn't worked the night before."

"Then some other night."

They were interrupted by a reporter. "That's her! The one he kidnapped. Where's the little girl?"

"C'mon," Carl said, helping Liz up. "Let's get out of here."

Someone shouted, "Did you shoot the suspect, Ms. Hanlon?"

Liz stopped. This was an answer she wanted on record.

"No, I did not."

Reporters nosed around her like sharks in shallow water.

"Who started the fire?"

"Where's the little girl?"

"Did the dead man kill Gina McCurdy?"

Liz stopped and looked directly into the camera. "Brad Gerrick, the deceased, was Gina McCurdy's lover," she said. "Gerrick had a gun, he was aiming it at me and was about to fire when Rocky, our bartender, swung a baseball bat to knock the gun from his hand. He swung to protect me, and in doing so, he killed Mr. Gerrick."

"What was your relationship with Brad Gerrick?"

"I had no relationship with him."

"Why was he chasing you?"

"He was looking for something he thought I had."

"Did he find it?"

"No."

Another reporter called out, "Are you saying that Gerrick was the killer?"

"And what about Danny Amata? Did Gerrick kill him too?"

Liz raised her head and stated, "I think it's safe to say that the murderer has been found."

Lt. Wahlberg looked up sharply. "She can't say that!"

Liz flashed an optimistic smile at the camera. "This whole ugly mess is over. We can put it behind us now, and begin to rebuild our lives. And speaking of rebuilding, I want to add that construction will resume tomorrow morning at Germaine's West. Six o'clock sharp!" She let the applause fade and added, "Sonnie Tucks has been working hard to restore Germaine's West, and like the saying goes, the show must go on!"

She and Carl inched their way through the crowd, ignoring the rest of the questions.

Thirty-Five

At four-fifteen the next morning, Liz slowed in front of Germaine's and turned the corner onto Camden Street. At the end of the short block, she parked under the same bushy tree branches that had been hanging over the road as long as she could remember. At this pre-dawn hour, the neighborhood was still, the full moon giving the events of these last two weeks a surrealistic feeling.

She'd packed a full bottle of Jack Daniels, and an assortment of meats, cheeses, fruit, and bread. Picnic food. She tucked her jeans inside her knee-high boots, grabbed the bags, and started up the street toward the club.

At the edge of the bushes that lined Germaine's back lot, she lingered. Danny had always assured her there was no danger. Streaks of moonlight illuminated the area, but there were no signs of life. "Elvin?" she whispered hoarsely. "Are you here? It's Liz Hanlon. I'm a friend of Danny's. I need to talk to you."

Tree branches rustled delicately in the mild breeze.

"Elvin?"

Silence.

She pushed back a few branches and stepped inside, zeroing in on the ground before taking the next step. Images of coiled snakes made her long to turn back, but she pushed on through the next set of branches.

"Elvin? I've got something for you. I heard you like Jack Daniels. Got a whole bottle, and some food too. I went by Martini's Deli on the way. C'mon, Elvin," she said, her tone almost pleading now, "I'm here alone. I won't disturb anything. I just need to talk. Please. You've got to be here."

Something moved in the distance. A rapist who hangs out waiting for women to run around alone at night? A group of punks waiting for someone to jump at the bank's ATM machine?

Branches moved. Too high for an animal, not really a comforting thought.

"Elvin?"

A short, stout man in a dingy pea-green jacket emerged, pushing heavy foliage out of his way. "I don't believe it," he said. "I never thought I'd see you here!"

Elvin was not how she'd pictured him.

He watched her, sizing her up.

"I'm Liz. We've never really met. Danny always told me I should come by."

"I know who you are. What brings you to my private castle?"

His manner of speech was remarkably clear, even sophisticated. She noticed a familiar accent.

She held up the bottle. "I was wondering if we could talk."

"You thought you had to bring a bottle of booze for me to talk to you?"

One minute and she'd already insulted him. "Danny said you liked Jack Daniels, so I thought maybe a gift. I brought some food, too. Are you hungry?"

"I'll have some. Over here," he said, leading her down a path that had been made by repeated footsteps.

An old quilt was spread out with half a dozen pillows leaned against tree trunks. A few of the comforts of home.

They set the food out picnic style. He produced a cardboard cup from a canvas bag, poured the scotch, and handed the bottle back to her. "Only have one."

"No problem." She took a sip from the bottle. "Elvin, there's something I've got to know. About the night of Gina's murder."

"It's about time someone came around to talk to me."

"What do you mean?"

He helped himself to a hunk of cheese. "I make no secret of my whereabouts. Everyone knows I live here."

"Meaning the cops should have known you saw what happened that night?"

"Should of."

"And did you?"

"I saw a pickup cruise in and drop her off by the back door, then take off again. Same routine a couple more times."

"Start from the beginning," she said. "Tell me as if I know nothing about that night."

"Raining like hell," he said, showing her the tarp he kept wadded up with some clothes.

"I was dozing, when about quarter to five, here comes this truck."

"What kind of truck?"

"Brown. Nothing special. Gina gets out at the back door, goes inside. Instead of staying there in the lot, the truck turns left on Camden, and parks half-hidden under those big overgrown trees up there."

The same place she'd just parked to stay out of sight.

"Then what?"

"I didn't think anything of it at first, but then I kept hearing the sound of an engine idling. After awhile the pickup came back. The driver's antsy, he's leaning over like he's trying to see inside the club."

"When was that?"

"'Bout twenty minutes later."

"Go on."

"He hangs there a minute, then gives it up and goes back to his same spot under the trees."

"Then what?"

"He waits."

Elvin opened one of the roast beef packages and pulled out two slices, stuffing them both into his mouth. "Hmm, you brought the good stuff." He went on, "Then the guy does it all over again awhile later, pulling near the door to check, then going back up the street. I figure he's waiting for Gina, but she never came out."

Elvin was backing up everything Brad had said.

He finished one sandwich and started building another.

"Me, I felt sorry for this guy, you know?" he said. "He drops his girlfriend off and waits for her, but he's got no way of knowing that while he's cruising back up the street, turning around to park, someone else is inside, maybe doin' her, who knows?"

"Who, Elvin?"

"Couldn't say."

His face was turned down as he made another sandwich.

"Yes, you can. You saw plenty. C'mon, tell me."

"She's already dead."

"I know, talking won't bring her back," Liz said, "but the person who killed Gina also killed Danny. That's two friends, Elvin."

He looked pained. "I wish I could say for sure, but I only saw the brown pickup movin' in close a few times, then back out again. The guy who ran out was moving way too fast."

"What guy?"

"Don't know his name. He looked like someone who's here a lot, but I don't know."

Suddenly the long sleeved shirt and leather boots felt like a sauna wrapped around her. "This guy runs *out* of the club?"

"Right. He's gone about a minute, and he comes back driving this ratty old white pickup. Parks it near the back door, runs back in to get something."

"A white pickup?"

"White. With primer showing on the hood, bunch 'a tools and crap in the back. He jumps out, leaving the engine running. He goes inside, then comes out in two seconds, this time half walking, half carryin' someone. He stuffs'em in the front seat—"

"Wait a minute! Carrying someone? Gina? Was he carrying Gina?"

"No, someone small. Could'a been a kid. He closes the door,

319

runs around and jumps behind the wheel, jams it in gear, and hauls ass."

A small person. Liz felt sick. "Then what?"

"I fell asleep until the cop cars are blasting their sirens loud enough to wake me up again."

"And Brad didn't come back after that?"

"The brown pickup driver? No."

"Back up a minute. In between the time Brad cruised by the back door and the time the ambulance came, who else went inside?"

"Just the guy with the beat-up white truck."

She popped up and started dusting herself off. "Thanks, Elvin. You have no idea how much help you've been."

"Either that or I've created major shit for someone."

"The killer did that himself."

He capped the bottle and handed it back to her. "No, you keep it," she said.

Elvin nodded. "Thanks."

She turned to leave, then turned back, about to speak.

"I got sick of M.I.T." he said.

"Boston! No wonder I recognized the accent. You're from Boston."

"New Hampshire. My parents insisted I go to M.I.T., which I did for five long semesters. Then I took a break."

He looked up sharply. "You never felt like you needed a break from everything and everyone?"

"Oh, yeah."

"No nerve?"

She smiled. "Guess not."

"I'm just taking a rest for awhile."

He folded up the rest of the empty roast beef wrapping and placed it neatly in a container.

"Thanks again, Elvin. Danny was right. I should have stopped by sooner."

He walked with her through the beaten-down path. At the edge of the brush she turned to thank him again, but he was gone.

●

Back at her car, Liz pulled off the leather boots and changed into her running shoes. She got behind the wheel, dialed Sonnie's number, and waited until his sleepy voice came on the line.

Thirty-Six

Liz shone a flashlight into the bottom drawer of Sonnie's desk and withdrew the .38 he kept there. She recalled feeling uncomfortable when he'd told her about it; now she stuffed it inside her belt and covered it with her shirt. She leaned back in a desk chair to think. And to wait.

Thirty minutes later, metal tools clanked in the lounge as they were dropped at the foot of the brick wall. A flashlight beam was placed to illuminate its far right corner.

With the sharp edge of a crowbar in place, a man threw his upper body weight against it several times, unable to pry the bricks loose.

"Good thing you made some noise just now. Without your cologne I might have missed you."

Tony spun around.

She faced him from the doorway. "You know, that brick you're chipping away at will come out a lot easier if you wait and let the construction guys do it."

Indignation flashed in his eyes. His mouth twisted, his jaw set firmly into an ugly shape.

She stepped forward into the light. "Of course, if you did wait for the construction crew, you might have a fight on your hands. It would be hard to convince them that all that money is really yours."

Flustered, his gaze darted. Beads of sweat formed on his brows. "What are you doing here?"

"I'm watching you bury yourself. I suppose we both want something tonight, don't we, Tony? I want to know how you could bring yourself to commit murder. And you just want the money."

His jaw sagged. "Murder? I could never—"

"You did. It was all over that money you chiseled years ago from a couple of mob guys who helped you get started in business. You worked hard, built yourself up. You had the big name, but after awhile you realized your debt would never be paid in full. So you started nickel'n dimin' from them. Problem was, they figured it out!"

Tony gaped at her, astonished. "Good God, are you on something?" His body underwent a quick adjustment while he regained outward composure. She didn't want to think about what might be going on inside.

"And those two years you were gone," she said. "Silly me, I thought you were trying to do the honorable thing! Trying to avoid being forced into business with them. It took me awhile to realize you were running to save your own ass! How am I doing so far, Tony?"

With the toe of his boot, he pushed the tools closer together. "This is madness," he snarled. "I hand you the most desirable career in the world—a lifetime opportunity other singers would fight over—and this is how you repay me?" He picked up the hammer and chisel, and began chipping away at the bricks.

Against the rhythmic pounding, Liz had to raise her voice. "You let them torture Archie for that money."

His pounding slowed, then picked up speed again.

"You had to know they'd go after Victor Markham, too. Yet you never turned it over."

"Where are you getting this absurd information?" he railed at her.

"From someone who was there. The money's in the wall, isn't it?" she pressed, finding it particularly telling that he did not ask who she was referring to.

She thought of Joey Tucks and how he had remodeled the room when he took over. "The bricks were loose when Booker had the place. You put the money behind a couple of them, assuming you'd get it out when you came back into the country. But then Joey gave the place a facelift, and you couldn't get to it!"

"Sonnie would have gambled away every penny if I hadn't.."

"Don't tell me you hid the money to save the show! Sonnie gambles a little, it's true, but when we get those bricks chipped away, the cash that comes out is going to be old cash. Twenty-five years old."

Cautiously, she withdrew Sonnie's revolver from her waistband, but he surprised her. He turned his back on her, continuing to work on the bricks. Several pieces of mortar flaked off and fell to the floor.

"The white pickup belongs to your gardener, doesn't it?" she said. "The rubber boots, too. All that preparation, I'll bet you wanted to kick yourself for letting Gina in on it."

"It is *my* money!"

"And you were going to buy her love with it. You gave her the scrapbook so she'd know you were rich and powerful, and for that, you expected what? True love? Bet it drove you nuts to find out she had a partner!"

He turned an expression on her that reminded her of the blaze at Brogino's. "I loved her. Because of that, you think I murdered her?"

"No. Because you were seen."

"I was not."

"You were.

 He blurted, "They were in on it together! It was a scam!"

"Imagine! One con out-doing another! The nerve."

"They were—"

She pressed, "Who Tony? Who's 'they'?"

"Her boyfriend! That drummer of yours! They planned to steal everything I'd worked for. Once he knew about the money, I knew he'd never give up."

"You twisted son of a bitch!" she screeched. "Danny was the gentlest soul I know. He didn't need your money! Gina's partner was a ruthless scumbag named Brad Gerrick! *You killed the wrong man!*"

For a moment her words rocked him, but he picked up the chisel. "I loved Gina."

"She didn't want many people to know that, especially her mother, Irene McCurdy. You knew her as Irene Markham."

At the mention of Gina's mother, all traces of the gentlemen disappeared. "That woman was a bitter old drunk twenty years ago. She hated everyone."

"Her instincts seem to have been right."

He whirled on her. "When I met Gina, her last name was McCurdy, not Markham. I had no idea who she was. But she certainly knew who I was! She moved in on me like a panther hunting its prey. All she cared about was paying me back for something that had been out of my control."

"What happened to my Uncle Victor was completely within your control! First him, then his daughter!"

"I didn't kill her! The old lady did! She was insane. She did it!"

Liz thought of the fragile woman she'd seen earlier. "My aunt is embittered, and she drinks heavily, but she would *never* hurt her own daughter."

His looked seemed demonic to her now. It sickened her to think that she had once found him attractive.

"It was an accident," he said. "The old woman came at me."

"With what? She's barely five feet tall."

"With her bare fists! She was screaming and pounding on my chest. Gina picked up a wrench and jumped between us--

"So you shoved her out of the way."

"I tried to get it out of her hand, but the old lady kept throwing punches, kicking me in the shins! Her hands were flying everywhere. She swung at me and hit Gina. Gina went down, her head slammed against the boards," he said. "I tried to save her, but it was no use."

"So you forced Irene out of here and loaded her up on

tranquilizers!"

"I got her out of here before the police came."

"She didn't care about herself! She wanted to save her daughter!"

"I tried to save her daughter," he screamed, then swung around and slammed his tools again, this time working more furiously.

"Don't hurry," she said dryly, exposing the revolver. "I lied. The construction workers aren't coming till tomorrow. I made that announcement to see if the killer would bite. And here you are."

One more shove and a large chunk of brick dislodged, creating a gaping hole. Her eyes darted toward the open cavity. As they did, Tony spun around and slapped a vicious backhand, knocking the gun from her hand. As it sailed across the dance floor, he slapped her hard across her face and sent her sprawling onto the floor, the gun out of reach. A trickle of blood oozed from her mouth.

He raised the crowbar and lunged at her. She lurched to the left, throwing him off balance.

She was reaching for the pickax, but he grabbed the crowbar. She jerked right, then left, just as he brought it down. It sliced into the leather seat of a nearby booth.

Liz leapt to her feet, grabbed a two-by-four, and swung it at him, but not fast enough. He caught it and slammed it against her waist, knocking her over the bar where she flopped like a rag. She slumped down between two stools.

The room went black. She blinked, fighting the urge to give up. She shook her head, working to stay alert, then got to her knees.

She was facing the barrel of the .38 she'd taken from Sonnie's desk.

"Get up," he ordered. "We're going out the back."

She rose, then pretended to pass out, falling, then rolling quickly across the floor.

Keep moving. He can't hit a moving target.

She rolled till she touched something sharp, reached out her hand and grabbed the hammer. She slammed it hard into Tony's shin.

He groaned, starting to collapse, then struggled to his feet, the gun pointed at her. "Drop it," he ordered, limping on the wounded leg. "Get up."

His face was the color of boiling lobster. He cocked the gun, she dropped the hammer and started for the back door.

In the half-light, she stepped on the tip of a long wooden slat. It flew up, she caught it in her hands, spun around and swung it at him with all her force, knocking him to the floor. The gun flew from his hands, into the shadows. She charged at him. They wrestled arm-in-arm, twisting on the floor like street fighters. She rammed a knee into his stomach, but he grabbed a clump of her hair and yanked her head back as he hunted for the gun with his other hand.

Bent backward, pain radiated down her spine. She could not move.

"Get up," he ordered.

"I can't—"

Tony's fingers were knotted in her hair. He started to stand, pulling her with him.

The front door smashed open. Sonnie Tucks threw on the overhead lights and bolted into the room. He stopped at the edge of the lounge and aimed a pistol at Tony.

"Let her go!" Sonnie ordered.

Tony glared; no one moved.

"I had to see for myself," Sonnie said, shock and disbelief

on his face. "See if my old buddy would really do this to me."

Tony tightened his stranglehold on Liz and pressed the gun barrel to her temple. "I have to do this," he said to Sonnie, his tone quiet, threatening.

Sonnie's aim never wavered. "We were kids together, Tony, let her go."

"You know I can't. Drop your gun, Sonnie."

Liz's scalp was on fire. "Do it, Sonnie," she croaked.

No one moved. Unable to stand the pain, Liz tightened both fists, twisted against him, and rammed them into Tony's groin. He doubled over, moaning. She jumped away.

Tony recovered quickly and raised the .38.

"Sonnie!" she screamed.

Sonnie fired.

Unharmed, Tony sprang forward as Liz grabbed the two-by-four, hurled it with a shoulder-twist, connecting with Tony's chest. He dropped the gun, she raced for it, seized it. He flew at her, dragging her down. He pounded at her, but she held onto the gun, trying to raise it between their two bodies. She was staring into his face when she squeezed the trigger.

Tony collapsed on top of her. She struggled free, then sat staring at his motionless body. Blood oozed down his front. Liz's hands and clothes were covered with it.

Sonnie touched a finger to Tony's neck. "He's dead."

Liz moved away from the body, still catching her breath.

Sonnie threw his arms around her. "Jeezus. Are you alright?" He examined the bruises welling up on her face and neck. "You need a doctor."

She touched her hand to her scalp. Clumps of hair came out in her hands. "I could use some ice."

"Cops're on their way."

"How do you know?"

"I called'em right after you woke me up."

"So that's what took you so long to get here? I thought maybe you stopped to have your tires rotated."

"Wise guy." He pulled her close. "My favorite wise guy. Sweet Lord, Liz. If anything had happened to you—"

"You either."

"Your instincts, boy, they were right on. How did you know? I mean, I should have noticed."

"He was your friend. You weren't looking."

She heard sirens in the distance.

"My dad's information tied it together. He remembered when Tony was broke, then one day he met some guys. Soon he was rollin' in cash."

"Why didn't he ever tell you?"

"He figured it was ancient history. Tony and I had lost touch. No reason to ruin the memory of a boyhood friendship."

"To tell you the truth," she said, "I didn't know for sure until I talked to Elvin."

The sirens grew louder. Liz walked over to peer inside the cavity left in the wall. Something glistened. She yanked on a corner brick. "Help me pull this brick the rest of the way out."

Sonnie took the chisel and gave it a shove. The brick crumbled.

"This is it," she cried, pulling the chisel out of his hand and knocking the last piece loose. "Look!" She dug through the debris and pulled out a canvas bag with one side ripped open. Dozens of gold coins fell out.

"That cagey bastard!" she cried. "He converted the cash into gold coins!"

The sirens screeched to a halt in front of the club.

"Quick. Let's get it out here," she said, scrambling to withdraw more bags. "I want to see how he did it."

"This is unbelievable," Sonnie muttered, pulling out bags two at a time.

In all, there were fifteen bags. Liz tore one open by its drawstring, then reached in and let the coins slide through her fingers.

"He thought about inflation even back then," she repeated in disbelief.

"No one can accuse Tony Perdusian of being stupid."

They pushed the heavy bags together in a pile.

"Can you imagine what this is all worth today?" she said.

"No wonder he couldn't wait to get this place remodeled."

She started to calculate their value. "There's got to be— there must be five million dollars here!"

Thirty-Seven

Sonnie entered Liz's hospital room with another vase of cut flowers. He set them on the table next to her, and picked another square of chocolate off a nearby plate.

Her eyes opened, and she saw that his had lost their blood-shot look. The puffs beneath them were nearly invisible. He looked well-rested, healthy. Like a man with renewed vigor, and a sense of purpose. "How 'bout saving some candy for the patient?" she said.

He smiled. "Thought you were asleep." He gestured toward

the wheelchair near the door. "Doesn't look like you're going to be a patient much longer."

She shifted impatiently in the bed. "They kept me overnight to make sure there were no internal injuries, but I thought I'd be out of here by now. What's taking everyone so long?"

"They've just had a shift change. Your doctor will probably be around soon to sign you out." He chomped down on another bite of chocolate. "You can't possibly eat all this yourself."

"They're good, aren't they? Reggie made them. The woman works magic in the kitchen."

"They're great, but not as great as the sight of you in one healthy piece."

She leaned back. "It all feels like a dream. I wish it were."

Sonnie eased down onto the edge of the bed. "I know. What's that they say? Life turns on a dime."

"It does."

"Marilyn sends her best."

Liz blinked. "Oh?"

"She's in New York. I talked to her, let her know what happened. We've split up. For good this time."

"I'm sorry you have to go through that."

"No. We don't belong together. Never did. We're not even close friends, let alone lovers. I guess she was having an affair right out in the open so I'd take the first step."

He walked to the window and watched the late afternoon sun. "I told you I talked to the attorney about the concerts, didn't I?"

"Yes! You said we're going ahead, but how can we do it without Tony?"

"The money belongs to the investors, and they're still a go. We'll replace Tony with another producer. It'll be tough, but we can do it. You up to it?"

"Of course. Seems strange, though, to come through this, and wind up with a TV show. How's my aunt?"

"I talked to Carl this morning. Her lawyer is using 'extreme anguish' as part of her case."

"I'll never believe she went there to kill Tony. I think her rage just took over."

"Looks that way. She drove her own car that night, then left it parked on the street and forgot about it. Tony took her home."

"And loaded her up on pills," she snorted. "Guess he forgot about her car, too."

"Cops would never have matched Irene's prints if that car hadn't been towed."

"So Tony wasn't so smart after all," she said. "By the way, do you mind if we stop to see her on the way to the recital tonight? If I ever get out of here, that is."

"Sure. I'm glad you don't have to miss it."

"Sherice would never forgive me."

He walked to the foot of her bed. "Speaking of musical events, I've got two tickets to the Hollywood Bowl next week."

"You bought tickets to the Bowl right in the middle of our broadcast dates? Just a tad optimistic, aren't we?"

"Man cannot work twenty-four hours a day without some kind of recreation. I know I'm not very knowledgeable about music, but I've been wondering if you'd find a guy like me too dull, or too boring to be with—"

"Oh, no you don't," she said, throwing back the covers. "You're not pulling that vulnerable little boy crap to check the waters before you jump in."

"What little boy crap?"

"Where you diffuse all the sensitive points first so I've got no reason to say no."

"No to what?"

"To whatever you want to ask. As if finally being able to pay my rent on time would make me value superficial things instead of the important things like real love! I base my decision on genuine attraction."

"Are we genuinely attracted to each other, Liz?"

"Well, I mean people need common goals, shared dreams."

"And do we share those things?"

She walked to the closet. "You can't just come out and ask that kind of question."

"Why not? You just fried my ass for not being direct. Now you're doing the same thing."

She stepped around him to gather her things, place them into her overnight bag. "It's not the same thing."

"Then that's a yes?"

"What's a yes?"

"You'll go with me to the Hollywood Bowl next Friday. I'll pick you up at five. We'll have a picnic in the park before the show. I'll bring the wine. Unless you're afraid you can't handle more than one glass."

"Is this a ... a date?"

"Only if we go together. If not, I don't think you could call that a date."

Wise guy.

"So. Do you think you can?" he asked.

"Can what?"

"Handle more than one glass of wine."

She paused. "I'll pace myself."

Thirty-Eight

Liz leaned on Sonnie's arm as they entered the busy squad room. She spotted Carl standing in the doorway of the interview room. They waved and started toward him.

He gave Liz a hug. "You're looking pretty perky for someone who's just spent the night in the hospital."

"The side's a little sore, but my scalp is the real problem," she said. "I'm still losing hair."

"You were lucky," he said, seriously. He looked at Sonnie. "You, too."

He nodded. "Neither of us are ever going to forget that. How's your aunt?"

Liz peeked through the glass, into the interview room. "She's just sitting there, staring straight ahead," she said.

Carl shook his head. "She's got no fight left in her. Adrianne Smidley's going to take her case. She's a hell of a defense attorney, but Irene seems bent on self-punishment. She asked to see you, Liz." He checked his watch. "Me, I'm on my way to pour coffee for tired parents."

"Oh, the recital," Sonnie said. "She conned you into it, huh?"

Carl made a wry smile. "Watch out, she's good at it. See you there." He headed for the exit.

Liz's hand was on the doorknob when Sonnie stopped her. "You go in alone," he said, taking a seat on a bench. "Irene'll be more comfortable. I'll be right here."

"I could be awhile."

"I'm not going anywhere."

"While you're waiting," she said, "see if Wallpaper knows anything about Nuke."

●

Adrianne Smidley wore a dark plaid blazer with a long, pleated skirt that made her appear shorter and rounder than she was. She had a cherubic face, silver-white, wavy hair, and a reputation for being a defense attorney who could deliver an "innocent" verdict for her clients. She had been sitting with Irene McCurdy in the interview room for two hours, but had been unable to elicit much response from her. She set a steaming cup of tea in front of Irene and sat down next to her just as Liz came through the door.

Liz hugged Irene. "Aunt Irene, is there anything I can do?"

"Oh, Lizzie," Irene murmured, grabbing onto her.

"We're going to get the truth out," Liz said, trying to sound hopeful. She sat across from her.

Irene's eyes raised to meet hers. "I'm not sorry he's dead, you know."

Adrianne interjected, "I've instructed your aunt that she does not have to say anything at this time, but she wanted to talk to you."

"Lizzie's family," Irene said. "I want her to know."

The words that flowed from Irene's weak voice were uncontrived, making the passion behind them poignant, and powerful.

"Don't expect me to pretend I'm sorry he's dead," she said. I'm not. I shoulda killed him twenty years ago. My baby girl would still be alive. But I'm not a killer. That's not why I went there that night."

"Why did you go?" Liz asked, gently.

"Gina was so happy when she'd found him," Irene said, her eyes filling with tears. "'I'm gonna nail that bastard,' she told me. "'I'm gonna do it for you! I told her, no! Don't go near him! If he finds out who you are, he could do to you what he did to your father! But she didn't listen. She said she was gonna put the screws to him. Get his millions, and expose him for the murderin' cheat he was!" Irene lowered her eyes, shook her head. "I could never stop her once she'd made up her mind, even when she was a little girl."

Adrianne asked, "So you went there to protect Gina?"

Irene nodded. "She had it all set up—where and when they were going to meet. He thought she loved him!" she scoffed. "At first she planned to get the money, and circulate enough stories about him to ruin his reputation, rip the bottom out of his career.

"But then," she said, raising sad eyes to Liz, "you came into the picture. She could see how much the concerts meant to you and Sonnie, so she told Tony she'd do him a favor. She'd leave his career in tact, but she wanted what he'd stolen from us years ago. The money that was rightfully ours."

"So you waited till everyone was gone?" Adrianne prompted her.

"Yes. I hid in the ladies room. Finally, I heard someone pounding on the bricks. Over and over," she said, cupping her hands over her ears. "Like the night they beat Victor's hands. Louder and louder, till I was nearly mad from it! I knew it was him."

Irene's breathing quickened and tears filled her eyes. "I knew Gina would be there soon, so I snuck out, and slipped under one of the booths. I was just going to watch, but he turned on Gina like a madman when she told him who she was. Scared the hell out of me. He turned into a monster. He picked up a big metal tool and charged at her. I jumped out. Couldn't help myself. The same man who'd murdered my Victor was about to kill my daughter!"

"What happened when he saw you?" Liz asked.

"I don't know," she wailed, "we were all pushing against each other. I was fighting hard, would'a killed him if I could."

Irene's tears turned to gasping sobs. Liz wrapped her arms around her, sending a pleading look at Adrianne.

"Let's stop for now," Adrianne said.

●

Liz felt numb when she left the interview room. She had confidence in Adrianne Smidley's abilities as a defense lawyer, but Irene's words worried her: "Victor's gone, now Gina's gone. The rest doesn't matter."

Liz sat down next to Sonnie in the squad room.

"I talked to the lieutenant about Nuke, Liz."

His somber tone alerted her. "Oh no—" She leaned back onto the bench.

"He didn't make it. I'm sorry. I know you two got to be friends."

"Aw, no. Not Nuke. I mean, he was so—Nuke was like a rock."

"The blade hit an artery. It was just too late."

"But he saved my life," she muttered, remembering the empty elevator shaft. "If he hadn't reacted when he did, I'd be dead."

She let herself sink into Sonnie's embrace. "One minute he's laughing at me when I tell him he drives like an old lady, and then ... aw, why'd it have to be Nuke?"

They sat on the bench a long moment.

"You know, I never even found out his real name," she said. "He said if I could keep a secret, he could, too!"

"Newton."

"No!"

"Wahlberg saw the death certificate. His name was Newton James McPhearson."

"Nobody names their kid *Newton*. No wonder he wouldn't admit it."

Thirty-Nine

The parking lot of Joseph P. Marienthal High School was jammed. Inside the auditorium, parents offered their children last minute advice on public behavior, most of it being largely ignored.

In the lobby, long tables were set up for refreshments, and manned by volunteers.

Carl stood behind a 40-quart coffee maker, looking uncomfortable in a full-length white apron.

"Ah, I do love this picture of domesticity," Liz teased, as she and Sonnie approached.

"Service is my life," Carl said.

"Yeah, right," Liz laughed.

"Did you hear the woodwind ensemble?" he asked. "Walter's walking around beaming."

"He should be proud," she said.

"Oh, he wanted me to give you a message, Liz. Something about Sherice's brother Jeffrey having gone into the Navy about a week ago. You know what he's talking about?"

"The Navy. A good place for Jeffrey. Thanks," she said, about to head backstage when she heard Walter's voice over the microphone, announcing the second half of the show.

"Quick!" she said, grabbing Sonnie's arm. "They're starting. Let's slip into the back row."

In the darkened auditorium, they found isle seats as Sherice walked onto the stage, composed, self-assured.

"Look at her!" Liz whispered. "She's amazing."

Sherice stood by the piano as she had at the rehearsal. This time, she announced that she had originally planned to play a traditional piano piece called *Two Hearts*, but was also prepared to perform a standard jazz song requiring her own improvisation.

"I only have time to play one," she said, "so I'm putting it to a vote. If you'd like to hear *Two Hearts*, please applause."

A lukewarm applause accompanied several chuckles.

"Or would you rather hear *Satin Doll*, by Duke Ellington, with a really good improv chorus," she said, her enthusiasm making her choice obvious.

The room broke into cheers for the second.

"Good!" She sat down at the keys, took a big breath, and

began the song, tapping the heel of one patent leather shoe to the beat.

"Listen to her!" Liz cried, louder than she'd meant to. "Her playing is flawless! Her changes are right, the rhythm flows—the kid grooves!"

Forty

By ten in the morning, the band was set-up on the stage, the sound check complete. Liz walked over to Frankie, the drummer Miles and Elliot had chosen to replace Danny. "This must be tough," she said, "replacing somebody as well-loved as Danny, but I think you're going work out just fine."

Liz had stayed completely out of the decision making process, saying that the shock of losing Danny was too much; she could never be objective.

"I can't do it," she'd told them, "and it wouldn't be fair to them." They'd argued that her input was essential, but until yesterday's rehearsal, she had refused to even meet the newcomer. Liz had arrived before the guys, and greeted a slender woman of five-foot-ten unpacking drums in what had been Danny's spot on the stage. The new drummer's girlfriend, she assumed.

"Oh, now I really feel like a jerk," she admitted when she realized her mistake. "Frankie, as in ... Frankie."

Frankie Langstrom was used to the gender confusion. She laughed. "You'd think my parents would have thought of that."

Liz also noticed that neither Miles nor Elliot had bothered to inform her that their new drummer was a striking, light-haired female beauty. "They probably figured I'd accuse them of picking you for your legs," she confided to Frankie over coffee later. "So they just avoided the whole subject. Anyway, I'm glad you're here."

●

The V I P table was centered in the front row at the foot of Germaine's stage. Sonnie had set the special table aside for Carl, Reggie, and Paige.

Media equipment filled the aisles and hallways. Tables were pushed closer together to accommodate the equipment, but the place sizzled with such excitement that no one seemed to mind the cramped quarters. Customers waited in long lines outside in hopes of getting a seat later. As Sonnie had hoped, the chance not only to be on television but to be part of music-making history, brought throngs of people.

Liz was onstage, wrapped in the energy of harmony and

rhythm. The cameras zoomed in on them. Miles showed off his on-stage charisma, the audience responded. Each player demonstrated his own special characteristics, something Liz always encouraged. "Don't hold back, thinking I need to be the star of the show up here," she'd told them at rehearsals. "This is a cooperative effort. The better we are individually, the stronger the band."

On the last note of the set, they locked in with the crowd. They brought the volume down...down...to a whisper, letting the clapping and foot-tapping create a slow boil.

They kept it up. Elliot improvised over the groove, exploring new territory on and off the strings of his electric bass. A short teaser out of tempo, then a quick switch back. The crowd cheered, totally absorbed. Frankie joined in on the hi-hat, building the intensity, taking listeners on a rhythm cruise. The clapping grew stronger, lights came down. Heads turned, conversation hushed.

Eight bars, sixteen, thirty-two. Stronger, vibrant. Miles stormed in with rich arpeggiated chords climbing up each scale tone. Higher. Tighter. The listeners intensified the pulse with their clapping, the band coaxing them on. They took the volume up, higher still, until the song climaxed with Liz holding one long, high note over Miles' lush chord.

The floodlights snapped off. A split second of silence. Applause thundered through the lounge. Liz was beaming when the spots flashed on again. They bowed, raced from the stage, the applause still resounding behind them.

Outside, a small green sedan circled the block around Germaine's, then parked two blocks away. The driver, a young man, pulled a basket of flowers from the back seat, locked the car, and walked down the sidewalk and into the club, inching his way through the waiting crowd. At the hostess' desk he flashed an identification badge from a local florist, and announced that he had a delivery for Liz Hanlon. He was to hand the flowers to her in person.

"That's not possible," the hostess told him. "She's busy being on television right now!"

"Then I must see a manager," he said, stiffly.

Irritated, the hostess picked up the phone and paged Sonnie. Ten minutes later he pushed his way through the chaos. He took the flowers and handed the boy a tip. "You could have left them for her."

"My instructions were to hand them to Ms. Hanlon."

"Right. I'll see that she gets these," he said.

The boy left. Sonnie hurried back down the corridor to leave the flowers in the office with the others. About to turn away, he wondered who had instructed the boy to hand them to Liz personally? And why send them so late into the performance? Florists were certainly closed by now. He pulled out a small red card from the bouquet.

His hopes for a perfect evening were dashed when he read the inscription on the card:

You're even beautiful on television.

He dropped the card and charged back down the hall, shoving customers out of the way as he raced out to the street. He peered up and down the sidewalks, but the delivery boy was no where in sight.

The End

Mystery & Music!

The love, passion and revenge continue when Liz Hanlon performs her original compositions on the

High Notes Are Murder
Soundtrack

Available Now On CD

Hear each suspenseful event portrayed in music!

Order now and save $1.00 with this coupon
Original Price: $7.95 • With this coupon only: $6.95

Soundtrack includes the following titles from Barbara Reed's previous recording, *This Was Meant To Be*:

- *The Child In You*
- *This Was Meant To Be*
- *The Tear Returns To Me*

.... Copy or Cut here to order ....

Please send me the *High Notes Are Murder Soundtrack CD*

Discount with this coupon: $1.00

Price per Soundtrack: $6.95	Quantity ____	Total:	$_____

Please send me the novel *High Notes Are Murder:*

Novel Price: $11.95	Quantity ____	Total:	$_____

Please send me *This Was Meant To Be*

Available on cassette: $8.00	Quantity ____	Total:	$_____

Subtotal:			$_____
Tax: CA residents add 8.25%Add:			$_____
Shipping & Handling:			
SET: One book & one CD:	Add:	$ 4.75	$_____
One book only:	Add:	$ 4.25	$_____
Each additional book:	Add:	$ 3.50	$_____
One CD or one cassette	Add:	$ 1.55	$_____
Total:			$_____

Name: _____

Address: _____

City: _____ **State:** _____ **Zip:** _____

Your Email Address: _____

Mail check or money order to: **Rare Sound Press**
P. O. Box 15028
Long Beach, CA 90815
Voice Mail: (714) 780-8349 • Fax: $562) 494-8986
Our Email: bworkman@raresoundpress.com